Tearing Down the Wall

Tracey Ward

ACKNOWLEDGMENTS

Thank you to my husband for digging me out of plot holes, my family for supporting me, my friends for cheering me on and reading every rough draft, my editor for pointing out when I'm wrong but somehow still making me smile, and my fans for loving these characters just as much as I do.

To die would be an awfully big adventure.

J.M. Barrie, *Peter Pan*

Chapter One

"What do we do?" I ask Trent, my voice barely above a whisper.

In the flickering firelight his eyes watch me intently, but I know he's somewhere else. His mind is outside the room, out on the streets, gauging the distance and weighing our options. We both listen to the crunch of feet on loose gravel, the scuff of shoes on asphalt. The drag of the blade over rough ground. When he finally sees me again, I know we're in trouble.

"We wait," he tells me, his voice too loud.

"Shhh!" I shush him violently, glancing nervously at the broken windows. So far they're still pitch black. They may be coming, but they're doing it in darkness.

"It doesn't matter, Joss. They know we're here."

"So we're just going to let them kill us? Eat us for dinner?" I demand. I sit up, going into a crouch and scanning the room for something, anything. "Screw that, Trent. If I'm going down, I'm going down fighting."

"If we don't fight and we don't run, we may be able to talk our way out of this."

My eyes snap to his, shocked. "Are you serious?"

He nods slowly. The footsteps are coming closer. They're almost here and my heart is ready to implode.

"I've seen it happen. I've seen people taken prisoner by them before."

"Pft," I scoff. "They were probably saved for a midnight snack. Kept warm with beating hearts and eaten later on."

"Maybe," Trent agrees with a shrug, "but what do we lose by trying?"

I chew on the inside of my lower lip as I debate this really stupid plan. But he's right and I know he's right; I'm just fighting it like crazy because I don't want to be taken prisoner again. I also don't want to die, and I really, really, really don't want to be eaten.

"Okay, but you're not doing the talking," I finally tell him. "You'll get us killed immediately."

He raises a skeptical eyebrow, but just like I know he's right, he knows I'm right. He doesn't fight me.

"Agreed. But you won't do any better. You're not exactly Miss Congeniality."

"No, I'm not," I admit reluctantly. My eyes go immediately to Ryan. "But you know who is?"

"You better wake him fast. They're here."

I pounce on Ryan, shaking him violently until he grumbles and moans, his hands flailing weakly to make me stop. But I'm relentless because I'm terrified and I know he's our only hope. I shake him harder only to be greeted with more grumbling.

"He's out cold," I say, exasperated.

"You'll have to—"

"Knock, knock," a voice sings from outside.

A pale face appears in the broken window, grinning when he sees me.

I nearly scream. As it is, I die a little inside— like Wesley in *The Princess Bride,* tethered to the machine stealing years off his life. That's what this world is doing to me: killing me slowly one terror at a time until I'll be the oldest seventeen-year-old ever to walk the earth. I'll think I have years left to live if only I can keep my guard up, keep the monsters at bay, but then one morning I won't wake up because my heart will have given out. And I won't blame it one bit.

The face disappears from the window. The second it's gone, I wish it was back because at least then I know where one of them is. I can hear more people milling around outside the walls. They run their hands along the exterior, tapping lightly as they move, until the entire building feels like it's humming. The walls are closing in on me and I'm panicking hard. My breaths are coming in short, painful gasps and my skin is nothing but a drowning victim under the sweat breaking out over every inch of my body.

I'm scared of zombies. I'm scared of the Colonists. After the gun in my face, I'm a little scared of the Vashons. But I have never been so afraid of another living being as I am right now. I always knew I was disgusted by them, repulsed by their willingness to devour another human being like the monsters that stole everything from us all, but I never knew how deathly afraid of them I was. They're human but inhumane. Living but dead inside. It's a double-threat enemy I'd hoped to never face.

Yet here they are now in force.

"Trent," I say urgently, not sure what I'm expecting from him. I think I want him to have all the answers and make this go away. I want him to know everything now. In fact, I encourage it. But what I get in response to my plea for God-knows-what surprises me.

Just as there's an eerily polite knock on the door behind me, Trent pulls a stick from the fire and lays it on Ryan's bare arm.

"What the f—" Ryan cries, jerking into a sitting position.

He blinks several times, trying to clear his eyes. He looks pissed and I don't blame him. If Trent ever tries that with me, I'll make him eat that hot poker.

"We have company," Trent tells him.

Ryan freezes as he listens to the sounds around him: fingers tapping on the building. Faces start popping in and out of the windows, some just passing by, some stopping to smile grimly before moving on. There are women in the group; somehow that makes me sicker.

The knock sounds at the door again.

"Who is it?" Ryan asks Trent.

"Your neighbors," the man outside the door

4

answers. "We need to borrow a cup of sugar."

"To make their People Pies with," I mutter.

I hate to admit it so I won't, not to anyone but myself, but I feel better having Ryan awake. I feel less certain that I'm going to die tonight.

He frowns at me now, his warm eyes dark in the dying firelight.

"Cannibals?" he whispers.

I nod, my mouth tightly strung in a grim line.

He curses under his breath then jumps slightly when the knocking starts up again.

"Little pig, little pig, let me in," the man sings mockingly.

"Trent thinks you can talk to them," I whisper to Ryan. "He's seen people talk to them and not end up dead."

"Not right away, at least," Trent corrects.

"What do I say?" he asks incredulously. "Please don't eat us?"

"Maybe don't lead with that."

"Lead with what then? The weather? Ask about his kids?" Ryan demands, whispering harshly.

"Maybe start with opening the door," I suggest.

Ryan takes a calming breath, then nods his head.

"Weapons hidden, give nothing away," he mutters to us as he stands.

Ryan, I think it's important to note, was our reigning poker champion in prison. Even Trent, with his robot's heart, wasn't able to beat him. Trent has no tells, no emotional outbursts or giveaways to exploit. Ryan, on the other hand, has many, but most are lies. He's an incredible actor—

5

or a liar, depending on how you see it. I think it's one of the reasons he does so well in the Arena. He has a charisma, an easy kind of charm that pulls you in and makes you trust him. Even as he's taking all your money.

My blood is rushing in my ears as he turns the door handle. I think someone says something from outside but I can't hear it, not over the sound of my own fear and panic pounding in my ears. Ryan nods, steps aside, and a man dressed entirely in black walks in. He gives the small room a once-over, his eyes barely falling on Trent and I. It's something I'm a little insulted by. He's looking for threats but I just got passed over like I was nothing. Like I'm an office chair or a roller skate.

The man's skin is painfully pale. His dark hair is a shock against it where it droops over his forehead, looking clean and shiny. This is how I judge people in the apocalypse: do they have a shower and do they use it? Yes on both counts for this guy, meaning they're living relatively well. No one showers first and drinks water to survive second.

"So," he says quietly, turning back to Ryan with a stern eye, "who are you and what are you doing here?"

"We washed up on the shore here and weren't prepared to travel at night," Ryan says, his voice surprisingly deep and strong. "Not through this territory."

"Not through *our* territory."

"No. Colonists' either."

"And how do you know we're not Colonists?"

"You knocked," he answers wryly.

The man grins. It's not as horrifying as I thought it would be. Not like when Trent does it. It seems more natural. Easier. Like he does it all the time. I remind myself that the truly horrifying thing about the cannibals is that they look just like everyone else—right up until they're pan-frying someone's calf muscle over an open flame. Then you can feel it in your bones, smell it in the air that they are wrong.

"You were on the ships then? You're Colonists."

"No," I blurt out. I snap my mouth shut the second I say it, but it's already done. All eyes are on me now.

"Really?" the man asks, stepping toward me.

I see Ryan tense beside him, but then another man steps inside the door to block his path. The first man looks at me intently. I don't feel as terrified as I thought I would meeting his stare. His eyes are strange, too large and too dark, but they're not crazy. Not as insane and empty as I expected.

"Yes, really," I say, worried my tone is too sharp, but I'm not great at censoring myself. I clear my throat. "We're not with the Colonists, and before you ask, we're not with The Hive either."

"Are you sure? That was a Hive boat you sailed out on."

I swallow, glancing quickly at Ryan. How do they know about the boat?

"Did it sink?" the man asks. "We lost sight of it in the chaos."

"Capsized," Trent says as a matter of fact.

"And you left it like that? Uh oh," he tuts, feigning concern. "Marlow won't like that. You'll be indebted to him now. That's never a good place to be."

"You know Marlow?" I ask.

"I know of him. Never had the pleasure of making his acquaintance."

"You're not missing much."

He grins again. "So I hear. Clear something up for me, would you? You sailed to Vashon Island on a Hive boat, but you're not with The Hive. You clearly aren't with the Vashons because here you sit, on the opposite side of the Sound. You say you're not with the Colonies and I'm inclined to believe that. So if you're not with The Hive, the Vashons, or the Colonies, who are you exactly?"

"No one," Ryan says, his voice dead.

I'm surprised by his answer but then I remember that it's true—that I did that to him. He's no longer a Hyperion because he betrayed them for me and that's going to eat him up inside. That was his family—a piece of his life with his brother—and I've taken that, giving nothing in return. But he's not no one. Even standing in an empty room without a weapon or cent to his name, he's so much more someone than I'll ever be.

"Well, whoever you are, you need to come with us."

"And if we don't?" Ryan asks.

"You will."

It's not a threat exactly, it's more like a truth. One I feel in my gut. He's right, we'll go with them because we don't want to die and it doesn't even have to be said that that's what will happen if we resist. We all know it. I can feel it and they can probably taste it and there's no sense in denying it.

I stand slowly. Trent does the same in my peripheral but I keep my eyes on Ryan. He's watching me rise and I'm worried that I can't read his face. He's gone into Arena mode: he's a fighter now, dead and calm inside. I envy him that. I recognize that trick as one I used to be able to perform, but my skills have slipped or fallen entirely away and I'll never be able to do it again. Even now as I look at him I can feel emotions swirling inside of me. I feel scared, anxious, protective, angry. And it's all for him.

We're led outside into the dark and the cold. We leave our fire burning inside and I have the fleeting, ridiculous thought that we should put it out before it burns the building down or draws someone to it. But it's not my home and the moths are already here. The damage has already been done.

I fall in line behind Ryan as we head out the door. I'm startled by the sudden silence, the cease of raps and taps on the outside of the building. It's so perfectly synched that the lack of sound unnerves me as much as it did when it started. I'm beginning to think these people share a brain.

"Weapons," someone ahead of Ryan says curtly.

I unhook my knife and toss it to the ground toward the shadowed voice that demanded it. Then I slowly pull my ASP free, running my fingers over it lovingly as I ache inside. I just got her back. How many times can we be separated before it's the last?

I glare at the man in front of us, holding up my ASP for him to see. "I want this back."

"Toss it with the others," is his cold reply.

"Do you understand me? I want it back."

"When?"

"When we leave."

"Who said you will?"

I suppress a shiver along with the urge to whip the weapon out to full length and crack it against the guy's face. He's taking shape as my eyes adjust to the darkness. He's not that big. He's actually almost my height, not that much meatier. I'm not used to fighting the living but I'm suddenly curious how I'd do. The more I can see of him, the more convinced I am that I can take him. But I can't fight all of them and neither can Ryan or Trent, so I slowly lower the baton to the ground where I let it fall with an echoing clatter.

"I'll leave," I tell the guy as I stand up straight, "and when I do, you're giving that back to me."

I can't be sure, but I think he grins.

"This way," the lead guy says, taking off without looking back.

As the cannibals fall into formation around us I realize I've misjudged their numbers: there are more than I thought. They seem to materialize out of the darkness as we move and I'm glad I stowed the urge to fight. Even if we were twice as many, we'd never have fought our way out.

I keep my eyes on Ryan's back, his broad shoulders leading me forward and blocking out the world ahead of us. It makes me nervous. I'd rather be the lead, see where I'm going. Know what I'm walking into. I'm going on a lot of faith following blindly behind him like this, especially with Trent and all his height pacing so close behind me. I start to feel caged and crazy. I'm surrounded on every side and I can't see and I want to run or fight or scream, but I keep it locked inside. I keep my eyes on Ryan and I remember sleeping beside him. I remember him between me and walls, me and doors, me and danger. I remind myself what it feels like to press my back against his and trust that whatever is coming behind me is irrelevant. It's already dead because he's there.

I remind myself to trust him the way he trusts me. All the way.

Chapter Two

We walk through the streets silently without any light. I've done this before—it's not that big of a deal in a neighborhood you know, but I don't know this one. Not at all. Not even a little. I don't come south of the stadiums. To move through this area is to be close to the Colonies, and while I can see their lights blazing closer than I feel comfortable with, I know the real trouble is what you don't see. Not until the van rolls up on you silently and people snatch you off the streets. But the way the cannibals walk us brazenly through the dark, I wonder how much of a threat the Colonists are to them. Maybe the Colonists give them as much space as the rest of us. Maybe no one likes the idea of being eaten for dinner, least of all by someone living.

Without a word, Ryan stops. I slam into the back of him, and as his hand reaches back to help stabilize me, I wait for the impact of Trent to sandwich me between them. It never comes. I feel clumsy, blind, and a little helpless. The helpless is what pisses me off the most.

"Why did we stop?" I ask, brushing Ryan's hand away.

Before he can answer there's a sharp screech of metal on metal. When I break formation to look around Ryan, my gut clenches.

One of the cannibals is using a horrifying hook weapon as a giant crowbar to pull a manhole cover up out of the street.

Funny thing about manholes—I don't go down them. It's dumb. Tight quarters, no idea who or what is in there with you, perpetual darkness. It's a black hole to nothing. The descent inside could be five feet or five thousand years—there's no way of knowing. I'm no wimp, I'm not afraid of the dark, but I'm also not a fan of it, either, and this thing is all darkness. All endless depths of black midnight with all manner of nightmare waiting for me at the bottom.

"Are we seriously doing this?" I mumble to Ryan as the first of the cannibals is swallowed up by the Great Nothing.

"Looks like it."

"Can I tell you a secret?"

"Sure."

"Promise not to tell?"

"Course."

I take a quick breath as the leader watches us, waiting. It's our turn.

"I'm scared," I whisper to Ryan.

When he looks down at me I wish I could see his face better, but I'm also glad it's too dark. This admission is huge for me. I'm not even sure why I told him. Not like he can do anything about it—but it helps somehow, having him know.

"Me too," he replies.

"Me three," Trent agrees.

Ryan I believe, but Trent not so much. Still, I appreciate the solidarity.

"I'll go first," I say quickly.

I step away from them before Ryan can stop me, because I know he'll try. I'm not surprised when his hand shoots out to grab hold of me. I saw it coming. I dodge it easily, slipping away toward the cracked can of no-friggin'-thank-you yawning in front of me. I don't give myself time to think about it. I don't let myself go full terrified toddler, imagining all of the things that could be in this hole waiting to grab my ankle and yank me down to Hell. I dive right in, swinging my legs inside and slowly climbing down, being careful as I feel the slippery, slimy coating on each step.

I slip down farther and farther until the meager light from above starts to fade away and I have that claustrophobic feeling you get in an unseen, wide open space. The area around me could be boundless or it could be tiny. There could be walls everywhere just waiting for me to walk straight into them and bash my nose on their cold, wet surfaces. All I know for sure is the circle of light above me, the ladder under me, and the endless black around me.

"One more step," a voice warns softly, scaring the crap out of me.

I pause for a second, letting my nerves calm and my senses take over.

They're to my left. It's a woman. Her voice didn't echo much at all so I'm assuming the space down here can't be too big. I let go of the ladder and instantly feel dizzy. My eyes are adjusting to the dark, picking up on what small light is coming in from up top, but it's not going to be enough. I can't get my bearings on anything. As I slowly take a step toward the voice, I wonder how much she can see. Is her eyesight that good in the dark or does she have all of these caverns and tunnels memorized?

"Stand over here."

"Where is 'here'?" I ask irritably.

"To your left three paces."

I put my hands out and shuffle-step three paces to the left. My fingers brush a rough wall, cold and damp. It feels like algae is growing on every surface down here and the air tastes wet and weird. How do they live like this without getting sick all the time?

The light coming in from above is blocked for a second by another body making its way down. It's moving too quickly to be one of the guys. They're staggering us: sending in one of their own, one of us, one of their own. It's smart. Annoyingly so. It also reminds me of the Colonies and my anxiety/anger ratchets up a notch.

Trent comes down next, another of theirs, then Ryan. No one says a word once we're all assembled. I can hear breathing and shuffling bouncing off the walls, making it feel like people are everywhere. But how many could there really be? Outside this hole I saw at most ten of them. But inside, trapped in an enclosed space with all of their lips and teeth, it feels like there are a million. And they're all hungry.

I jump when there's a loud crack followed by a scraping sound. Someone has sparked flint, lighting a torch off to my right. I watch the firelight play off the sheen on the walls, dancing like diamonds faceted in every surface, when what I'm really looking at is slime. The ground has an obsidian, oily coating on it that glistens with rainbows in the light. I worry that it actually is oil. One dropped spark from that torch could send this entire place up in flames in an instant.

"This way," the guy with the fire says, his voice surprisingly gentle. Almost welcoming.

There's an otherworldly feel to this place. As though when I came down that manhole what I really did was slip down the rabbit hole into Wonderland. I'm not so sure I prefer it to Neverland. I knew the rules there. Down here with these people… well, it feels like anything goes.

We walk for half an hour before I see light glowing at the end of the tunnel. It's yellow and clean. Warm. The temperature has been rising, the moisture disappearing from the air. This is where they live. Where they sleep.

Where they eat.

We walk into the light through a blown out section of wall. It looks like they demolished it to break from these tunnels into another section. The area here is wide open, like a large basement, which makes me wonder where exactly we've walked to. Without any landmarks from up top to guide me, I'm completely lost. The walls are exposed brick and broken plaster, but as we move through this open space, the eyes of more cannibals watching us curiously from unlit corners, I see wood support beams. We come into a narrower passage, almost like a hallway, and I pass a window frame looking through into another large room.

"Where are we?" I whisper despite myself.

"It looks like an underground city," Ryan mumbles behind me.

"Since when is there an underground city in Seattle?"

"Since 1889," the man ahead of me answers without turning.

We pass by a pristine brick archway leading into a small, well-lit room with a burning fireplace and three beds pressed against the walls.

"That used to be part of a bank in the 1800s. This was all ground level back then."

"How did it end up underground?" Trent asks curiously.

I glance back to find his eyes scouring the walls, taking in every detail. His hand brushes along a wall to feel the wood of a door frame, the brick of a pillar. It's a new, strange mystery and my robot is deeply, passionately in love.

"There was a fire. Thirty-one blocks of this area were destroyed. When they started to rebuild they decided to re-grade the streets in this area, since they were built on tidelands and were constantly flooded. The roads were raised twelve feet. In some places they went up thirty. What was street level in a building became basement or underground, where we are now. There were skylights like these," he points to a metal mesh of

17

squares in the ceiling, some of them still housing small, cracked cubes, "up to the ground level to let in natural light. The entire underground was shut down in 1907 when people panicked over the bubonic plague. Most of it was condemned or absorbed into building basements and shut off. This is the last of what's left."

"And this is where you live? All of you?" Ryan asks.

The guy half turns his head to look back at us, his face pure shadow. "Tour's over," he says, his voice losing its friendly tone. "We're almost there."

They take us down a long, narrow alley—with more broken down storefronts that lead into bedrooms lining the left side, and high crumbling walls lining the right—before turning sharply into one of the rooms. Inside is another wood-burning fireplace carved into the wall, venting somewhere above ground in the cold night air. There's a round wooden table, a couple of mismatched chairs around it, and three men standing in a corner talking heatedly. They pause when we enter, all eyes falling immediately on me, Ryan, and Trent.

A guy just barely my height steps forward, making me want to step back. There's a shine to his eyes. It's unnatural and strange. Foreign in the wild.

It's hope.

"Is this them?" he asks, his tone hushed.

"We think it might be," our tour guide answers noncommittally.

"Where's Andy?"

"I'm here."

There's shuffling in the hall as a man pushes

through the people guarding us. He's tall, his complexion darker than most of the pale, white skin I've seen down here so far. He strides into the room, scanning everyone inside and taking inventory. The move reminds me of Trent.

"Well?" the short man asks him anxiously.

His eyes meet mine, staying there for longer than I like. But as I look at him I start to wonder if I don't recognize him. It's too dark in here to be sure, but I swear I've seen him before.

"It's them," he says, his voice deep and firm.

Well, all right, he apparently knows us.

"Wonderful," Shorty says happily.

The guy walks farther into the room to stand beside Shorty. His eyes stay with me the entire time. His stare is starting to make me uncomfortable but I don't dare look away. I'm an animal from the jungle. I can play the staring game all day long.

"This is perfect," the short man says to himself, clasping his hands together and smiling. "I'm so glad to finally meet you all."

"Do we know you?" Ryan asks, his voice uncharacteristically cold.

"Not yet, but we have so much to talk about. We'll know each other very well soon enough."

My lips curl back in disgust. "We have nothing to talk about with you."

The short guy flinches. His teeth flash, and it may be a trick of the light but they look shadowed and sharp.

He steps toward me. The room shifts with him. Shadows build, growing too tall beside him, an army of darkness waiting to answer his call. A

19

cavalry of devils.

"Oh, my dear girl," he says, his voice going hushed, taking the entire room with it. Everything is pinpointed down to this small man with the quiet voice and the dangerous gleam in his eyes. "I believe you're wrong. We share the same dream."

"I really doubt that."

"You're wrong."

"What dream could we ever have in common?"

He grins darkly. "Revolution."

Chapter Three

I'm sitting down to dinner with a table full of cannibals.

It sounds like the beginning of a bad joke—one that ends with something about passing the salt and then everybody laughs, only I'm not laughing. I'm also not eating, definitely not anything of the meaty, protein-packing variety. I wouldn't even trust a glass of milk, and I. Love. Milk. Love it. The Colonists almost had me selling my soul to them for it. But with the Colonists, believe it or not, I trusted the source more than I do here.

These people will eat your toes while you watch, so it doesn't seem outside the realm of possibility that the milk on this table came from a person, and while that's fine for babies, there's something very sickening about the thought of it now.

"Please, dig in," Shorty says from his seat at the head of the long rectangular dining table.

Shorty's name is Elijah. I should probably start

21

thinking of him as that, but I feel like names humanize these lunatics and I don't want to soften my image of them. They're polite, more hospitable than my mom on Thanksgiving, but I don't like it. It's creepy. Creepier than if they came at me covered in living human blood with bits of warm tissue dribbling from their lips. This right here, this is like Halloween in reverse. This is monsters and ghouls dressed up as preachers and soccer moms.

We've been joined by a couple of new people, but I can tell by the seating that the important ones are Andy and Elijah. Andy seems to have almost a celebrity status with the rest of the group. People smile at him, clap him on the shoulder; the few women I've seen look at him a little too long. He's a decent enough looking guy from what I can tell in this light, but good looks and a charming smile can't account for the reaction people have to him. It doesn't explain why Elijah has him sitting directly to his right at the table.

Elijah smiles patiently at us. "You're not eating."

"I'm not hungry," I tell him dryly.

"You're not hungry or you're not hungry for what we have to offer?"

"Does it matter?" Ryan asks from across the table.

"Quite a bit."

I push my plate away slowly. "I've never been hungry enough for what you call food."

Elijah's smile changes. He holds it steady but the tightness around his eyes makes it different. It makes it angry.

"Waste not, want not," he sings softly.

I shiver down to my toes.

"What did you mean by us sharing a dream?" Trent asks, his curiosity knowing no disturbing crimes-against-nature bounds.

"We want what you want: freedom from the Colonies."

"How are the Colonies even a concern for you?" I ask.

"They're a concern for everyone."

"But they're afraid of you."

"We're afraid of the daylight," he replies bitingly. "Imagine being a child and never playing in the sun. We've made monsters of ourselves, monsters trapped in the dark. It was our only defense. Our numbers have always been too small to fight with and we knew early on that the Colonies would be a problem. They were corrupt from the start."

"So we've heard," I mumble, thinking of the Vashons.

Elijah nods in understanding. "We aren't the only ones who saw it coming. Some ran and hid, some found the numbers to defend themselves, and some made a deal with the devil."

"What deal did you make with him?"

"Not us. The Hive."

It shouldn't surprise me, but it does anyway. Marlow obviously hates the Colonies just like he hates the Vashons, and I think I get why: they're bigger than he is. He thinks of himself as a king and it's a huge blow to his bloated ego that there are people out there stronger than he is. He'll never control the kind of numbers the Vashons and Colonies are working with, and it eats away at him. He hates them for it.

I suddenly wonder if he hates them enough to pit them against each other.

"Did Marlow tell the Colonists we were talking to the Vashons?"

"Yes," Andy answers. "He sent word to them immediately after Ryan won the Blind."

This is the first time Andy has spoken since he IDed us. As his voice cuts through the room, I notice how familiar it is.

I narrow my eyes at him, trying to get a better look. "I know you, don't I?"

He smirks. "Ryan knows me better."

"He's a guard in The Hive," Ryan confirms with a small nod. "He's one of Marlow's closest men."

My eyes go wide with shock. "You're the one who brought us in to see Marlow. The one who didn't search us. I was carrying an ASP and a knife in that room."

"I figured," Andy says easily. "I was hoping you'd use them."

"You want Marlow dead?"

"I wouldn't cry over it."

"So wait. Are you Hive or are you…" I trail off, not sure what to call them. I don't know if 'cannibal' is an offensive term.

"I'm a member of this tribe."

"Then you're what? A spy? For how long?" I ask incredulously.

"Seven years."

"Do you have spies in the Colonies?"

"No."

"Would you tell me if you did?"

"No."

"So you're probably lying?"

"Anything is possible."

Ryan sits forward, catching Andy's eye. "What deal did The Hive make with the Colonists?"

Andy glances silently at Elijah, an unspoken question passing between them. Elijah nods.

"The Colonies have always been obsessed with two things," Elijah explains. "Cleansing the world of the plague and recruiting more people into their flock. At first they talked about the plague as divine retribution. They said everyone infected and dying outside the walls they hid inside were getting what they deserved. They felt they'd been chosen to survive. But then not everyone agreed with them and their numbers started to shrink. That's when they miraculously got word from God Himself that they were meant to save as many people as they could. When willing members dried up, they started the roundups. They used to be one meager group hiding inside a shopping mall, but they kept expanding—and as they did hey needed more bodies. More laborers. The Hive made a deal with them that they would give them people in exchange for goods. I don't know what Marlow gets in every payment, but I would bet it's mostly crops. They're a group of gamblers, pimps, and thieves. They're not known for their farming skills."

"Where is The Hive getting people? You can't just make them out of thin air," I complain.

Trent snickers behind me. I turn to glare at him. "What?"

"You've lived alone for too long."

"What are you laughing at?"

He leans back in his seat, looking entirely too comfortable considering where we are. "Ryan, you want to field this one?"

"Joss, think about it," Ryan says patiently. "How would The Hive be creating people to sell?"

I blush as it dawns on me. "The stables."

"Exactly."

"They're selling babies?!"

"Yes," Elijah answers bitterly, the disgust I feel written on his face. "There's no contraception anymore. Pregnancies are a real risk, and with the women in the stables... *working* as often as they do, babies are going to happen. A lot."

"Are these women giving their children up willingly?"

"Not all of them," Andy tells me tightly. "I've seen them stripped from their arms just moments after they're born. The women fall apart, the babies are screaming. It's not easy to watch."

I glare at him. "But you still do it."

"I can't stop it. I might be able to save one but then my cover is blown and years of work are lost. Wasted."

"So instead of saving one, you save none. That's noble."

Andy's eyes flash as his jaw clenches. "I saved your boy here after his show in the Blind. That crowd wanted to tear him apart and I got him out. I can't save everyone but I do what I can."

"However you need to work the math to sleep at night," I spit, but I wonder why I'm doing it. I actually understand and I'm grateful that he got Ryan out. I'm just appalled by the idea of selling children to the point that I can't see straight. I'm angrier than I've been in a long, long time and I don't have the real villain here to shout at so Andy will have to take the abuse.

"Joss, calm down," Ryan warns.

"No way! Captain Hook is selling Lost Boys, Ryan! It's jacked up!"

Elijah frowns. "Captain Hook?"

"She's very into *Peter Pan*," Trent explains casually. "It's endearing."

"The point is, we have to do something about this," I demand.

"That is precisely the point, yes," Elijah agrees. "From what Andy heard in your meeting with Marlow—"

"Captain Hook," Trent corrects.

"Shush," I whisper to him, exasperated.

"Hey, it's your thing. I'm only trying to help."

"Help by being quiet."

"You do realize that you're Peter Pan in this scenario, right?"

"What?" I cry, turning to face him. "No, I'm Tinkerbell."

"Hardly. She was a seductress. Spritely. You're too manly for that."

I sigh. "I hate you sometimes."

"But you love me most of the time. That's what matters."

"Andy heard us talking about the Colony in the

north," Ryan says, getting us back on track.

Elijah nods. "He told us what you had planned, what you asked from The Hive. He also told me they had no intention of helping you, no matter what happened on your trip to Vashon Island."

"No surprise there."

"So we'd like to take you up on your offer."

"Our deal with Marlow was that we'd bring the Vashons in to fight with us," Ryan reminds him. "We didn't get their help. We barely made it off their island with our lives."

"They think we betrayed them to the Colonies," I agree, feeling oddly sad at the thought of the Vashons hating us.

They're the closest thing to my kind of people that I've seen in a long time. After hearing Sam talk about it, I could see living there out in the open and the free. No zombies, no Colonists, no Hive. I could sleep soundly at night in a warm, dry place without worrying about waking up to find a Risen in my face or a Lost Boy in my bed. But that strange dream died when the Colonist boats rolled down the river and Ali put a gun to my head.

"We aren't worried about the Vashons," Elijah assures us. "We'll join our numbers with yours to fight back against the Colonies. To take back the surface."

"Our *numbers* are three," I tell him, gesturing to Ryan and Trent.

"For now, yes. But once you've taken down the Colony in the north you'll have more."

"Not many more. Those aren't fighters. Those are Colonists. Maybe not the die-hard, uber-religious crazy ones, but they're still soft. The three of us, a few of you, and whoever we can get to put up a fight from the MOHAI aren't going to be enough to take down one of the stadiums."

"And once one is down, the others have to fall quickly behind it like dominoes," Ryan reminds us. "We can't give them time to call for help from the other Colonies."

"Wherever the others are. No one knows."

"We do," Elijah says simply.

I blink, surprised. "You know where the other Colonies are?"

"We know where one is. The one in the south, near the shore. They have boats there that they use regularly. We assume there's another Colony across the water, but we don't know exactly where."

"How many are there?" I whisper to myself, starting to feel hopeless.

"There's the one in the north where you were held," Ryan says, counting, "the two stadiums, one in the south, and now one across the water. So five."

"That we know of."

"Yeah."

I start to panic a little inside. When all of this started I never intended to get involved beyond fulfilling my promise to the people in the MOHAI: I'd bring them help if I could and I'd get them free. From there I figured it would be between them and The Hive what happened next. I never planned on being part of it—the Colonies were their problem—but the deeper I sink into this mess, the more I see that the Colonies are *everyone's* problem: the

Hive's, the Vashons', the cannibals', the Hyperions' Crenshaw's—even mine. Very, very much mine.

So now here I am amassing an army of my enemies, exposing myself to all of the people I've lived in fear of for the larger part of my life, and I'm talking about taking down more Colonies than I ever knew existed. This is insane. It's impossible.

"We'll need more people," Trent says quietly. He's still reclining, comfy and at ease, but his eyes are piercing. "We'll need to talk to the others in the Hyperion to see if we can recruit more bodies. We'll need to visit other gangs as well. The Elevens. The Pikes. You," he says, looking directly at Andy, "will need to blow your cover. Start shopping for help."

Andy stares back at him impassively. There's a tension passing between them, one that I don't understand but I'm pretty freaked out by. The way Trent is eyeing Andy… it makes me happy Trent likes me.

"This is what I was planted for," Andy finally agrees. "I have some connections I can tap into. There are always people unhappy with the status quo."

"They're going to need to be pretty angry if we want them to go against The Hive," Ryan warns him.

Andy grins knowingly. "Oh, they're a very angry bunch. Trust me."

I don't. I don't trust this guy that has probably sat at a table full of Hive members just like he's sitting with us now, smiled that same smile, and spoken those same words. He's a traitor, and it doesn't matter if he's betraying the trust of a man I hate or not—he's still willing to look people in the face and lie to them about absolutely everything. I don't trust your average person even on a basic level, so this guy is setting off all kinds of alarms inside me.

"How many people can you rally to make a move on the northern Colony?" Ryan asks Elijah.

"At least twenty men and women from our guard."

"It's not much."

"It's more than none at all," he says, carefully reminding us just how many people we've successfully recruited from The Hive and Vashon Island.

Ryan nods in silent, grudging agreement.

Elijah stands suddenly, gesturing for the rest of us to do the same. We do, though I'm not sure why, and the ease with which he commands the room bothers me. He leads Trent, Ryan, Andy, and I down one of their dark, strange hallways to the room where we first met him. Large white tubes have been brought in and propped up against the far wall. He and Andy immediately begin examining their tops.

"Do we have that area?" I hear Elijah mutter thoughtfully.

"We have everything," Andy answers confidently. He looks over his shoulder at me. "Where exactly up north is the Colony you were in?"

"On the shore. In the old MOHAI building. It was a museum. The Museum of—"

"History and Industry. Yeah, I know. Here it is."

He pops the cap on one of the tubes and pulls out a large scroll of paper. When he spreads it out on the table, the faded blue paper a mess of white writing that makes me dizzy, I nearly gag. More maps. It makes me think of Captain Hook and his whorehouse. It makes me oddly angry.

"This is a map of the sewer systems and storm tunnels," Elijah explains. "We have street maps too, but the best route for making a move against the Colony is by the underground. They'll never see it coming."

"That area is swarming with zombies," I warn.

"Yes, everywhere is lately."

"Not like up there. They have barricades to lock most of them in as a natural defense."

Elijah looks at me pointedly. "We can handle the Risen."

I nod silently but inside I'm thinking he's using a Colony word. Is he like me and it became part of his vocabulary as he adjusted to this life? He's old enough to know where that word started, but does he remember?

Or is he like Andy? Is he playing both sides?

"We'll move on the smallest Colony immediately," he says.

"How soon is immediately?" Ryan asks.

"Tomorrow night."

"No," I say firmly.

He looks up at me with a mix of surprise and annoyance. "And why not?"

"Because it's impossible. Because we don't

have a solid plan yet. Because we don't know how many people we'll be able to gather from the gangs." I look him hard in the eye. "Because I don't know you. I don't trust you. I don't want to make deals with and fight alongside vicious, rabid animals."

Andy snaps up, his posture going rigidly straight. I ignore him. He worries me, but not right now. Not when I've got Ryan and Trent beside me. I'm still afraid—I should probably watch my back when I think I'm alone—but I don't feel vulnerable right now. It's a heady drug knowing the Boys have my back.

"You don't know a damn thing about us," Andy seethes.

"Lucky me."

"We don't need her," he tells Elijah. "We know where the northern Colony is now. Get her out of here."

I grin at him. "All you gotta do is show me the door."

"Right this way."

"Stop, both of you," Elijah barks impatiently. "Andy, we need her because the location of the Colony isn't enough. She's connected to them. They know her. They won't work with us—they're terrified of us—but they'll follow her."

"She's nothing but a mouthy brat. She'll get people killed. *Our* people."

"And you'll have dinner for a week," I tell him with disgust. "What are you complaining about?"

He shakes his head, his mouth a tight line of compressed anger. "Get her out," he snarls. "Get her out of my sight."

"She stays," Elijah tells him, his voice quiet yet firm. "But I'll make a deal with you."

"I get to kill her when it's over?"

I smirk at Andy even though my stomach is a tight knot of dread. I feel Ryan and Trent close ranks around me. It's a half step each but it's a warning—one I really hope Andy heeds.

"No," Elijah tells him. Then he looks at me and I see the anger Andy is so openly expressing buried deep inside this small man. The firelight is in his eyes where it burns hot, livid, and…happy? He smiles faintly. "You get to educate her."

Chapter Four

My education is a true learning experience—I'm sitting at a desk and everything. It's a reminder of something I barely got to experience back in life pre-apocalyptic wasteland, and if this is anything like the real deal, I'm not sorry I missed out on most of school.

Trent and Ryan sit on either side of me. They're also in old, broken down school desks that were probably jacked from an abandoned elementary school because they're about three sizes too small for all of us. The room we're in is a legit classroom with a blackboard, chalk, a tattered world map, the alphabet and numbers counting up to one hundred painted in brilliant colors on the plain walls. And bones. There are bones, clean and shockingly white, stacked up neatly in a corner underneath a chart with a picture of the human skeleton. Beside that is a very beautiful painting of a bunny in a meadow.

It's the weirdest room I've ever been in.

"What you know about us, or rather what you think you know about us," Elijah says patiently, standing at the head of the classroom, "is a lie."

Andy stands next to him, his body tense, his eyes hard on mine. I keep my face carefully blank as I stare back.

"Do you or do you not eat human flesh?" I demand coldly.

Elijah pauses. Andy's jaw clenches tightly.

"Yes," Elijah admits.

"Then you're animals and there's nothing else I need to know."

"There's more to it than you realize."

I break my stare with Andy to shoot Elijah a bitter look. "I don't care what else there is to it. You're no better than the zombies outside. You're insane. You're inhuman." I take a breath, knowing I shouldn't say what I want to say, but self-control is not my thing lately. I've been through too much, I'm flying wild and loose with all this change, and I feel my heart in my throat as I spit out my next words. "You're disgusting."

I feel Ryan tense next to me. He knows a fight is coming. I know it too. I'm insulting monsters inside their home and it's a great way to get yourself killed; but we're probably going to die anyway, so at least I'll die honest.

"Shut up, Joss."

My head swings to Trent. "What did y—"

"I said shut up," he repeats. He looks at me with complete calm. Complete irritating as hell calm. "I want to hear what they have to say."

"Why?"

"Because I like to understand things."

"What's to understand? They eat people."

"But why do they eat people?"

"I don't care why!"

"I do, so shut up."

"Quit telling me to shut up," I growl.

"I will when you quit talking."

I sit back in my chair hard, staring straight ahead and shaking my head angrily.

"What about you do we misunderstand?" Trent asks Elijah.

Elijah nods to Andy, his entire demeanor changing as he looks at Trent. He's much more relaxed. He almost looks pleased.

Personally, I'm pissed.

"We do ingest human flesh," Andy begins, his angry eyes still locked on mine, "but not for the reasons you think. We do it out of respect, and most importantly, we do it out of love."

I fight to stifle a snort of disbelief.

"When the disease first took hold, the world was chaos. People were killing each other to stay alive. They abandoned each other, they turned deaf ears to pleas for help. It was humanity at its worst, but eventually things calmed down. People started to realize they needed each other to survive. Some realized they needed to work together, some realized they could enslave others."

"The Colonies and The Hive," Ryan says grimly.

"Yes. We realized the same thing the Vashons did: people like us—people willing to live together and help each other—needed to hide to stay free.

But we didn't have the numbers the Vashons did. They were better fighters. They had better resources."

"Why didn't you join with them?" Trent asks.

Andy's mouth pinches tightly. "We weren't invited."

"Can't imagine why not," I mutter.

He ignores me entirely. "We were everyday people then, just looking to survive. But that was the problem. We were too average. We had nothing to contribute to their island, so they didn't want us. They slammed the door in our faces."

Andy's voice has grown more and more bitter until he's spitting the words out like venom. Any anger he has toward me doesn't hold a candle to the hostility he feels toward the Vashons.

"We were locked out," Elijah agrees calmly. "Forced to live here on the outside in the wild with the growing gangs and the Colonies running out of control."

"Why didn't you join with the Colonies?" I ask. "If you were scared of everything else around you, why not willingly be locked inside their gates? At least you'd be safe."

"Why don't you join with them?" he counters. "Why did you escape?"

"Because I refuse to live as a prisoner."

"You were a slave. They all are. And we're exactly like you—we refuse to live that way."

"When and why did you begin to eat people?" Trent asks.

His tone amazes me. There's no judgment. None at all. From the sound of it, he could be asking them when they first learned how to ride a bike instead of when they decided to go full Hannibal on their family and friends.

"A couple of years after we were locked out of the Vashons' palace," Andy tells him. "We were threatened by other gangs and the Colonies with their roundups. We were made up of mostly families. We weren't great fighters. We were parents—parents who would do anything it took to save their children. That's why we moved underground. We hid from the Risen and the gangs, but they found us. We knew we had to do something to keep them away. We tried laying traps but they never worked. We were hiding in the sewers like rats and they still attacked us, still stole from us and killed our people. We were dwindling and dying out and all we could think was who would take care of the kids if we were gone? They'd be next to die. They'd starve or they'd be taken in by the Colonies and raised as slaves. Or worse—they'd be taken in by The Hive and the girls would…" He takes a deep breath, his eyes fixed far off on the empty wall behind us. When he speaks next his voice is soft. "We couldn't stand it. We definitely couldn't let it happen. That's when we came up with a plan. We tapped into a defense we hadn't considered before."

"Fear," Ryan says quietly.

Andy nods. "And what is everyone afraid of?"

"The zombies."

"The Risen are monumentally stupid, something that makes it relatively easy to escape them if you know what you're doing. They can't strategize, they don't have any thought—not beyond eating human flesh. But what if they did? What if they worked together? What if they could plan and plot? What if they were organized killers?"

"They'd be horrifying. No one would be safe from them ever."

"So that's what we became. It didn't take much. We were seen killing an intruder via ingestion one time and the rumors flew. The warnings went out and the attacks slowed. A few more times to drive the point home and the attacks all but stopped. We were monsters but we were safe."

Via ingestion. What a lovely, clinical way to say they gnawed on a person's living, kicking, screaming body until they died one of the most horrible deaths the world has ever known.

I feel bile burning the back of my throat.

"I understand how it's an act of love," Ryan says, "because you did it for your children, but how is it respect?"

Elijah sighs. Whatever he's going to say, he knows we aren't going to like it. "We eat our dead," he tells us gently.

I sit forward and put my face in my hands, breathing deeply. I can't. I can't deal with this place and these people. They are so far beyond insane that they can't even see crazy anymore. It's a pale light beyond the horizon. A star still burning in the sky eons after its last ember has died out.

"Why?" Ryan asks, his voice tight.

"To ingest them is to take them with us. To carry them on in our lives as part of us. They maintain us. They keep us alive and we keep them close to us forever. It's done very ceremoniously. It's not much different than taking communion. Jesus himself said that his body was the bread and his blood the wine. He encouraged people to ingest him into their bodies as a religious rite."

"It's not the same thing at all," I say, my face still in my hands, my voice muffled against my palms.

"It's exactly the same."

"I see Joss' point," Ryan agrees, carefully remaining neutral. "With communion a person ate a Ritz cracker and drank some grape juice. It was symbolic. What you're talking about is… it's pretty different."

"It's sick," I groan. I lift my face, dragging my hands down it roughly. "You're telling me that if a kid's parent dies, you make them *eat them*?"

"No," Elijah says firmly. "Children are not allowed to participate in the burial ceremony until they're eighteen, and then it's their choice. No one is required or forced to do it."

"Burial ceremony," I chuckle to myself. I feel like I'm losing my mind in this place.

"Joss," Trent begins.

"No, uh-uh. Don't tell me to shut up again. I listened. I heard their side and you know what I'm taking away from all of this? They bury their dead in their bowels." I stand abruptly, unable to sit in this room with them anymore. "School is over. I'm done. I'd like to leave now."

"And where will you go?" Elijah asks, his voice hard. "Who will you look for help from now?

Will you try to save your friends in the northern Colony or will you give up and try to forget about them? If that's your plan, you should be asking yourself who the real monster is in this room."

I stare at the floor. I stare at the floor and I try to remember to breathe, but I feel trapped. Trapped by the truth, by these walls, by the cage I've built for myself with my promises and high hopes for a world we all gave up on years ago. That filthy word that lights the way and draws me like a moth to a flame, to my doom, but I can't look away and I can't ignore it. I can't ignore him.

I look at Ryan to find him already watching me and I feel it swell in my chest—hope. The rest of the men in the room are watching us and I feel the weight of the world on my body, crushing me down into powder on the floor. I could stay there. I could become part of the dust and the earth under their feet to never be bothered again. Never be burdened. Never be expected to be something I'm not.

Or I could finish what I started. I could try. I could become something more than the sum of my broken, fragmented parts, and maybe it will never be perfect or beautiful, but it will be me. And it will be strong, because I don't know any other way to be.

I swallow hard as I take a reluctant step forward. "What's the plan?"

Trent slips past me, going to stand next to Andy as though the guy had not just told us that he eats his cousins for Easter dinner.

"We haven't decided yet how exactly we're going to go in," Andy tells us.

"By water?" Ryan suggests.

"It's too obvious," Trent disagrees. "They'll be watching the water for sure. We have to go for something less conspicuous."

"We can't go in on the roads," I tell him. "They have that zombie swarm trapped around their front gates. We'd never get through without being noticed. Or being eaten."

Trent raises his eyebrows. "You made it through."

"Barely," I remind him, holding up my injured arm.

"So if we can't go in by land or sea…" Ryan says suggestively, looking to Elijah.

He nods. "Underground. We don't know that area, but if the tunnels aren't caved in we should be able to make it. We can come in from under the building."

I scowl at the map they're all looking at. It means nothing to me. "What are we going to do? Pop up in a toilet?"

"I know I said you were too skinny," Trent tells me, "but you're not that skinny."

"Why is it that it sounded like an insult when you said I was skinny but it still sounds like an insult when you say I'm not?"

"I'm gifted."

"You're insulting."

"I told you, if you want compliments go to Ryan. I'm no good at them."

"You're not even trying."

Trent shrugs. "It's probably why I'm not good at them."

"You don't want to see him try," Ryan warns me. "It's unnerving."

"When have you seen it?" I ask, surprised.

"Market day."

"A whore, Trent? Really? First of all, gross. Second, you don't have to flirt with them. You just hand them money."

Trent shrugs. "I was shopping for a discount. If you don't haggle you may as well stay home."

"How will we get in from underground?" Ryan asks Elijah.

"A building like that will have a basement. We'll find a way in there. We may have to dig our way in, or we may get lucky and find a large drainage tunnel. We won't know until we get there."

"Then what? Once we're in, where do we go from there?"

All eyes shift to me. I hate the spotlight but I sigh deeply and try to remember the layout. "From the utility room in the basement we have to go upstairs. It opens up into a back hallway full of storage and a mass shower room that they use for cleaning the newbies."

"That's where they took you when you first got there?" Ryan asks, his voice unusually hushed. Controlled.

"Yeah. I was showered, stripped of my weapons, and given very basic, very thin clothing to wear. They used the threat of the cold and the zombies outside to stop us from running."

"But you did anyway," Elijah says. I can't be sure because I don't know him, but I think there's a small amount of respect in his tone.

I avoid his eyes. "I didn't have a choice."

"Why not?"

"How did you manage to escape?" Andy asks harshly.

Him I have no problem looking at. Glaring at. "What does it matter?"

"However you got out, maybe that's a way we can get in."

"It's not. You can't reverse engineer what I did to get out."

"And why not?"

"Because you're not a necromancer," Trent tells him coolly.

Andy smirks slightly. He knows I killed to get out. Psycho thinks we're even now.

"Who'd you kill?" he asks.

"It doesn't matter."

"Was it someone who trusted you?"

"No, she never liked me."

"Surprise, surprise," Andy sings dryly.

I feel my blood boil. "Why are you asking me this anyway? You know how I got out. You were there in that room when I told Marlow all about it."

"I heard what you told Marlow, but who knows if that's the truth. I'm still having a hard time believing Vin willingly handed over that ring to you, or that he had any plans of coming out of that place and going for help. My thinking is, Vin would have gotten out and went home. He would have forgotten about all of you by lunch time."

"That was my thinking too. And his."

"Is that why you killed him?"

"*I didn't kill him*," I say emphatically. My palms are sweating. I'm itching to come at him with my fists to explain to his face what he obviously doesn't understand.

"And we all believe you," Andy tells me calmly, obviously not believing anything about me.

The feeling is mutual.

"I'll send a scout team out immediately," Elijah says, taking control of the room again. "They'll check the tunnels, see what we can do about getting in through the basement. Once they report back we'll have a better idea of when we can make our move. Until then, I recommend we all rest. Andy, you need to return to The Hive before sunrise. Joss, Ryan, Trent, we'll put you up for the night. I don't think it wise you go above ground."

"Is that a suggestion," Ryan asks cautiously, "or a demand?"

"You're not prisoners here," Elijah assures him.

"In that case, I'd like to leave," I say. "I won't sleep here."

"Joss, I think he's right," Ryan warns.

"No."

"I'll walk her there," Trent offers.

"We should stick together."

"Then come home," I beg Ryan. My tone surprises us both.

I can feel my face flushing and my heart racing even though I'm not really sure why. But when Ryan steps forward and takes my hand, I know it's about him.

"All right. We'll go home."

"It's your choice," Elijah says reluctantly. He turns to Andy. "Lead them out through the tunnels. Get them past the stadiums." He eyes us warily. "Will you come back tomorrow night?"

"When?"

"At sunset."

"We'll be here," Ryan promises, stepping forward and offering Elijah the hand that had just held mine.

Elijah shakes it firmly, a small smile on his lips. "Excellent."

Chapter Five

After dragging us through a long labyrinth of tunnels, some I'm pretty sure we doubled back on to confuse us, Andy brings us above ground just outside the stadiums. He did what Elijah told him to do, he got us past them, but he didn't give us much of a buffer. I don't really care. The farther he is from my home, the better. I don't need this guy or anyone from the cannibals or The Hive knowing where I live. Trent and Ryan knowing is enough. Probably more than.

"Well, good luck," Andy tells us, already moving to leave us behind.

Then he stops mid-step, listening. It only takes a second before I hear what stopped him. The shuffling. The groaning.

Ryan and I wordlessly whip around to face the crowd moving in behind us. Happy to have my ASP back (I made a point of getting it from the same guy who took it), I whip it out to its full, deadly length. They're coming from up the street, emerging from the shadows by degrees. Writhing black rising from nothing.

"How many?" I ask Trent and his eerie eyes.

"No more than seven."

I nod confidently. "We can handle this."

"Are you leaving or staying?" Trent asks Andy.

He looks down the street, maybe to confirm Trent's count or to buy time, but for what I don't know. It's an easy question.

"I can't be seen with you," he says tightly.

"Then go."

"I never run from a fight."

"We don't need you," I tell him sharply.

I flex my hand on my weak arm. It hurts less than it did before. I'm starting to wonder if I can use it.

"I should go."

"Then go!" I snap, casting an angry glance over my shoulder.

My eyes meet his and I can see the frustration in them. If he leaves I'll count him a coward even though I understand why he can't stay. He's right— he can't be seen working with us. Especially since Marlow has it out for us right now. I still judge him when he turns to go, though.

"You should lay off him," Ryan tells me.

"Are you serious?"

"We need to work with him."

"It doesn't mean I have to like him."

The first of the zombies is on us. Ryan steps up. I see a flash in the moonlight across his knuckles, lightning quick. The zombie goes down.

Ryan has his Death Punch on.

"You don't have to hate him every second either," he says, shaking his hand out.

I lash out with my ASP, swinging wide and connecting with the skull of what looks like a woman. She drops to the ground but continues to moan: I didn't hit her hard enough.

"I'm not," I grunt out as I smash down on the woman's head, "good—at hiding—my feelings!"

Ryan smoothly sidesteps a zombie before driving home his spiked fist into the base of its skull. I'm green with envy when it drops instantly. I'm sweating from killing one and he's managed two with barely any effort. I love my ASP, but I'm wondering if I don't maybe need a Death Punch too.

"She doesn't like him because he's a liar," Trent says. His voice is coming from the dark farther down the street. I see a blur of movement, a flash of metal, hear a distinct *thump*. I don't know when he moved into the thick of the fight, but he's thinning it quickly. "She doesn't trust him."

"Okay, I get that," Ryan agrees. "But she should take it easy. We don't know who he's lying to."

"That's my point!" I cry. "Is he a spy for the cannibals or The Hive? Or both? Is he playing everybody? I don't like liars."

"It's because you're not good at doing it," Trent says.

He's emerging from the darkness where the zombies had been hiding, only he's alone. I glance around anxiously, looking for the rest of the Risen, but there are none. When I do the math, I'm a little nervous.

"Did you just take down four by yourself in the time it took me to finish one?" I ask him incredulously.

His shadow shrugs at me. "You're injured."

"I'm almost healed."

"You were talking. You were distracted."

"Stop making excuses for me. You're a killing machine, you freak."

"This is why he can't fight in the Arena anymore," Ryan says.

"He's not allowed to?"

"It's not financially beneficial to Marlow, so no," Trent explains. "I'm not invited to."

"Why? Because you're too crazy good?"

"Too efficient," Ryan corrects. "The fight's over before it starts. People go there to see a show. Trent doesn't give it to them."

Trent comes to stand in front of us. Whatever weapon he used is stowed now. Maybe it was just his fists, I don't know. I wouldn't be surprised.

"They tell me to kill zombies, I kill zombies. I don't know how else to do it."

"People want to be afraid you'll die."

"I'm not going to die."

"Someday," I tell him. "We all will someday."

Trent grins down at me. "Sometimes I forget."

"We should get moving," Ryan reminds us.

We make our way through the dark streets that are growing lighter every minute. Even though it hasn't been the longest night of my life, not by far, it has been one of the strangest. The closer we get to my building, the more anxious I am to get inside. I want to lie down on my bed and fall asleep in the familiar smells, sounds, and feels of my own home. I try to figure out how long it's been since I slept there, but the best I can remember is that it's been days. Too many days with too much time spent surrounded by people I can't stand. In the last month I've been exposed to almost the entire wild, to every person I spent the last six years hiding from and a few I didn't even know about, and my little reclusive heart can't take it. Ryan promised we'd go back to the cannibals' tomorrow night and I know we have to, but a big part of me wants to tell them to suck it. We'll find another way. Only there is no other way and I know that.

When my building looms gray in the distance against the lightening sky, I run to it. I can't help it. Without a word I break into a sprint, leaving the boys behind. They'll be fine. They don't need me. No one ever has.

I'm surprised when I hear their footsteps pounding close behind me.

We burst through the doors, up the stairs, and they're on my heels now. I can both hear them and feel them. Ryan laughs loudly, his voice bouncing around the walls and against my face until I'm smiling as I run, breathless and crazy, bounding up the stairs two at a time. I hear them scuffle behind me. They're fighting. Racing. And I'm winning.

When I stumble through the door to my loft, panting for breath and nearly giggling, I don't know myself anymore. I don't know this girl with the breathy laugh and the Lost Boys behind her. I don't know her at all, but I think I like her.

"Trent, you can—"

"I'm sleeping on the roof," he interrupts. He's barely out of breath. Robot freak! "Do you have a spare blanket?"

I point to my pile of cloth on the floor, the one I pretend is a bed. Since sleeping on a real mattress, I'm a little ashamed of the lie I tell myself every night. I wonder if I'm spoiled now. Maybe I'm the princess Taylor accused me of being, but if I am it's his fault. Real mattresses with real clean sheets? It's just mean.

"So no," Trent says. "That's fine. I'll be all right. Goodnight."

"Wait, you can take one! I have a couple sleeping bags!" I call after him.

He's already heading toward the roof hatch.

I turn to Ryan for help. "He doesn't have to sleep up there."

"He likes it."

"No."

"I do," Trent's disembodied voice calls from the hatch.

It snaps sharply shut behind him.

"He does it all the time in the Hyperion," Ryan explains. "He seriously does like it. He doesn't like walls. He gets cagey. He also doesn't get cold much, so don't sweat the blanket for him—but I'll take one."

"You get cold easily?"

"I'm a dainty flower. Also, it's drafty by the door."

I watch him walk to my 'bed' and pick up a thin, threadbare blanket. It's yellow. I don't know why that makes it sadder to me, but it does.

"You don't have to sleep by the door," I tell him faintly.

He turns slowly, looking at me with his large, golden eyes that see too much. "Where would I sleep?"

"Don't."

"Don't what?"

"Don't make it harder for me than it already is."

He grins slightly, but then he nods. "Okay. Sorry. And yeah, if you're okay with it, I'll sleep next to you. I wasn't sure you'd want to now that we're here."

I smile. "You mean now that we're out of prison?"

"Is it weird that I don't feel any freer now that we're out?"

"Is it weird that I felt better in the Vashons' prison than I did as a guest at the cannibals' table?"

"You really hate them."

I roll my eyes. "And you don't? They're disgusting."

"They're different," he replies diplomatically.

"The bad kind, not the interesting kind. Except to Trent. He seemed *fascinated*," I say sarcastically.

Ryan goes to the door to drop the security bar across it, locking us in for the night.

"Better to act fascinated than disgusted if we're going to work with them. I don't like the way Andy was looking at you."

I nod in agreement. "He'll kill me if he gets the chance."

"See, I don't feel like that worries you as much

as it should."

"Eh, I've made it this far. Trick is to never trust anyone. Never let your guard down."

He sits down by the bed and begins unlacing his shoes. "Are you going to sleep with your knife on your hip?"

"I'd be stupid not to."

"Should I be worried I'll wake up with it in my gut the way I woke up to your elbow in my face?"

I wince, remembering the damage I did to him on Vashon Island. It's reflex, I can't control it! But I do feel bad about it.

"Maybe," I reply weakly.

Ryan chuckles. "I'll take my chances. I'll keep my knife on me too, just so we're even. Just in case you get handsy."

"I won't."

"Not even a little? I'll pretend not to notice."

"Maybe you should sleep by the door after all," I grumble, heading for the bathroom.

"Come on, I'm kidding!"

I don't answer. I do my business slowly, freaked out by the strange feeling of not being freaked out. Trent is on my roof and Ryan is in my bed, and that's okay. I'm eerily fine with that. Not even just fine. I'm… happy.

When I come back out I find Ryan lounging on my bed. He smiles up at me, golden brown from hair to eyes to skin, and there's so much of that amber glow that it's stupid. He's ridiculously beautiful to the point of being annoying, but I still like it.

I plop down across from him. "So we're siding

with the psychos, aren't we?"

He sits up slowly, his arms coming to rest on his legs and his hands held loosely together. "We don't have another choice."

"I don't like it."

"No one does, and that's your problem: you think because we're willing to work with them that we like them. I don't. They freak me out but we need their help, and if we were seriously willing to do business with The Hive, we're desperate enough to do business with these guys."

"I don't know about that."

"Joss," he says emphatically, "we're pretty freaking desperate here. Do you want to free your friends or not?"

"They're not really friends," I reply weakly.

"They were a few days ago."

"A lot has changed since then."

"Enough to make you change your mind about saving them?"

I bite my lip, worrying it between my teeth as I stare at his face. "You died," I say quietly.

His expression softens. "Not completely."

"Close enough.'

"It doesn't change anything."

"It does for me."

His mouth tightens slightly. "What are you saying? You don't want to try to save someone, basically everyone, because I got hurt?"

His voice is becoming agitated. He's annoyed with me.

"How's your shoulder?" I ask pointedly, feeling just as annoyed.

I still worry about that injury on him. I still wonder if he'll get a fever someday soon and I'll have to end him. It's another reason I avoided people for as long as I did: it wasn't just because I got sick of watching them die—I got sick of being the one to beat down their reanimated corpses.

"It's fine. I'm always getting hurt, Joss. I got hurt before I met you and I'll get hurt again in the future. So will Trent. So will you. Look at your arm. You think that doesn't kill me to see every day? But you can't let that stop you from doing what's right. This isn't just about the people in the MOHAI. This is about everyone. Everyone trapped in the Colonies, everyone living in the wild afraid of the roundups."

I clench my hands together tightly, feeling my chest pinch and my skin go clammy. "You're wo—" I try, but the words die on my tongue. It's just too... much. It's all too much. I stare down at my hands, finding the words easier when I'm not looking at his face. "You're worth more to me than everyone else on the earth combined."

He doesn't answer. The room feels tight in the confines of pure silence. I keep my eyes fixed on the growing sunlight flickering over the skin on my hands, the scars and scrapes highlighted in deep shadows until my own flesh looks foreign and strange. I feel different. I feel afraid of my own body, unfamiliar in my own skin. I feel like I'm becoming something or someone I'm not sure I know how to be.

Ryan moves. He's on his knees in front of me, his face hovering over mine and his eyes filling my vision. He's all I can see, all I can hear, and the room suddenly feels like it doesn't exist. Nothing exists beyond his face and the places where his skin touches mine. His hands are warm and dry on my arms, my shoulders, my neck, my chin. He pulls me toward him until my lips meet his and my eyes fall closed. I forget how to breathe, so he breathes for me. In and out, slow and even with the beat of his heart. I can feel it under my hand where I've rested my palm on his chest.

Thump-thump…thump-thump…thump-

It skips a beat when I rise up on my knees in front of him, my body coming in line with his. He freezes, inside and out, just for a second. Then his heart is racing, taking mine with it, and his tongue brushes across my lips as his hands lower to my waist. He pulls me against him until I can't feel his heartbeat under my hand anymore. I feel it everywhere—I feel *him* everywhere—and it's so thrilling and so claustrophobic I want to scream. I want to pull him to me until it hurts and I want to push him away so I can run down the halls until I find stairs up and out, into the air where I can breathe. Where I can find the shadows to hide inside that will keep me safe from everything I'm so afraid of. I fight with myself to stay put, to hold onto him, to find out how much I can take, while my instincts are telling me to run—that there's more to fear in this world than zombies, cannibals, Colonists, and gangs.

Suddenly I'm under the boat again, with no breath and my heart in my throat. I'm in the water and he's drowning. I can't save him. He's slipping from my fingers. I keep going under for him but I can't get him free and Trent isn't there to help me and Ryan is fading. His heart is failing as I'm failing him. He's dying. He's gone. It's so real I can hear the water lapping against the hull of the boat. I can see the bubbles against my eyelids as they get smaller, fewer. As they burst against the surface, his life leaving him in tiny increments that I'm powerless to stop.

His pale face in the darkness. My heart slowing with his, confused and lost. Uncertain where to go without him. It aches in my chest and I know.

I love him.

I love him and I will lose him.

I pull my mouth from his and clamp it shut tightly, worried he'll hear the sob begging to escape. I hug him to me, clinging to him in a way I haven't done since the night in The Hive when I was so relieved he was alive I lost my mind and threw my body against his. He holds onto me, his breath uneven in my ear and his hands splayed out on my back.

"If I say it," he whispers, "will you run away from me?"

I know what he's asking. I know what he's thinking about saying because it's exactly the same thing I'm thinking right now. It's the same thing that's scaring the crap out of me and making me an emotional mess that could fall apart at any second. It's a dangerous thing to think or feel, but it's even more toxic to say. It's a truth that I can't handle— not yet, maybe never. It's one more thing that will change the way I look at the world and live my life and it could be the last thing—the big final thing—that gets me killed. Or worse: it could kill him.

"Yes."

He sighs, his hands moving slowly up and down my back. "Joss, I—"

"I said I'll run," I interrupt, my voice firm as my fingers clench his shirt in tight fistfuls of anxiety. "I will go full Olympic sprinter on you. Road Runner style. I will burst through the wall like the Kool-Aid Man to get away."

He chuckles. "Okay, okay. I wasn't going to say it. Calm down."

"I can't, Ryan. You can't say it. Please don't say it."

"I don't need to say it because you obviously know it."

I press my forehead against his shoulder, hiding my face in the crook of his neck.

"And I know it too," he breathes, his voice deep in my ear.

In my blood.

"We'll side with the psychos," he whispers against my skin, "we'll free your friends, we'll take down the stadiums, we'll destroy the Colony in the south, we'll dethrone the guy pulling all the strings, and then..."

"Then what?"

I feel his hand running over my hair, smoothing it along my neck. His fingers brush my skin. "We'll be free then—all of us. Isn't that enough?"

"No."

He chuckles softly. "What else is there, Joss?"

I lift my head, look in his eyes. Then I kiss him.

I kiss him like I'm losing him, because I feel like I am—and even though that's crazy, even though we're closer right now than we've ever been, I still feel it. I have a sick, sinking feeling that he's a punishment. He's a promise dangled in front of me only to be ripped away; I just don't know when yet. I've never wanted anything the way I want him. I've never needed anything this way. He's my weakness, my soft spot, and I love him and I want him but I fear him and I hate him. I should run. I should get away before I've fallen too far and it's too late to turn back, but I think I passed the point of no return a long time ago.

Win or lose, live or die, I'm with him all the way.

Chapter Six

Twelve hours later, as the sun is disappearing behind the ragged Seattle skyline, I find myself once again going down the rabbit hole. We aren't sure exactly how we're going to meet up with the cannibals again, so we go to where Andy brought us above ground and hope for the best. What we get is an entourage. Six cannibals are waiting for us and it feels creepily similar to the first time they took us underground just last night. A lot has changed since then. I see them differently now. I understand they aren't bloodthirsty vampires luring us to their lair to suck the marrow from our bones, but it doesn't mean slipping down into that dark unknown isn't still a little freaky.

I assume that we're going to be led back to the main chamber where the cannibals all live to get another lesson in eating your loved ones, but instead we're immediately taken in the opposite direction. Even underground, I know where we're headed.

North.

"So this is really happening, isn't it?" I mutter.

"Looks like it," Ryan replies. He looks at me sideways as we slosh through the two inches of standing water in this tunnel. At least I hope it's only water. "Are you ready?"

"As I'll ever be, I guess."

"Are you worried?"

"About what?"

"About going back."

How does he do that? How the hell does he know I'm nervously chewing the inside of my cheek raw at the thought of going inside the MOHAI again?

"Maybe," I admit reluctantly.

"I don't blame you."

"Are you worried?"

"Yep."

"About what?"

"Getting this close to a Colony. You spend all your time avoiding them, it feels pretty stupid walking right into one."

I can't stop the chuckle that escapes my lips and echoes through the tunnel. Ryan smiles down at me.

"What's funny?"

"I think I'm relieved."

"Relieved you're not the only one who thinks this is stupid?"

"Bingo."

"For what it's worth," Trent chimes in behind me, "I think it's stupid too."

"That's pretty comforting actually," Ryan says.

I shake my head. "So if we all think it's so

stupid, why are we doing it?"

"Because," Elijah's voice breaks out from ahead of us in the darkness, "something so idiotic could never be predicted."

"Are we crawling in through the toilets?"

Elijah comes fully into view, the light from a torch lit behind him giving a grim line to his face. He's smiling. "Like little baby crocodiles," he says happily.

"We can't go in through the basement," another guy says, all business and stern stares. Oddly enough, I kind of like him. "There's no clean way to get in quietly. The walls are too thick—we'd have to blast and there goes our cover. But we lucked out. There's a drain. One nearly the size of a manhole. We'll remove it, climb up and in. It's that easy."

"What kind of drain is that room in?" I ask, feeling sweat break out on my neck under my hair.

"A large shower room."

"Ugh," I gag, feeling surprisingly sick.

Flashes of the first day at the Colony flip through my mind: the creepy thorough cleansing I got, the rough scrub of exfoliates, the smell of the harsh soaps, the lice shampoos, the bitter smell of bleach on the floors and the walls.

Caroline.

I feel Ryan's hand on my elbow. "What's wrong?"

"Nothing," I reply, pulling it together. "It's not my favorite room is all."

His grip tightens gently before he releases me.

"You'll go in with my people," Elijah tells us,

gesturing to the sixteen men and women he's brought with him. It's not the twenty he promised, but if you throw our three into the mix it's close enough. "You'll hold back, wait in the shower room. They'll do a sweep. They'll take control of the building. When it's done, when it's safe, they'll bring you out in the open."

"Why aren't we going up with them?" I ask irritably. "Shouldn't I be front and center in the fight where the Colonists can see me? I thought that was the whole point."

"You're too valuable to risk. Containment first. You're there for negotiations, not fighting."

"Ugh," I groan again.

Elijah sighs with annoyance. "Something else bothering you?"

"No," I lie.

"Will you wear that sour expression when they see you or do you think you can manage to look at least a little bit more pleasant?"

"If I did, they wouldn't recognize me."

Some of the cannibals exchange uneasy glances. I'm losing what little faith we've somehow managed to gain from them.

"Ryan will do the talking," I assure Elijah. "I'll be quiet."

"Silent would be better," someone mutters in the darkness.

"It'll be fine," Ryan promises them.

We head off down the tunnels after that, parting ways with Elijah. He's headed back home to tell his people how perfectly this plan will go. How in sync we all are and how excited he is for the future.

They'll buy his lies, gobbling them up like sweet meat treats, because he's a good leader and his words can cover up the scary truth that is me.

"Where have you been?"

I scowl to my left. One of the cannibals has crept up beside me, somehow quiet even walking in the water. His face is pale and bright against the dark interior of the tunnel. It sticks out sharply above his black clothing, making it look like his head is floating six feet above the ground. He's looking down at me with dark eyes and a small smile that gives me chills.

"What do you mean?"

His smile broadens. "I mean, where have you been hiding?"

"With the Westies," I lie, grabbing the first gang name out of the air that I can think of.

"No, no, no," the man sings quietly, shaking his head. "You don't look like a whore. You don't talk like a whore, and you definitely don't walk like a whore. You weren't with the Westies."

"How do you know I wasn't someone's private pet?"

His answer is a long hard stare. He doesn't blink.

"I was alone," I finally admit reluctantly.

I look away and pick up the pace. Ryan is a few feet ahead of me, talking quietly with one of Elijah's men. I'll feel better when I close that gap.

"Really? How did a small thing like you make it out there alone?"

I shrivel inside when he matches my pace easily, his long legs striding through the water that I feel like I'm thrashing through. He has a hulking grace that's seriously annoying, and the way he talks... it's weird. His tone is too even, the cadence of his voice almost a constant sing-song.

"I managed."

"All alone," he muses. "It's exciting, isn't it?"

"Too bad it's over," Trent says. I glance over my shoulder, surprised to find him walking directly behind me. He's watching the tall cannibal with dark interest. "She's joined the Hyperion. She's no longer living alone."

The tall creeper doesn't acknowledge Trent. I feel his eyes still on me. "How lucky for everyone."

Trent pushes against my lower back firmly. I stumble forward a little but I turn the trip into a jog. It only takes a second before I'm walking beside Ryan again.

"—dark in the basement. We couldn't make out much through the crack in the wall," the young cannibal is telling Ryan.

"Is that why you decided we couldn't go in that way?"

"That and the walls were too thick. Making that one crack to look through took forever and it was way louder than we planned. Once we could see in, we couldn't see enough. Couldn't get a read on how many were working down there."

"Two," I tell him.

He looks me up and down quickly, seeming surprised to see me show up all of a sudden. "You know that for sure?"

"I know that's how many used to be working in that room. Now I don't know for sure."

"They could have strengthened the watch on the place since you left," Ryan tells me. "I know I would have."

"So you're the one who got out?" the kid asks me.

He's shorter than Ryan—younger, too—with the cannibal pale skin and gleaming eyes they all have. His dark black hair looks glossy like ink in the torchlight.

"Yeah, that's me," I admit, feeling weird.

For a hermit, I've got a lot of notoriety going on. I liked it better when I was a ghost.

"You're lucky. My sister was taken. She never came out."

"I'm sorry, man," Ryan tells him.

The words come from his mouth so easily, so earnestly. Even if I'd said the exact same thing, I doubt it would have sounded half as genuine as Ryan. Not because I don't mean it, because I really am sorry. That sucks, there's no doubt about it. It's because I'm awkward as hell and it taints everything I do. Trent is right about me: I don't like liars because I'm no good at lying. I don't understand how to do it, so how can I ever hope to spot it when other people do it?

"I'm sorry," I mutter.

"Thanks, but we've all lost someone, right?" the kid replies nonchalantly. "At least I know she's probably alive. That's better than most people get."

"Quiet," someone whispers from up ahead.

Everyone stops to listen. My hand flexes around my ASP and I become painfully aware of the bodies around me. If zombies are in these tunnels, I don't think I have the eyesight to tell the difference between a living and a dead—not in the split second you get to make that kind of choice. Plus, I don't care for how close the tall creeper is. It feels like he's hovering.

Once the water noises are dead and the only thing I hear inside the tunnels is the gentle sound of living people breathing, I can hear the outside. There's a manhole not far ahead of us. Dripping down in through the small holes punched through the weathered steel are the moans and groans of a true horde. Suddenly it all comes flooding back to me—the night I escaped. The night I ran through their ranks, blind and freezing in the disorienting dark. My heart starts to hammer but I keep my breathing even. I make sure no one knows.

It's been over a year for most of us since we heard that sound. Lately the zombie pop has been dwindled down so far you don't come across large groups anymore. Just stragglers. Loners like me. But out here, close to the MOHAI where they've herded the dead, you can get a reminder of the old days. It's the new nostalgia. No more 'Remember when we had hot meals every night?' or 'Warm showers with soap and water every day? Crazy!' No, now remembering is horrifying. 'Remember when you couldn't walk down the street without being swarmed? Remember when you saw someone die violently every single day? When people were screaming in the dark? Remember when the streets were red with blood and even the Seattle rain couldn't wash it away?'

Those days are coming back again. I would

trade every hot meal, every warm shower I've ever had or even dreamed of, to keep those days away.

"It's the barrier around the gate," I whisper. "We're close."

A few heads bob in agreement. We're about to go inside the walls. It won't be long until we're at the building, and it suddenly bothers me more than I'd like to admit that I'm not going in all the way with them. I don't know what their version of taking control of the building looks like, but I worry it's more violent than it needs to be. They don't know what it's like in there, how many of the people inside aren't actual Colonist supporters. That doesn't mean they won't fight to save their lives if an unknown enemy bursts inside in the dead of night, though.

The group starts to move again.

"Wait," I say, stepping forward and talking too loudly.

Everyone looks at me sharply.

"Keep your voice down," a woman tells me.

"You can't kill anyone."

"What are you talking about?"

"This isn't a 7-Eleven. You can't go in there and start snacking on everyone. No one dies."

The woman looks at me in disgust, and that is so messed up it's almost funny to me—because yeah, I'm the disgusting one.

"They're Colonists," she spits out.

"They're prisoners. They're victims of the roundups. Most of them don't want to be here. They've been separated from their families and I guarantee that *you* are some of those families."

"Our orders are to take the Colony."

"And we'll do that. Peacefully."

"You can't be serious," a guy says incredulously. "Nothing is done 'peacefully' anymore."

"And that's why we're almost extinct. No killing, and he," I say emphatically, pointing to my creeper still staring at me, "doesn't even go inside."

"Bryan?" the guys asks. "Why? He's one of our best fighters—that's why he's here."

"I don't like him. He doesn't go in."

"He goes in. We need him."

"As much as you need me?"

The guy gives an exaggerated sigh before he exchanges a quick look with the woman. "What do you think, Macy?"

"I don't know," she says uncertainly. She looks angry, but in the end she shakes her head tightly.

"Fine," the guy says reluctantly, turning back to me. "Bryan will watch the tunnel."

"And no killing."

"If they attack us—"

"If one person dies, I'm out. I'm on their side."

Macy throws her hands up in frustration. "This is ridiculous, Kyle."

"This is how it is," I tell her. "Take it or leave it."

"Maybe we'll take this place and leave you behind."

I start to back away slowly, putting my hands up in a gesture of 'go ahead.'

"Stop," Kyle tells Macy and I irritably. "We've come this far. We're not turning back and we need her. At least for a little while longer."

"Let me know when we're done with her," Macy says darkly.

"Deal."

"You'll have to get in line," I tell her with a smile. "Andy has called dibs on killing me."

"He gets to have all the fun."

"Not too late to back out on this," Ryan warns me quietly, watching the pair openly threatening my life.

"You heard them," I tell him, spinning my closed ASP in my hand. "We've come too far to turn back now."

It's actually comforting to know pretty much everyone wants to kill me. It's what I'm used to. Picking and choosing between my enemies and my friends—that's exhausting. One miscalculation can get me killed with my guard down like an idiot. But this, knowing everyone wants to see me die, that's an equation I can understand.

It's easily half an hour later when we finally stop. The cannibals are a well-oiled machine, leaping into action without a single word or sound. They form a three-person human ladder to get underneath a large drain—one I can only assume is the drain in the center of the shower room. The rock around it in the ceiling of the tunnel has been roughly chipped away, leaving jagged edges around the gaping hole. I watch in amazement as the person on top of the people ladder, the young guy Ryan and I had been talking to, makes quick work of the drain. I hear it pop up and clatter quietly to the floor in under a minute.

After hoisting himself inside, the young kid leans over the hole and helps pull me up with him. Once I'm in, I'm sick to my stomach. It's damp in here. They used this room tonight. Whether it was on newbies or the weekly member showers, I don't know.

Ryan and Trent come up next, followed by the rest of the cannibals. Everyone but Bryan. Even with the cement floor between us, I still feel like that dude is too close.

I play the obedient princess when Kyle and Macy give me stern eyes and signal us to wait in the showers. Ryan and Trent fall in beside me and I feel even weirder with them standing like knights at my side. When did I get valuable? Since when do I matter so much to so many people?

We watch as the cannibals slip out of the room, silent as the shadow of nothing and gliding on air. They think they're not fighters, and maybe in the beginning they weren't, but they're pretty freaking ninja now.

There's nothing but silence for a long time. I count it out, listening to my heart, and I think it's about twenty minutes before one of the boys breaks the silence.

"This place is big," Ryan mutters beside me. His eyes are roaming over the room, taking in the shelving with the clean towels and the closed cupboards that I know are stocked full of the best soap I've seen in ages, the ones you don't get to touch until after your 'cleanse.'

"You've only seen one room."

"And it's big. What about the rest of the

place?"

I shift on my feet. "It's big."

"Called it."

"There's an airplane inside. A fake tree. A foot car."

"What's a foot car?"

I shrug. "It's a pink car shaped like a foot. They told me it's a toe truck, then they laughed. I didn't get it."

"I don't either."

We both look at Trent. He's not listening.

"How long are we waiting?" he asks, staring at the darkened doorway.

"Until they come get us. That's the plan."

"Are we sticking to that?"

I glance down at the hole in the center of the room and I wonder if Bryan can hear us. I'm guessing yes. Yes, he can.

"I don't want to," I admit.

"Then why are we doing it?"

"Just because I don't want to do something, it doesn't mean it's not the right thing to do."

"It usually means it *is* the right thing," Ryan says.

I look at him sharply. "What does that mean?"

"I didn't mean it about you specifically. I meant in general—screw it, you'll be mad no matter what. Let's just move on."

"With me mad?"

"I'm learning to live with it."

"I personally like it," Trent tells me with a smile.

"Lucky you," Ryan grumbles.

I fully turn on him. "And what does *that* mean?"

"It means we're wasting time. What's the plan?"

"We wait here."

"That's their plan. What's our plan?"

"We don't have a plan. We never do. We just kind of do things and see where that takes us. So far, it's made us more enemies than I can count and landed us almost dead a few times, so maybe we should follow their plan and wait here."

There's a commotion from upstairs. A crash, a shout, the sound of furniture being shoved across the floor. The cannibals could be fighting the Team Leaders—the Melanies and the Carolines that I didn't kill—and that would be good. That would be what they're here for.

Or they could be fighting the innocents. The women from the sewing room. The guys from the barns. The girls from the greenhouse. The kitchen crew. The workers. The stolen. Nats. Vin.

I break into a sprint, tearing through the doorway toward the stairs. It's dark in here—too dark, more so than I've ever seen it, but I'm used to the dark. I hear Trent and Ryan behind me just like they were when we ran to my building. When we were laughing and I had fun and felt so free.

I bound up the back stairs to head straight for the dining area, where I'm pretty sure the noise is coming from. As we get closer, I hear plastic clatter to the floor and then another shout rings out. It's a woman. I run harder, bursting through the door and running right into someone's back.

We both go down. I hit the cement floor on my shoulder, my body weight landing on my injured arm. Suddenly I'm seeing stars. I think I even cry out. I don't know who I ran into but they're up off the ground instantly and towering over me as I clutch my throbbing arm. They raise their own arm, a long, dark thickness extending off of it that could be a bat or a rolling pin. Either way, they're planning to bring it down on my face. I use my legs to sweep theirs; it's easy on this slick floor. They go down again and this time they stay there for a second, groaning. I don't give them a chance to recover. Quickly, I rise up on my knees and come down on their face with my fist.

A warm spurt of liquid on my hand tells me I've broken their nose. Their pained scream tells me they're not getting back up right now.

Ryan and Trent run in, do a quick survey of the situation, then jump over me and my fallen enemy to go deeper into the room where the fight is still going on. I roll up onto my knees just in time to see a fistfight come to an end. Ryan pulls one figure off another, spins him around, and drops him to the ground on his stomach. I hear an "oof," the rushing of air leaving their lungs, then coughing. Trent has taken hold of the other figure and pinned his arm behind him until he dropped to his knees. I can hear him groaning against the pain he must be feeling in his shoulder. I'm praying Trent doesn't dislocate the guy's arm, because I'm not good with joint injuries. If I hear that distinct *pop,* I might vomit.

Instead, I hear a snap from the hallway. I spin around, my hand forgetting that it's hurt and gripping my knife secured to my hip. My other hand clenches around my ASP, still coiled and small against my body, begging to come out and play.

Bright, unnatural light pours in from the hallway, highlighting three tall figures standing there. They don't move for the longest time—too long to be comfortable. No one speaks. I barely breathe. I'm bathed in the light, blinded by the glare, and I can feel it from the tension in the air that the person looking at me knows me. But whether that's good or bad is still up for debate. If this is one of Caroline's friends, I'm dead and I know it.

When one of the figures moves, I'm wound so tightly I almost weep. He steps into the doorway, light spilling in from behind him, blotting out his features. There's no way to tell who it is. No way to recognize him beyond his build and the way he moves, but that's all I need. I know it in an instant. I know it in the way my stomach bottoms out, my heart screams in my chest, and the greatest sense of relief I've felt since Ryan opened his eyes in the water under that boat courses through my veins.

When he speaks, his voice deep, vibrant, and alive, I can't hide the smile on my face.

"'Bout fuckin' time, Kitten."

Chapter Seven

"Vin."

"Where the hell have you been, huh?"

My smile drops into a scowl. "What do you mean 'where have I been'? I've been out in the wild busting my butt to bring back help!"

"Took you long enough to come back."

"At least I came back," I snap hotly. "You'd be sitting in The Hive right now laughing it up with Marlow and pretending this place never existed."

"Which is what you should be doing. Did you even go to Marlow? Who are these people you brought into my house?"

I stand up sharply. "*Your house?!* Have you gone native?"

I see the shadow of Vin shake his head in frustration. He gestures to one of the figures still hovering in the doorway. "Hit the rest of the lights, would you?"

The dining room lights snap on, making me blink rapidly, trying to adjust. The room is a mess, with tables knocked over, chairs shoved across the room, plastic plates scattered everywhere. But there's no blood. Well, yeah, okay, there's a little blood from where I broke someone's face, but there's no mortal wound amount of blood and that's what matters. I don't recognize the guy that Trent is holding onto, but Ryan has taken down one of the cannibals that came in with us. The person on the ground at my feet, however, is very familiar. So is the busted up shape of her face.

"Hey, Lexy," I tell her wryly. "Long time no see."

She presses the back of her hand to her bleeding nose. "Good to see you're still a bitch."

"Good to see you still can't fight."

I turn back to Vin, surprised to find him with short hair again. It had almost grown out the last time I saw him. He almost looked like a Lost Boy. Now he looks like a... well, a Colonist.

"What's going on with you? What do you mean, 'your house'?"

"I run this place."

"No."

"Yes."

"No."

He grins. "Yes. What happened with Caroline kicked off a fight. By the end of that night everyone had heard that she was dead and I was as good as. Things were tense after that. Three days later someone snuck in. They tried to kill me."

"Who?"

"The Leaders, who else?"

"No, who specifically tried to kill you?"

79

His eyes go cold, dark. "Breanne."

I nod slowly. "She's dead, isn't she?"

"She knew better."

"She should have, yeah."

"All right, I answered you, now you answer me. These people aren't Hive, so who are they? Pikes?"

"No. They're cannibals."

I'm surprised when he laughs long and hard. "Are you serious?"

"Yeah," I reply hesitantly.

"Wow, Kitten. I don't know what I expected, but it wasn't that."

"Did they hurt anyone?"

"No."

"Did you hurt them?"

"Would it bother you if we did?"

Maybe. "No."

"Hmm," he hums, not believing me. "They're fine. Caged, but fine. My guys took them down easily."

"What guys? Since when is there anyone here willing to fight?"

"Since always. They were just looking for someone to follow. I found another Hive member after you left. Couple of Westies. They had just brought in those Elevens before you bailed. You were worried they were your boy..." His voice trails off as he looks over my head to Trent and Ryan behind me. His face lights up. "Ryan Hyperion? Are you kidding me? That's your man, isn't it?"

"Stop," I mutter, knowing it's useless.

He steps around me to go to Ryan and Trent. I'm surprised when he offers his hand to Ryan, then pulls him into a half embrace.

"Good to see you, man. I've watched you fight in the Arena. Your brother, too. That guy made me a lot of scratch. I'm sorry about what happened to him."

Ryan nods, his expression guarded. "Thanks."

"So you're the guy Kitten is all hot and bothered over? Nice."

I groan, letting my head fall back until I'm staring at the ceiling. "Why do you have to make everything sound dirty?"

"Speaking of," he says, turning back to me. I meet his gaze as he looks me over slowly, then whistles softly. "You're still a Benjamin, Kitten. I'm a little less impressed with Hyperion here. Or disappointed, depending."

"Depending on what?"

His response is a sly grin.

I want to punch him, but what I feel the most, what knocks the angry hot wind out of my sails, is the fact that I also want to hug him. I hadn't realized it until now, but I've missed him. He's obnoxious, he's frustrating, he's rude, he's cocky—but he's Vin, and for some strange reason, I like him. Probably for the same reason I like Ryan and Trent. They're honest. Annoying as Vin may be, he owns it. He is what he is and he's not at all sorry.

"So you're the King now, huh? The new Marlow?"

He shakes his head, his face falling serious. "No. I'm more like the president."

"I don't remember enough about life before the fall to know the difference."

"A king is unchecked power," Trent tells me. "He can pretty much do what he wants. A president answers to the people. Supposedly."

"Why supposedly?"

"Depends on if he's dirty."

I look Vin up and down. "This one is dirty."

He smiles at me as he closes the gap between us. "Not as much as I thought I'd be."

"But a little more than they'd like you to be."

"They who?"

"The people."

"Nah, the people love me."

"What about Marlow?" Ryan asks.

Vin doesn't flinch. He also doesn't turn to look at Ryan. He stares at me, his eyes intense and strange. He looks almost angry. "Marlow loves me too," he purrs.

I narrow my eyes at him, not buying the everything-is-cookies-and-cream act. "Sounds like everybody loves you," I reply quietly.

He nods in silent agreement.

"But will they still love when you won't give them what they want?"

"And who am I denying in this scenario?"

"That's kind of my point."

"Ask what you're asking."

"You know what I'm asking. You know what I'm *saying*. These people want to be free. Marlow wants both them and the building. You can't please everybody, so who will you make angry? Who isn't going to love you in the morning, Vin?"

He leans in close, his breath hot on my face. He smells like candy—like sugar and sweetness, which is just about the weirdest thing ever, but that's not what worries me. It's his eyes and his words. They're both hard and cold, like ice. "Same as always," he whispers against my skin. "Whoever I screw."

***

"Your pimp is going to screw us," Trent tells me.

We're standing in a small office tucked in the back of the building. Vin has taken it over, putting all of the wasted equipment in the corner—things like filing cabinets, telephones, computers, and inspirational posters telling us to hang in there and be determined to succeed. Thanks, random guy in a stiff-looking suit. I'll be sure to keep in mind your advice the next time I'm cornered in the dark by flesh-devouring dead.

The cannibals have all been captured and put on lockdown somewhere in the building. I'm not sure what Vin has planned for them and I want to say I don't care, but I do. I told the cannibals not to hurt any of the Colonists, and now that we're on the flip side of that, my anxiety is still there. I guess I don't want bloodshed of any kind, a fact that's pretty surprising to me. Ask me a few months ago if I cared whose blood was on whose hands and I would have told you that I hope they all kill each other and leave me alone forever. But now here I stand in a building filled with cannibals, Colonists,

Hive members, and Lost Boys, and suddenly I've lost my edge.

"Yeah, I know," I mutter.

"Don't call him her pimp," Ryan snaps at Trent. "He's *a* pimp, not *her* pimp."

I glance at Ryan, surprised by his tone. "What's your deal?"

"Nothing."

"It's something."

"He's jealous," Trent says.

Ryan shakes his head in disgust. "Dammit, man."

"What are you jealous of?" I ask, completely confused.

"He's jealous of Vin."

"Trent, seriously, shut up," Ryan barks.

I frown at him. "Why are you so angry?"

"I'm not angry."

"He's jealous," Trent repeats.

I touch Trent's arm, hoping he'll get the hint to shut his mouth for two seconds. "Why are you jealous of Vin?"

"I'm not."

"He—"

I slap Trent's arm hard. He finally gets the hint.

"I'm not jealous, all right?" Ryan tells me. "Or maybe I kind of am. It doesn't matter."

"It does to me."

"He was obviously happy to see you."

"Because I brought help."

"That's not why he was happy to see you. And there's all that Benjamin talk and the way he looks at you."

"He's a pimp. It's what he does."

"I want him to stop."

"He never will."

"Then I'll never like this guy."

"You and nearly everyone else left alive. He's not very likeable."

"You like him," Trent points out.

I close my eyes, wishing I could slap him again. "I do, yeah."

"Why?" Ryan asks.

"Because he's my friend," I say weakly, feeling small talking about this. I'm exposing a chink in my armor. They already know I care about them; now there's this Vin crap on top of it. If they find out I'm stressing over the welfare of a room full of cannibals they'll probably take me out back and shoot me in the head because this pony has gone lame.

"A friend who's going to screw us," Trent points out.

"Maybe."

"And you still like him?" Ryan asks, amazed and annoyed.

I shrug, feeling uncomfortable. "It's hard to explain."

"If you have to choose sides, him or—"

"You," I say firmly, looking him dead in the eye. "I will choose you. No question."

Ryan grins slightly, almost grudgingly. "That's not what I was going to ask."

"Oh. What were you going to ask?"

"Him or the cannibals?"

"You. Still you. Whatever side you're on, that's

where I am."

"Even if I side against him?"

I chuckle. "I assume you will. Look, I'm not good at reading people or dealing with people. I also don't have that selfless thing going that you do, so you're my moral compass. I'll follow you wherever you tell me to go."

Ryan raises his eyebrows in surprise. "That's a lot of faith."

"I was ready to put my faith in Vin once. Compared to that, you're a lock. Besides, Trent is stupid smart and he'd follow you to the ends of the earth, so it seems like a safe bet."

"Unless you go to Canada," Trent inserts.

Ryan balks. "Why would I go to Canada?"

"My point exactly. It's cold. I don't like cold."

"We should go down to California."

I shake my head. "Droughts. Fires."

"Oregon?"

"How is that different from here?"

"Idaho?"

"That's a worse idea than Canada."

"You're determined to hate everywhere, aren't you?"

"Why does it matter? Are we going somewhere?"

"I don't know, are we?"

I look at him skeptically. "Are we?"

"Are we?" Trent asks.

"Maybe," Ryan answers softly.

My stomach churns as my gut tightens. I don't know what this means for him or for me or for Trent. Is he seriously thinking about leaving here?

We don't know what the world outside of Seattle is like. It could be better, but it could definitely be worse. There could be more compounds like the Colonies, there could be bigger and badder gangs. There could be more zombies than we've seen in years or there could be wide open spaces, empty and thriving with life—real life, that doesn't moan or groan.

It also makes me wonder why we're doing all this. If he wants to leave, why don't we just leave? Cut and run. This thing is in motion but there are plenty of bodies ready and willing to carry it out to the end. It doesn't have be us. They need me to bridge this gap right now, but after that I'm useless. The cannibals have all hinted at that fact. We could leave tonight and never look back. Never remember.

But I know it's a lie. I know I would always wonder. I would wonder the way the ring still resting on my finger felt heavier the longer I was away. I worried for Vin and the rest of the people in this building every second of every day, and no matter how hard I tried to distance myself from them, I never really left. A part of me was still with them here in this building, trapped and burning to be set free.

"No matter what we do or where we go," I tell them softly, "we see this through to the end."

Ryan nods. "Of course."

I look up at Trent to find him staring out the door and down the hall. I can't tell what he's looking at. The long hall is dark and filled with Colonists milling around, waiting for whatever is going to happen to hurry up and happen. Nothing looks unusual to me at all. Whatever has his attention, though, it has it strong. I don't think he's blinking.

"Trent?"

"I'll play follow the leader until it's done," he replies, his voice dead.

I frown at Ryan, confused, but if I'm looking for answers I'm looking in the wrong place: his face is a mirror of mine. I'm about to ask Trent what he's looking at when Vin appears at the end of the hall. People say hello to him as he passes, and generally bask in the glory that is Vin. Women smile, men step aside, and I can immediately see why they fell in line behind him so easily: he has *it*. It's the same thing that I don't have. Never have and never will. The same thing that Ryan has that Trent doesn't—charisma.

"Thanks for waiting," he tells us as he comes inside and closes the door solidly behind him.

"What else were we going to do?"

He grins. "I'm glad you're back, Kitten. I've missed that."

"Missed what?"

"Your bluntness."

"What happened to the Leaders?"

"See, there it is. Right down to business."

"What happened to them?" I repeat.

"What do you think happened to them?"

"They're dead," Ryan guesses.

I shake my head. "No, they're not dead. They're in prison."

"Why would you think he'd spare them?"

"Because it's what I would have done. They're a liability but they're valuable, but the big question is what are you going to do with them?"

"It's already happening," Vin confirms. "We've been using them to keep up communications with the other Colonies. We rotate them. Put each of them on the radio at different times to keep up appearances that everything here is business as usual."

"How long do you think you can keep that up?"

"Not much longer," he admits, taking a seat. "We've been buying time, that's all. It's not a permanent solution by any means."

"What's your plan then?"

"You."

I can't help but laugh. "Me?"

"You were always the plan. Well, except for when I was the plan. You're what we've been stalling for. We've been waiting for you to come back with reinforcements. You were supposed to come back with The Hive, but I guess you had other plans."

"You mean Marlow had other plans," I say sharply, bristling at the implication that I didn't do my job. "We went to him. I stood in the center of his filthy lair and I told him everything. I even showed him your ring, and do you know what I got in return?"

"A ride up a brown creek without a paddle?" Vin asks knowingly.

"Winner, winner."

"I'd like it back, by the way."

"What? The boat?"

89

"Hope you can swim," Ryan mutters.

"No, not the boat," Vin says impatiently. "The ring."

I slide it off my finger and toss it to him. He catches it easily. When he slips it on his own finger, I swear I see him relax. As for me, my hand feels oddly empty without it.

"So you brought me savages in place of soldiers?" he asks.

"I brought you what I could get. We even went to Vashon Island looking for help."

Vin sits up straight, suddenly very interested. "For real? You hit up the Vashons?"

"We tried."

"And how'd that go?"

"We ended up in prison," Ryan tells him frankly.

"And now they hate us," I add. "Colonist boats showed up out of nowhere so they assumed we were spies. We barely made it off the island alive."

"Colonists showed up how long after? Days? Weeks?"

"Days. There was a fight out on the water. The Vashons won. We barely survived it. The boat Marlow lent us sank, we ended up on the Colonist shore, and that's when we were found by the cannibals."

"And the cannibals took you in like the compassionate, social butterflies that they are?" he asks sarcastically.

I scowl at him. "No. They took us prisoner."

"You've been to jail a lot lately," Vin chuckles. "Do you want me to lock you up for the night? Will you feel more comfortable?"

"They took us to their city under the streets," I continue. "That's when they offered to help us."

"And why would they do that?"

"Because they hate the Colonists as much as anyone else—maybe a little bit more," Ryan tells him.

"They told us about the arrangement," I snap.

I shouldn't have brought it up, not now, but I couldn't help it. It was out of my mouth before I even knew I was saying it.

Vin looks at me blankly. "What arrangement?"

"The one in your stables. The one with the babies."

I've never been afraid of Vin, and there's no visible reason why I should be now, but there's something in the air that changes then. It becomes hotter. Tighter. I feel it burning and turning in my lungs, not filling the space the way it's supposed to. It's more like a living, angry, writhing thing threatening to strangle us all with each breath.

A scream cuts through the air and the tension. It's gut-wrenching, and for a brief, crazy moment I wonder if I made it. The tightness in the room and in my chest make it completely possible, almost probable. But then I hear running outside as Vin leaps from his desk and sprints for the door, and I know it wasn't me. It's coming from farther off in the building. Somewhere downstairs.

We follow Vin out of the office, down the stairs, and into the open sleeping area. He stops there, his eyes scouring every corner of the room like a wolf sniffing the air for its prey. The scream sounds again and we're on the move. I know where we're going now.

The showers.

Chapter Eight

When we reach the door to the showers we find a crowd already forming. Vin shouts once, just a bark of a noise, and the crowd immediately thins to let him through. I'm amazed by it, but the amazement is short-lived. When I enter the room behind him, my amazement turns to horror.

The floor is bathed in blood. Vibrant red. Living. Warm. The walls are sprayed in a mist of rusty red that's running down the gray surface, dripping onto the floor, and racing down to move toward the drain. It looks like the little rivulets are trying to get back to the source—to find their way home, but home is just a memory. The heap of red gore and white bone barely resembles a human body anymore. It's been gutted from the center, desecrated to the very edges.

At the edge of the mess is a woman I recognize from the sewing rooms. She's on the floor on her knees in the corner, as far away from the body as she can get. She's sitting silently with her hand against her mouth, her eyes watery and wide. Several people are sitting with her as she shakes uncontrollably.

I hear someone in the hall vomit on the floor—coughs and heaves, the splash of their dinner hitting the cement. Someone else gags. Footsteps run away. It's then that I realize just how sheltered these people are. There was a time when a sight like this was as common as bird poop; you couldn't turn a corner without coming face to face with this stuff.

"Who is it?" someone asks tremulously from the corner.

I look at the thin delicate wrist, one of the few sections of skin still intact. It's a woman.

"Can you tell?" I ask Vin.

He shakes his head.

Ryan steps up beside me. "This is the room we came in through. It was clear when we got here. Joss, Trent, and I were the last to leave it."

"Not exactly."

We all turn to look at Trent.

"What do you mean?" Vin demands.

"When we left there was a cannibal guard still inside the tunnel, waiting just under that drain."

"Bryan," I breathe, remembering my tall creeper.

"He was one of them?" Vin asks, pointing to the ceiling where the cannibals wait somewhere above us.

"Sort of," Ryan explains. "He was with them but he wasn't exactly like them. He was more… predatory than the rest."

"He freaked me out," I agree.

"Roll call! Rec room! Now!" Vin commands, turning sharply to the crowd at the door. "No one is left alone! Buddy system goes into effect immediately! Go!"

Everyone flies into action. Only Vin, my Lost Boys, two guards, and I stay in the showers. When we're alone, Vin turns to the guards, his eyes bright and hot.

"Lock this space down. That drain is a weakness. Seal it."

"Wait," I tell the guards, turning to Vin. "You can't do that. That's how we got in. How will we get out?"

"You'll take the water, same way you left before. You don't need to sneak in and out."

"Yes, we do. What if the other Colonies have eyes on this place? They can't see us coming and going over the water or they'll know something is up. This tunnel is our only way."

"You expect me to leave it open to the cannibals after this?" he asks angrily, pointing to the woman on the floor.

"Guard it, but don't seal it. We need it open."

"For what exactly? Where are you going?"

"It's not where I'm going, it's who's coming. Elijah, the head of the cannibals, will want to come here to talk about what we do next."

Vin steps up until he's towering over me. "And what do you think is happening? You think I'm allying with them now?"

"You need to team up with someone," I snap, not intimidated by him. "You can't keep this place by yourself. Word is going to get out to Marlow and the Colonies that this place is under new management, and when that happens you'll have angry armies knocking at your door. What are you going to do then? You'll lose this place so fast you won't even remember it, and any chance we had of being free will be dead."

He chuckles. "Still reaching for that star, huh, Kitten? Freedom?"

"Isn't that what all of us want?"

"It's a dream. A stupid one."

"You wanna be Marlow's stable boy forever?" I ask, aiming for the belt, or just below. "Do you want to answer to him for the rest of your life? You're not that old, Vin. You've got a lot of years left and you can spend all of them under another man's thumb or you can be your own man and live your own life free and clear of all of them—the Hive, the Colonists, even the whores."

Vin stares at me with hard eyes that give nothing away but I know he hears me. I know he wants that freedom because Ryan is wrong: we are alike. And deep down Vin wants it just as badly as I do.

"We have one chance," Ryan says, coming to stand beside me. "One shot at taking them out, but without this Colony we have nothing."

Vin steps back suddenly, rolling his shoulders. He glances back at the guards watching from behind him. Listening.

"We'll have a meeting," he says curtly. "We'll let the people decide what we do, both with the building and the cannibals."

"Are you going to kill them?" I ask anxiously.

He shrugs. "We'll see, won't we?"

***

It only takes ten minutes to round up everyone in the entire building—two hundred people plus the cannibal prisoners and three reluctant outsiders rallied into one location in under ten minutes. Vin runs a tight ship.

Ryan, Trent, and I stand against the wall in the common room watching people chat quietly as we wait for Vin to break the news. With how quickly gossip flies in this place, I assume everyone already knows. But do they know who they've lost?

Vin stands in a huddle with six other people— four men, two women. I don't recognize any of them. They're talking in hushed tones, the men and women holding pieces of paper that they were all pointing to at first, but now dangle limp and useless in each of their hands. Vin is standing in front of them, his arms crossed over his chest and his handsome face patiently serious.

"Did you know her?" Ryan whispers to me.

I shrug. "I don't know. I couldn't recognize her. I doubt it, though. I see most of the people I was even a little bit close to." I jut my chin toward the southern corner of the room where a big man stands next to an older redhead and a young brunette. "That's the kitchen staff over there. Aside from Vin and Nats they were my only real friends. They're the ones who first told me about the rebellion."

Ryan follows my gaze. I think Trent was

already looking.

"They made the pie?" Ryan asks, his face very, very serious.

I laugh. "Yeah, they made a pumpkin pie to bribe me. It worked. It was delicious."

"What are their names?" Trent asks.

"Oh, um," I stutter, thrown by the question. It's personal and it's coming from Trent. I expect battle stat questions from him: How much can they lift? What's their dominant kill hand? Weapon of choice? "The big guy is Steven. The redhead next to him is Crystal, and the brown-haired girl is Amber. The other ones I'm not sure about. I think one of the other guys is named John? Don? Dan? I don't remember. We didn't talk much."

"Where's Nats?" Ryan asks.

I scan the room but I don't find her. My blood goes cold. "I don't see her."

"They might not have everyone here yet."

"Vin would have recognized her," I say, voicing the fear coursing through my veins. "If it was her in that room, he would have known her."

Ryan only nods and I wonder who exactly I'm trying to convince—him or me?

Suddenly Vin steps into the center of the room. Without a word from him, without a gesture, the entire room falls into silent expectation.

"Whoa," I breathe.

"No doubt who the boss is here," Ryan mutters.

"As you all probably know by now, there's been a breach," Vin begins. He isn't even trying to raise his voice. He's speaking in a normal tone, just daring people to make a sound above him. "It's been contained. The intruders have been captured. Their intentions are still up for debate, but we'll get to that in a minute. The most important thing that has to be addressed immediately is one I'm sure you all know about by now. We've had a fatality in the building."

There's a scattering of gasps. Maybe a few people were somehow out of the loop, but for the most part the room is unaffected. They already knew the what. They want to know who.

"I've spoken to the Mayors," Vin continues, looking over his shoulder at the men and women he had been talking to, "and through roll call and head counts we've been able to find out who we've lost. It was Rebecca, from the gardens."

A wider-spread gasp runs through the ranks. There are tears immediately being shed and quiet sobs are peppered through the room.

"I know we're all very sad to hear about what happened to her. We're also very angry because her death could have been avoided."

"I heard it was a Risen attack," a man calls out.

"Are there Risen in the building?" someone else cries out fearfully.

Vin shakes his head solemnly. "It looked like a Risen attack but we're sure it wasn't."

"Then what was it?"

"Who was it?"

Vin glances at me for the briefest of seconds. Just long enough to make me sweat.

"It was a cannibal," he tells the room.

Chaos. Absolute freak out chaos. People seriously scream in fear. I haven't seen anything like it since the early days, and the sight of it now makes me shift on my feet nervously, eyeing the exits.

"Calm down, calm down," Vin says loudly, his voice bizarrely soothing. "The Guard is sweeping the building right now. If any other outsiders are still here, they won't be for long."

"Are these them?" a woman shouts, pointing angrily at the cannibals held prisoner.

"Yes," Vin confirms. "They're cannibals."

More chaos. There are curses mixed inside angry shouts. Some people move farther away from the prisoners, eyeing them cautiously. For their part, the cannibals stay perfectly still. None of them make a sound or move a muscle as a room full of people is whipped into an angry frenzy around them.

"Stop!" Vin commands sternly.

The Colonists quiet almost immediately.

"It's being taken care of. You're safe. I promise you. From what I've been able to find out so far, these are not the people responsible for what happened to Rebecca, though we are still looking into it and they will remain in custody."

"They should be killed!"

"Put them outside the gates! Let the Risen have them!"

Movement from the cannibals catches my eye. I glance over to find Macy looking right at me, her eyes pleading and watery. She looks terrified.

"Wait!" I shout. I've stepped forward into the center of the room with Vin before I even realize what I'm doing. When I do realize it, when every eye in the entire place is on me, I wish I could sink into the floor and disappear. "I—we have—"

I look at Vin, feeling frantic. He's watching me calmly, waiting. They're all waiting. All watching. I'm gonna be sick.

I swallow hard. "I brought them here to help you."

"You brought them here?"

"Why isn't she tied up?"

"She's one of us! She went for help!"

"She brought death!"

"No, I didn't!" I shout defensively. "I—We tried to bring The Hive, but—"

"The Hive? Rapists and druggies! That was your plan?"

"I'd rather she brought The Hive than the cannibals."

"She should have stayed gone. We'd be better off and Rebecca would be alive."

I can't tell for sure in the chaos, but I'm pretty sure that last shout was Lexy.

I look to Vin, feeling helpless, but what I find is nothing. He's staring at me blankly. No emotion, no support. No help. They're calling out The Hive, *his home,* as being full of rapists and drug addicts and he's just standing here, passive. Silent. He might as well throw me to these wolves. Without his support they'll tear me apart.

"You wanted help and that's exactly what she brought you!"

I whip around, startled. Ryan is striding across the room like he owns the place. He comes to stand directly beside me, his body nearly touching mine.

"My name is Ryan Hyperion!" he shouts, grabbing the attention of every last person in the room. They quiet again, even though there are still murmurs drifting through the crowd. "I was a member of the Hyperion gang, a fighter in the Arena of The Hive. I recognize some of your Guard. Members of the Elevens, the Westies, the Pikes. I even recognized Vin when we arrived. And yes, we brought them here." He points to the cannibals, all of them watching him intently. "We went to The Hive for help, but they wouldn't give it. We went to the Vashons for help, but they wouldn't give it. No one with the numbers we needed were willing to help us. To help *you*."

Ryan pauses to look around the room, letting that sink in. Reminding them that this was all for them.

"Then we found them. Your prisoners. The people you want to kill. The people who risked everything to free you."

"They killed Rebecca!"

"They were clear from the start that no blood would be shed if they could help it," he replies, stretching the truth just a little bit. "The man who killed Rebecca was acting alone and he should be held accountable for his actions, no one can deny that, but you cannot condemn them all for what one man did."

"He's a cannibal, like them. They're all dangerous. They should all die!"

"You're a Colonist!" Ryan shouts back. "You're all Colonists. You all kidnap and enslave. You should all be punished!"

The anger in the room is tangible. I want to thread my fingers through it as it weaves through the room, feel it ripple warm over my skin. It's that real. That visceral. Ryan has touched a nerve, but he's also hit home.

"They're people," he continues softly. "They're men and women just like you, and they want what you want. They want freedom from the Colonies. They want to live with their families in the open, unafraid. Like it or not, right now we're all beggars and we can't afford to be choosy. You don't have to agree with the way they live because, honestly, they don't agree with the way that you live, but they're still willing to work with you. I hope you have the common sense to work with them."

"The enemy of your enemy is your friend," Trent intones.

Ryan nods to the room. "The Leaders in the stadiums fear them just as much as you do. Take this chance to turn that weapon against them and take back what's yours—your lives." Ryan goes to stand beside the cannibals, turning his back on them and proving his complete lack of fear. "Talk to them. Hear them out. It doesn't have to be here. Send them away tonight, seal your doors, but don't turn your backs on them for good because they might be your only chance. The way things are right now, it can't last. You can't hold this building forever. Eventually the other Colonies will find out what's happened here or The Hive will get wind of it, and then where will you be?"

"Enslaved," Steven replies.

There's a rumble of agreement, grudging and

angry. But they're not dumb. They know what's coming and they know how fragile their situation is.

"They'll leave tonight," Vin tells the room, his eyes on Ryan. "We'll send them back to their home and we'll agree to talk about joining with them on one condition. They have to give us the man who killed Rebecca. We do with him as we see fit, no interference."

It'll never happen. Elijah will never allow it. Bryan may have acted outside the norm for the cannibals, I don't really know for sure, but I do know that family is everything to them. Bryan is one of them and they'll never give him up.

"Good," Ryan says. "That's good."

"But remember this," Vin continues. "This house will never be theirs. No matter what happens or where we go from here, they will never set foot inside these walls again. Is that clear?"

I meet his eyes, nod curtly. "Crystal."

"Get them out of here."

With that Vin leaves the room. I'm surprised by the abruptness of it, but I don't have time to worry about it. Immediately people are in motion all over the room and I'm worried about the cannibals. That's the craziest moment of my crazy day— worrying over flesh eaters.

Members of Vin's Guard appear in the doorway. They make quick work of rounding up the cannibals and ushering them out of the room, a room that's beginning to buzz louder and louder with discord. I'm starting to wonder if Ryan, Trent, and I shouldn't leave tonight too.

"Joss."

I jerk when I feel a hand on my arm, a hand attached to the quiet voice behind me. I'm pretty on-edge the moment, not really sure everyone in the room has moved past the 'lynch her!' phase, but I'm infinitely relieved and surprisingly happy when I turn to find Amber standing beside me.

"Sorry," she says with a sheepish smile, retracting her hand quickly. "I didn't mean to scare you."

"You didn't," I lie. I do it poorly, as always. I can see it in her bright blue eyes that she doesn't believe me. "How are you?"

"Good. We're all really good, actually. Well, except for tonight. The news about Rebecca is unbelievable."

"I'm sorry."

"We were worried for you there for a minute. Good thing your friend stood up."

"Oh, yeah, this is Ryan."

She smiles. "I heard. I'm Amber."

"Hi," Ryan says.

"I'm Trent."

We all look at him, Ryan and I both a little uncertain.

Amber goes right on smiling, not knowing the weird she's walking into. "Hi, Trent. I liked what you said about enemies and friends."

"It's a proverb. Fourth century."

"Oh."

"Arabian or Chinese. No one knows for sure."

"Well, it's cool. And fitting."

"You work in the kitchens."

Amber looks at me, unsure. It's not exactly a

question. "Yes?"

Trent doesn't say anything after that. He stares at her as though he's waiting for something. Problem is, none of us knows what the hell it is he's waiting for.

"Anyway," Amber says hesitantly, "we're so glad you're back, Joss. You were gone so long we worried we'd lost you."

"Yeah, sorry about that. Help wasn't exactly easy to find."

"You did your best and we're all grateful," she says, lying much more convincingly than I do. "We're lucky we had Vin while you were gone. He's really turned this place around. It feels so different now."

"Who are the Mayors?" Ryan asks. "Are they a council?"

"When we were a Colony we were split up into groups based on our jobs. The Guard, the gardens, the kitchen, you know. There used to be a Team Leader in charge of each group. When Vin overthrew the place, he put the Colony Team Leaders in prison and replaced them with our own people who work just like the rest of us, but they also meet with him. They're the ones called Mayors. They're a voice for each group."

"Wait, hold on," I interrupt her. "Did you say 'when Vin overthrew the place'? What? He did it alone?"

Amber beams excitedly. "Practically. They tried to kill him twice and he survived both times."

"And that made him valuable to you," Ryan says thoughtfully.

"Well, yeah. It's like what you said about the cannibals. If your enemy is afraid of it, you should use it as a weapon. After he survived the second attack when he was already injured, we were all convinced."

"Convinced of what?" I ask.

Ryan looks at me with a weird expression I can't quite read. It's almost worried. "They were convinced he was the one who would set them all free."

Amber laughs. "Maybe not so biblical as that, but yeah. We realized he was strong enough to help us finally take over. We'd all wanted it since the day we set foot in this place. Vin gave us the opportunity and the courage to do it."

"We have to leave," Trent says suddenly. "They're moving the cannibals. We should go with them to make sure they get out safely."

"Oh, okay," Amber says, sounding confused. She's probably wondering why we care if the cannibals live or die. Part of me wonders the same thing. "Good to see you again, Joss. I'm so glad you're okay."

I smile at her. "Thanks."

Amber blushes suddenly, her eyes going to Trent who has yet to stop staring at her like a lunatic. "Bye, Trent."

"Goodbye," my robot replies.

Chapter Nine

We go our separate ways, Amber heading out with the flow of Colonists and us following the cannibals back to the shower room. More members of the Guard have joined our group, some leading and more following, and I'm grateful that Ryan, Trent, and I aren't lumped in with the cannibals; we're allowed to follow freely behind the herd.

"All right, what's wrong?" I whisper to Ryan as we walk.

"With what?"

"With Amber's story about the overthrow. You didn't like it."

Ryan pauses, his eyebrows coming together in concentration. "It's not that I didn't like it, it's... I think it worries me. The sort of hero worship vibe I got from your friend could be bad news."

"Why?"

"Because it reminds me of what Sam told us about Westbrook and how the Colonies first got started. And also because it's not really true. In that story of him surviving two assassination attempts, where were you?"

"I was with him by the wall when Caroline stabbed him."

"I know that and you know that."

"Caroline knows that," Trent remarks.

"But Amber didn't mention it. Does she not know that you're the one who saved Vin that night?"

"I don't know," I reply, not sure what it matters.

"If you're being left out of that story, are more people being left out of the other story? The other attempt on his life? If he was already injured, I'm thinking he wasn't alone for that second fight."

"Okay, probably not, but who cares? He still survived. She's right—they tried to kill him twice and he survived both times."

"But why did they try to kill him? Why did Caroline do it the first time?"

"Because she was crazy and in love with him and she thought I was stealing her man."

"So it wasn't an assassination attempt at all. It was one person acting on jealousy. And the second time, why did that girl try to kill him?"

"Probably because Caroline was her friend and Breanne was kind of nuts. She went native the second we got here. She was insanely loyal to the Colony by the time I left."

"So neither attempt on his life was actually ordered by the Colonies or by the Team Leaders as a group—it was all personal and emotional, but that's not how the people here are looking at it.

They're looking at him as some messiah who their enemies tried to strike down but couldn't. It gives him this legend status and puts him on a pedestal. It's no wonder they follow him like they do."

I hadn't thought about it, but he's right—these people are looking at Vin as their savior, but he's actually nothing more than a gangster pimp with bad taste in women and a habit of getting shanked.

"If he gets them where they need to go, then what's the problem?" I ask, trying to convince myself as much as Ryan.

He shrugs. "I don't know. Maybe nothing."

"Are we staying here tonight?" Trent asks out of the blue.

"I'm not really sure," I reply hesitantly. "We'll have to talk to Vin, I guess."

"Do you think it's safe?" Ryan asks.

I want to say yes, of course it is, but after what happened upstairs just now I'm not so sure. Vin didn't turn on me, but he didn't exactly help me either. He left me to fend for myself, and something about that royally pisses me off. Whether we're staying here tonight or not, he and I have to talk.

"Probably not. It might not be a bad idea for us to sleep behind locked doors tonight, wherever we go."

"Careful what you say. I'll think you've grown to love prison life."

"I do miss the bathrooms. And the soaps."

"I miss the pillows."

"I miss the books," Trent adds.

"Was Sam right?" I ask him. "Could you have busted us out of there?"

"Maybe."

"Maybe or probably?"

"Definitely."

My jaw drops. "Why didn't you?"

"I didn't need to," he says like it's obvious. "You wanted to stay."

"How would you have done it?"

"Picked the lock."

"Is that easy to do?"

"No."

"Then how do you know you could have done it?"

Trent grins. "Because I did it."

"What? When?"

"While you and Ryan were sleeping. Sam was out cold too. I was up and I was bored so I picked the lock. Wandered around a little. That house was nice. Big kitchen. They had oranges."

"Are you kidding me?" I cry incredulously.

The guards ahead of us look back at Trent warily.

"No."

"Why didn't you tell us?" Ryan demands.

"You guys wanted to stay in that room and play by their rules until they let you talk to their council, so I played by their rules."

"Not really. You ninja-ed around their house in the middle of the night."

"Just for a few minutes. I told you, I was bored. Besides, if they had found out I could do that we'd have been killed or kicked off the island immediately."

"If you had been caught," I begin.

"But I wasn't."

"But if you had been—"

"But I wasn't."

"Oh my God," I grumble, closing my eyes briefly. "Ryan, I can't."

He rubs his hand on my back in small circles. "I know. Believe me, I know."

Luckily, before I lose my mind we reach the showers. The body has been taken out—probably to the gardens, which is kind of fitting considering where Rebecca worked—but her blood remains. There are two people in the room cleaning along with two guards standing nearby watching. The cleaning crew pushes pink-stained mops toward the hole in the floor, water washing away the red remains of Bryan's mistake.

It changes everything, what he did. This could have been easy. Well, easier. The Colonists didn't even have to know these people were cannibals. They could have been a random group of gang members we rounded up, something that would have gone over perfectly with the mixed company inside a Colony. But no, Bryan had to go and get hungry and murder some innocent girl and now we're all screwed—Vin included. This castle of his, no matter how sturdy it looks from the inside, is made of sugar. And the rain is coming.

"Warn Elijah to stay away," Ryan tells Macy as they approach the drain. "It's not safe to come here again."

"No joke," she mutters.

"I think we're all assuming the plan is off," Kyle agrees bitterly.

Ryan steps up to him, catching his eye. "Not yet. It's not over yet."

"They'll kill us if they ever see us again."

"If they ever see you *here* again."

"What's your point?"

"This place was meant to be a battle, but it's not the war."

"You really think they're going to fight side by side with us someday?" Macy asks, her tone disbelieving.

"I think very soon they aren't going to have a choice."

"You think the Colonies are coming," Kyle says.

Ryan shakes his head. "Worse. I think The Hive is coming."

"Marlow knows what we have planned," I mutter, catching on. "He knows Vin is here. He knows we don't have a prayer without him or the Vashons, and he definitely knows the Vashons told us no."

"It won't be long before he comes here. He'll rally a small army and storm this place, just like we did. The thing that worries me is what will V—"

"No," I blurt out, interrupting Ryan.

He looks at me with surprise on his face, but I shake my head firmly and shift my eyes to the guards; they're standing on the edges of the room, listening.

I don't know what Vin was doing up there in the rec room letting me drown myself in stupid, but I'm not willing to undermine him in his own house. Not yet. Not until I know what his deal is. Ryan must pick up at least part of what I'm trying to convey because he drops the issue immediately.

"Tell Elijah we'll send word on the plan," Ryan tells Kyle, offering his hand. "Until then, please ask him to sit tight."

"What about Bryan?" Macy asks suspiciously.

Ryan sighs. "Tell Elijah about Vin's demand, but I won't be shocked when he says no. We'll have to figure out a way around it."

Kyle hesitates only a second before taking Ryan's hand in his. "You got it. Good luck."

"You too."

We watch the cannibals go one by one down into the drain. The cleaning crew doesn't even stop their work. A thin river of blood and water pours through the hole on top of the cannibals as they leave. They'll be covered in blood when they get home, but they should count themselves lucky it isn't theirs.

"What's the plan now?" Ryan asks me when they're gone.

"You and Trent go look around. Mingle. Whatever," I say with a shrug, not really concerned what trouble they get themselves into. They can go set the display tree on fire for all I care. Things can't get much worse than they already are.

"What are you going to do?"

I angrily chew on the inside of my lip until I taste blood. "I've got a date with a pimp."

***

"Where is he?"

114

The guard—another Hive member, judging by the hornet tattoo on his neck—looks me up and down.

"Why?"

"Why what?"

"Why do you want to know where he is?"

"Why do you think?" I ask hotly.

The guy smirks. "For the same reason all the women look for him."

"Unless all the women here are looking to kick his ass, then no."

"That doesn't make me want to help you find him."

I turn away in frustration to head up the hall. "I'll find him myself, dick!"

"Roof."

I stop, looking over my shoulder at him. "Why?"

His smirk becomes a grin. "Why what?"

"Why are you telling me?"

"Because you're not a Colony girl. You're a wild girl. He likes wild girls."

"You're still a dick."

He laughs. "So are you, wild thing."

When I reach the roof, there he is—just as the hornet downstairs told me he would be. He's sitting on the edge of the roof, his legs dangling, his back to me. It's a dangerous position he's in, and no eyes on the entrance? It worries me more than impresses me.

"What's on your mind, Joss?" Vin asks without turning.

I sigh before going to sit next to him. The anger

I had building inside of me is dying out. Maybe it's because I'm tired, but it's probably because it doesn't matter. I'm still alive. The cannibals got out alive. One Colonist died—I genuinely feel bad about that, but it could have been worse. So, so much worse. All in all, if I survive to see the sunrise, I'll count it as a good night.

When I sit, I let my legs dangle off the edge of the building as well. Like a little kid. A little kid sitting three stories above the ground, tempting fate, begging it to take its best shot.

"Nothing much," I lie.

"Did they send you up to tell me to hand over the Colony?"

"Nope."

"Then why are you here?"

"Not for the company, that's for sure."

"Spill it," he insists.

I glare at him before looking away out over the black water. "Why'd you do it?"

"You mean why did I leave you hanging?"

"Almost literally, yes. I don't feel safe being here anymore."

"You shouldn't. You shouldn't feel safe anywhere. That's when your guard goes down and you die."

"Did you want them to kill me?"

"No."

"Then why didn't you help me?"

"Your boy helped. You don't need me, Kitten."

"Is that what this is about? Ryan?"

"Get over yourself," he scoffs. "No."

I throw my hands up in frustration. "Then what

is it about?"

"It's about this place," he hisses fiercely. "It's about this building and the people in it."

I stare at him, shocked. Then something slowly begins to occur to me: he's not actually angry. He's feral, like an animal. An animal protecting his territory.

"It's your house. You want to keep this Colony and I'm a threat to that."

"I took it. *I* did that. And I did it half dead."

I pause, feeling scared, but it's weird because I think I was already feeling it. It's not a new feeling; it's an uncovering. It's shining light on something that's been hidden in the shadows of my mind since I got here. I think I've known something was wrong since the moment I walked in the building.

Something is off, something is missing.

Someone is missing.

"When Breanne died," I begin, my voice whisper quiet, "you weren't alone, were you?"

Vin curses harshly under his breath. It's all the answer I need.

"Nats is dead."

He nods.

Tears sting my eyes, hot and angry. I will them back, I pull them inside, and I swallow the rough, salty tang down into my stomach where it burns like lava.

"How?" I whisper shakily.

The worst thing is that Vin doesn't give me a hard time. I'm emotional, I'm obviously nearly weeping beside him, and he doesn't say a word about it—that's how bad it is, how hard it's hitting him, and it makes it so much worse because it somehow makes it more real.

"She was standing watch over me after you left. I was in and out of it, sweating and aching, feeling like I was dying because I was. Sometime the next day I woke up to fighting. It was Nats and Breanne. On instinct I reached under my pillow for a knife. I always kept one there in The Hive, just in case. I was surprised to actually find one. Nats knew. She must have put it there. She fought Breanne hard, but the entire time she was asking her to stop. To remember we were family. I pulled myself out of the bed to help her, but I fell on the floor. I couldn't stand up straight. I was useless. When I looked up, Breanne had sunk a kitchen knife into Nats' chest. To the hilt." Vin coughs roughly, rubbing his hand over his mouth. "She pounced on me, but she was too excited. She didn't see my knife. I put it in her stomach three times, then I tossed her aside. I lay there on the ground with her and I watched her die. It took hours."

"Where's Nats now?"

"She's buried by the water. Breanne and Caroline are buried by the wall. I wanted to toss them to the zombies, but…"

"But what?"

He runs his hand over his face briskly. "I thought better of it."

"It would have been an aggressive move for this crowd."

"That's what I thought, but they were pretty eager to throw out that option tonight."

"You were already thinking of ruling this place

the second I killed Caroline, weren't you? Or was it when they asked you to go home and bring back help?"

He chuckles darkly. "I've been thinking about ruling this place since we walked in the door."

"You'll never be able to keep it. Not once word gets out that you have it."

"I know that."

"Marlow will want it and you'll have to give it. You owe him a lot."

"I don't owe anybody anything," he replies, his tone harsh.

I glance over at him to find his jaw clenched tightly, the muscles working under his skin.

"You care about this place, don't you?"

"I always watch after what's mine."

"This isn't like the stables, though. Those were Marlow's. This is real to you, isn't it? This place really means something."

He sighs heavily, the air sliding past his lips for what feels like eternity. When he finally speaks his voice is shockingly soft, all of the anger seeming to have slipped out of him.

"In The Hive people feared me. There were a few that knew me better than the others, ones who weren't afraid of me, but they were of Marlow. That entire place is run on fear. I never knew there was any other way."

"They respect you here, I can see it. I saw it in the rec room when you talked to them. They listened and it was because they love you, not fear you."

He nods. "It's different."

119

"And you don't want to go back to the old way?"

"I don't know what I want."

"I think you do."

"I'm surprised about your boy," Vin says suddenly.

"Oh yeah?" I ask, thrown by the change of subject. "Why's that?"

"Because he's Ryan Hyperion," Vin replies like it's obvious. "Kevin was a big deal in the Arena, and everyone—me included—was sure Ryan would follow him. He's a hell of a fighter."

I eye him shrewdly. "Is that respect I hear in your voice?"

Vin grins. "It might have crept in there."

"So you approve?"

"Yeah."

"Can't tell you what that means to me," I mutter sarcastically, but part of me means it. There's a weird feeling of satisfaction knowing Vin is impressed by Ryan. Ever since I met him, part of me has worried about Ryan a little. He's not exactly soft, but… I don't know. I think I worry he's too nice. I see it as a weakness.

"You're not gonna fight me about calling him 'your boy'?" Vin teases.

I roll my eyes. "What would be the point?"

"Are you admitting it's true?"

I feel my cheeks flush instantly hot and pink. I know he can see it. I know I have weaknesses of my own.

"Yeah," I grumble.

"What's with you?"

"I'm embarrassed!" I snap, feeling more annoyed than embarrassed at the moment.

Vin nods slowly, looking out over the water. "Yeah, I get that."

"Really? Then maybe you can explain it to me 'cause I don't understand it at all."

He doesn't answer at first. I think he's going to ignore my outburst, but then he's talking soft and low.

"It's because you're worried it makes you weak. You're afraid and that's embarrassing enough as it is, but what you're afraid of is even worse. You're afraid that you care. That you have something to lose. There's a lot of angry and a lot more ugly out there and most of it wants to destroy, steal, kill, or just plain ruin anything and everything we have the gall to give a shit about. So in a way, yeah, how you feel about him does make you weak and that's embarrassing for fighters like you and I."

He glances over at me, his face striking in the glowing yellow light of the fading sun. His eyes are strange to me. Maybe it's a trick of the light or maybe it's a trick of this life, but they're warmer than I've ever seen them. More genuine.

"It's dangerous for us to love anyone," he says, his voice deep. Husky.

Horrifying.

My stomach drops out. I'll go look for it later somewhere in the basement of the building beneath me, but for now I feel the hollow space where it's supposed to be. My pure fear and anxiety must register on my face because Vin laughs, shaking his head and turning away. When he glances at me sideways with that sly grin of his, the one that's pure hotness and sex appeal, I relax a little. He looks like himself again.

"Calm down, Kitten. I'm not in love with you."

"I—I didn't think—" I stutter, flustered and confused.

"Yes, you did. You definitely thought it."

I smack him hard on the arm. "Well, the way you said it was pretty leading!"

"I meant it the way it sounded. I love you."

I am so lost.

"What the hell is happening?" I ask weakly.

"I'm not *in* love with you, all right? Take it easy. I'm shockingly advanced. I can have a soft spot for a woman without have a hard one for her too, you get me?"

"Gross."

"So, yeah, I love you, Kitten," he says plainly. "And that's embarrassing for me but I'm dealing with it."

"You're dealing with it better than I'm dealing with Ryan."

"It's because it's different. The way you feel about him, it's soft and it's hard."

"Quit saying it like that."

"Quit being a prude. Sex isn't dirty." He winks at me. "Not unless you want it to be."

"I will leave," I warn him. "I will stand up right now and leave this place forever."

"No, you won't."

"How do you know I won't?"

"You won't because you missed me. You're happy being here."

He's right—I feel the most at ease I have in a long time. I feel centered. Safe. I feel like he doesn't want anything from me that I can't give or anything that I want to give but I'm not sure how. Being with Vin is… I don't know. It's good. Like being alone without being lonely.

"I'm right, aren't I?"

"I hate you," I tell him, looking away.

He nudges my shoulder with his. "You love me too, Kitten."

"*Shut up.*"

He slings his arm around my shoulders, pulling me in close to him. "Are you going to ask what you're dying to ask?"

"I don't want to."

"Why not?"

"Because you'll probably lie to me."

He chuckles, the sound vibrating through his chest and into my shoulder tucked against him. "You're tougher than that. Ask anyway."

"If it comes down to it, who will you side with? Me or Marlow?"

He sighs with his whole body. I feel his chest expand against my shoulder. His hand squeezes me to him once, hard and brief, before going lax again.

"I don't know."

I nod, not surprised and not mad. I'm not even a little bit hurt because I get it. I understand being torn between two choices, none of which seem like good ones. I get trying to find loyalty inside yourself when you've never needed to know it before.

Vin and I, we're a lot alike. We're loners at

heart. He may surround himself with people but he doesn't align himself with them. For as much as he connects to them, he may as well be alone. But now the world is changing and it's asking more from both of us. It's forcing people into our space, into our lives. Neither of us is good at being cornered or pressured. Odds are we'll lash out eventually.

Or run.

Chapter Ten

I leave Vin to sit on his perch on his castle, pondering its fate and his. From the roof I spotted Ryan down in the gardens so I make my way down to him. He's wandering around, checking out what's growing, even pulling a stray weed here and there like he knows what he's doing. The movement gives me a weird feeling of déjà vu.

"How do you know you're not uprooting a carrot when you do that?" I ask him.

He smiles when he turns to face me. "Carrots don't flower."

"Could be a tomato."

"They grow above ground. All these years on your own and you don't know much about gardening, do you?"

I shrug. "I was lucky. I had Crenshaw. Where did you learn?"

"Crenshaw."

"Seriously?"

"He's been teaching me for years. I've been

learning about medicine too. I had to with Kevin and what he did at the Arena. The stuff I brought you for your arm, he and I brewed that together."

"So that's what all the 'master' and bowing stuff was about at his house?"

Ryan nods. "I'm his apprentice."

"Huh."

"What?"

"Nothing. It's weird. He never offered to teach me."

"He didn't offer to teach me either. I asked. But he'd never show you anyway. He said you don't have the patience."

"When did you two talk about me?"

Ryan tosses the weed out across the open grass. "The day you were a jerk to him."

I tense at the memory but I don't argue with him. I was there, I know what I did. "I left you guys alone for like two minutes. Did you spend the whole time talking ugly about me while I stood right there?"

"'She doesn't have your patience, Helios,'" he says in a nearly perfect Crenshaw drawl that makes me grin. "'It is why I never bothered to instruct her.' That's how much we talked about you."

"That's it? Really? You didn't say anything about me at all?"

He grins. "I said you had other redeeming qualities that made up for your lack of patience."

"Like what?"

"Like strength. Intelligence. Bravery. Humor."

"Pft," I scoff. "I am not funny."

"I think you are."

"I think you're laughing *at* me more often than with me."

He shrugs. "You're still funny. And sweet, too."

"This is getting really far-fetched."

"What are you doing out here?" he asks, coming to stand in front of me.

I look at the edge of the field where it meets the water. Where the wet green grass turns to brown mud in a perfect rectangle that's just long enough.

The laughter he built inside of me slips away.

"I came to say goodbye to someone," I say hoarsely.

"Who is it?"

"Nats."

"I'm so sorry, Joss. Do you want company?"

"I'm not going over there."

"Okay. What are you going to do?"

"I never got to bury my parents," I blurt out, my eyes still on the mound. I can feel Ryan's surprise in the air around us, but he stays silent. Waiting. "I was too young to do it alone and I didn't go back into the house after it happened. I was hiding in my dad's car for a long time. Days. I probably would have died in there, but eventually a family found me. It was a mom and a dad and two kids. Both boys. They took me with them. It was stupid because I was worthless. I could barely walk I was so weak and I didn't speak a word. Not for weeks. The first time I spoke was to tell them zombies were in the building." I swallow hard, remembering how my throat hurt as I screamed, using my voice for the first time in too long. Using it too hard. Too late. "They all died. Even the boys. I didn't see it because I ran. I left them. I tried to warn them, but I left them. Two more groups took me in after that. Two more times I saw everyone around me die. Torn apart the way Bryan tore apart that girl in the showers. I stopped talking again. I got quieter. Faster. I started moving alone because packs will get you heard and get you killed. People are dead weight. Even me. I knew I was worthless to whoever picked me up, so I stopped letting them. I started running from people and zombies and animals. Everything. Nothing was safe. I knew I had to be smart. I had to be fast and silent. A ghost."

You need to choose whether or not you want to survive or you want to live.

"I didn't want to die, but I knew I couldn't live," I breathe brokenly.

Ryan stands beside me silently, his hand clasped around mine, somehow warm despite the cold air.

"Can I show you something I found?" he asks, tugging on my hand.

I nod mutely, reluctant to pull my eyes from the brown earth. I feel like I'm failing her. I won't go over there, I know that, but it hurts to think I'm abandoning my friend. She's the first person I've lost in years, and while we weren't that close, it still stings. It's still an opening of a wound that should have been closed forever a long time ago.

It's still a strike of flint, an itch in my veins that makes me want to run.

When I realize where Ryan is taking me, I want

to dig in my heels. I want to root myself like those carrots out in the garden, buried under the ground and oblivious to the burn of embarrassment that's building in my gut and on my cheeks. But I don't back down because he's right—I'm brave. And stupid. I'm beginning to think the stupid is getting stronger every day. Ryan doesn't see it that way, though. Stupid to me is what sweet is to him.

When he stops in front of the wall at the back of the building, I cringe. It's still there. The writing in white rock that I impulsively scrawled on the rough brick. The message I wrote to him in the hopes that it would find him someday. It was a moment of plain, simple honesty that was too big to keep inside at the time. Now standing here next to him, it seems too big to hide. It's always been too much, this thing with him. It always has been and always will be more than I can manage.

I miss your kiss.

"That's your handwriting, isn't it?" he asks softly.

He's doing me a favor by not looking at me. His eyes are fixed on the wall, his shoulder pressed up against mine.

"Yeah," I admit weakly.

"You wrote it before you got out?"

"Yep."

"Why did you write it?"

"Because I couldn't say it."

"Because I wasn't here."

"No. Because I'm broken."

I feel him look at me, but I stare straight ahead. My eyes are fixed hard on the 'm' in my message. They keep following the lazy roll of it—up and down, up and down. Like waves on the ocean.

"You're not broken, Joss."

"Yes, I am."

"You're alive."

I shake my head in silent protest.

"Every day when I saw your writing on the wall, I knew you were still out there. You were telling me you were still alive. Do you know what this message tells me now?"

I feel my chest tighten, my fear of the words I've told him not to say rising in my veins so thick they might burst. "No."

"Even in here, even in prison when they had you trapped, you didn't give up. You don't know how to quit. You don't know how to die. You may have been a ghost for six years, Joss, but you've always been alive."

I close my eyes, a wave of dizziness rushing over me. I'm not surprised when he kisses me softly, lighting me up inside like the sun rising over the river behind him. I'm grateful for it. His arms around me, his lips on mine—it steadies me. It pushes away that dizzy, sick feeling in my head and my heart until I'm standing straight. Firm. Solid.

Until I feel more like *me* as I'm wrapped up in him than I have in a very long time.

Everything is changing. Everything is different than it ever has been before. I've always felt like Ryan was taking something from me, stripping away the layers of shadow and shroud that I've covered myself in while trying to hide. To survive. And I let him. I grudgingly let him do it, and now that I'm standing in the sun beside the water with him holding me, seeing me, knowing me more than anyone has in my short, painful life, I feel less afraid and more alive than I ever thought I could.

***

We sleep for most of the day. My schedule is getting all turned around. I'm going nocturnal and I don't know how much I like it. I prefer the daylight. I like the warmth of the sun on my skin and light in the sky. I like seeing what's coming. Too many shady things happen in the dark for me to ever trust it completely. I read once that up in Alaska there are weeks in the summer where the sun never sets. I thought that sounded like heaven until I got to the next chapter. Turns out in the winter there are times where the sun never comes out. Hard pass on that noise. Alaska can keep their wonky hours.

Once we get up, Ryan and I join Vin in his office again to talk about where we go from here. Trent is MIA—he was gone before we woke up— but I know he's somewhere; he wouldn't leave Ryan on his own, and part of me is pretty convinced he wouldn't leave me either.

"Who do you have locked up?" I ask Vin.

He eyes me shrewdly. "Who are you looking for?"

"No one. It's just a question."

He stares at me, unmoving.

"Fine," I groan. "Melissa."

"Why Melissa?"

"I have my reasons."

"Penance? Forgiveness?"

"No."

"Yes. She was Caroline's closest friend. Do you have some things you want to say to her? Or more importantly, do you have some things you want to hear from her?"

"No."

"Yes."

"Stop that," I growl.

Vin sits forward in his seat, his arms coming to rest on his desk. "Melissa won't forgive you and even if she did it wouldn't help. You don't feel bad for her. You don't even feel bad for Caroline. You feel bad for yourself."

"No, I don't."

"Yes, you do."

"He's right," Ryan says quietly.

I stare at him, shocked. "Are you siding with him?"

"He's right," he repeats.

"Even your boy knows," Vin tells me. "And I bet if we brought your buddy Trent in here, he'd agree too. That dude has definitely killed a time or two, but you don't see him wandering around all sad-faced and begging everyone who will listen for forgiveness."

"That's not what I'm doing," I tell him hotly.

"Not yet. But if you go in there with Melissa, you'll start. She won't say it's okay, because for her it's not. You killed her friend. You gotta learn to live with that."

I shake my head in frustration.

"You told Hyperion here because you thought he'd make it all better, didn't you?"

I want to leave. I want to pull my knife, take my best shot at him, and shut his mouth.

"But he couldn't do it, could he? What'd he tell you, Kitten? That you'd never get over it?"

"I killed a woman."

"You'll never get over it."

Stupid freaking know-it-all pimp!

"You've done it, haven't you, Hyperion?"

There's a long pause, a silence that fills the room, expands then bursts, leaving it feeling empty and cold.

"Yeah," Ryan admits roughly.

"We all have. Anyone who really wants to live has done it."

"Doesn't mean I'm okay with it," I mutter.

"No one says you should be."

"This is pointless," I snap, sorry I brought it up. "We need to decide where we go from here."

"I told you, same as I told the people out there: we don't make a move with your friends until we get our hands on the guy who killed Rebecca."

"They'll never hand him over," Ryan tells him honestly.

Vin spreads his hands. "Then where we go from here is nowhere. Not with the cannibals."

"You're being impossible," I growl. "You know you don't stand a chance without their help."

"I also know everyone here won't work with those people, not in a million years."

"Not even if they get Bryan," Ryan agrees.

"Nope. It's just not going to happen. So I don't care that they won't hand him over. In fact, I'm counting on that."

"Because then it's their choice that you don't work together, not yours."

"We tried to be reasonable," Vin says in mock sadness.

I begin to the pace the room, unable to hide my frustration. "You've already been living on borrowed time here, using the Leaders you captured to put on a show. That can't last forever. Eventually one of them will get sick of prison and betray you, even if it means dying. Then what will you do? The Colony will be at your door in a heartbeat and your Guard can't hold them off."

"I could hand it over to Marlow instead," Vin suggests calmly. "Absorb it into The Hive."

"The other Colonies won't just let that go. They'll take it back."

"We'll find out."

I stop pacing, my eyes landing on his unnaturally calm face. "When?"

"Soon," he says quietly, watching me too. "In the next half hour or so."

"He's on his way, isn't he?"

"He's been spotted. He's bringing an army. Just like you said he would."

I square my shoulders, standing tall and defiant. "You don't think that I—"

"Why would I?"

"But you don't trust anyone."

Vin looks down at his desk where his hands are clasped together loosely. He's absently spinning his ring on his finger the way he does when he's thinking, only I wonder if it's as unconscious an act as I imagine. He pauses, pulling the ring from his finger and looking it over thoughtfully.

"Today is as good a day as any to start," he mutters.

"What's the plan?" Ryan asks curtly. "What will you do when Marlow gets here?"

"I haven't decided," Vin says on a sigh, slipping the ring back on his finger. "I'll open the doors. I'll let him in. I'll listen. From there, I don't know."

"Letting him in is pretty much letting him have this place," I remind him.

"It's better than letting the Colonies have it back."

"They'll probably take it back anyway."

"Maybe. But they have bigger things on their mind right now."

"Like what?"

"Like the mess you started with the Vashons."

I scowl at him. "We didn't start anything. Marlow sent us to them and—"

"He sent the Colonists there too," Ryan says.

"What?"

Vin is nodding at Ryan. "I think so. The timing is too perfect. He sent you there and days later the Colonists attack an enemy they've left alone for at least four years? Pretty convenient."

"But why?" I ask.

"Because he's not strong enough to attack them himself."

"The Colonists or the Vashons?"

"Take your pick. He hates them both. Now they're busy fighting each other."

"The Hive boat," Ryan says bitterly. "He sent us sailing down the river in the dead of night in a bright white boat, straight past the Colonies, heading for Vashon Island. He probably gave it a day, and then went to the Colonies and told them he'd been to a meeting with the Vashons. A meeting they called about joining forces and overthrowing them."

"It's not completely a lie," I say.

"But it was the other way around. It was him bringing the idea to the Vashons."

"Intent is everything," Vin agrees.

"So now Marlow has the Colonies fighting the Vashons, two of the largest forces left in the city. His two biggest rivals."

"And one of his closest men is on the inside of an undefended Colony building," I say, looking to Vin.

"He thinks he's coming here to take this place," he says quietly. "He has no idea it's already been taken."

"He'll kill people," Ryan warns.

"Not if I throw the doors open and go out to meet him."

"That's why you're opening the doors to him?" I ask skeptically. "To save the lives of the people inside?"

"Well, that and I don't want him damaging my home."

"You still think you can hold onto it?"

He stands suddenly, his eyes hard. Determined.

"Either I keep what's mine," he says severely, "or I'll watch it burn."

"And what happens to the people inside? The ones following you? Trusting you blindly?"

"We all have our own paths to follow," he replies coldly.

I scoff at him. "You're full of it."

"Usually, yes."

"You won't leave these people to die and you won't leave them to Marlow. You're not that selfish."

He raises his eyebrows at me. "Since when?"

"Since you tasted real leadership. Not control, not fear, not power. They follow you because they love you and you get off on that more than anything."

"I wouldn't say more than anything. I'm still a man, Kitten."

"Then act like one."

He grins slightly, eyeing me. "Gladly."

"Stop."

Vin and I both look at Ryan. He's standing just behind me, his arms crossed over his chest and his eyes locked on Vin. He's not himself—not the warm, funny guy I've come to know and love.

He's Arena Ryan, made of stone and fire.

"Stop talking to her like that," Ryan warns Vin, "or I'll show you what a man looks like."

Vin's grin doesn't falter, but his eyes change. They're amused. "I understand it's meant to sound like a threat, but I feel like you're flirting with me, Hyperion."

"You're not my type and she's not yours, so

back off."

"Is that how it is? You're finally staking your claim on her?"

"She's not a piece of property to be claimed."

Vin snorts. "That's cute, but it's a lie and you know it. Things aren't like they used to be. Resources are scarce. She's one of the rarest items I've seen in a long time and if you don't hurry up and mark your territory, someone else will and it won't be sweet and it sure as hell won't be pretty."

Ryan tenses. "It won't happen like that. Not as long as I'm alive."

"You're walking around with a diamond in your hand hoping a city of thieves will let you keep it. Once Marlow marches through that door, you won't be able to keep her any more than I can keep this Colony." Vin's voice lowers, softening slightly. "We're both about to lose everything. I'm willing to destroy what's mine to keep it from being taken. What are you going to do?"

Ryan stares back at Vin for a long time. I don't bother speaking up. I don't tell them I'm my own person and they don't need to defend me, that I'm no one's property, blah, blah, blah. They wouldn't listen to me, so why bother? And here's the real bitch of it: I don't know that it's necessarily true. I don't know that they're wrong.

I remember the way Marlow looked at me when I was in his Hive. I remember what it felt like to tell him I was a Benjamin, the reaction he had and the feeling it gave me in the pit of my stomach. I know what it means, I'm not an idiot. I understand what Vin can see, what Marlow wants, and what

Ryan will die to protect it.

"I'll kill Marlow."

I close my eyes, feeling defeated.

Ryan is completely calm, completely certain, and completely out of his friggin' mind.

"Ryan, you—" I begin tiredly, opening my eyes.

"Give me an opening and I'll kill Marlow."

I feel sick to my stomach, but Vin is grinning.

"Hyperion," he says slowly, "you got yourself a deal."

Chapter Eleven

"He's playing you!" I shout at Ryan.

My voice echoes off the hard, gray walls of the showers. We're waiting for the line to form outside—the line of Colonists being rounded up and sent away down the tunnels to hide from Marlow and his men. Vin has a lot of confidence in his ability to talk Marlow down from killing everyone inside, but he's not insane. Confidence does not equal a sure thing, so the entire place—aside from the Guard—is being evacuated. Trent seems pretty sure we can find our way out without getting lost and dying in the dark. As much as I trust his wicked sharp eyes and bizarre computer brain that probably mapped every inch of tunnel we've seen so far, I have my doubts. About everything.

Right now as I stand in front of Ryan shouting, I know people can hear us—especially the guards just outside the door—but I don't care. I'm angry and they can all know it. I hope they feel it, taste it. Choke on it.

To my surprise, Ryan laughs. "Of course he's playing me."

"Then why did you agree to it?"

"Because it needs to be done."

"You can't kill Marlow."

"He's a man. All men can be killed. Vin will find me the opening to make it happen."

"He'll screw you over is what he'll do."

"Not on this. He needs Marlow dead just as much as I do."

"Why do you need him dead?"

"Because it's the only way to make sure he never lays a hand on you."

"We could leave like you were talking about."

"You said not until this is over. It's a long way from over."

"I don't care what I said! We'll leave right now." I grab his arm, tugging on him hard. He's too strong. I can't move him. "Let's go!"

"No."

"Why not?"

"Because I'm not a coward."

"Well, I am. Let's go!"

Ryan smiles at me as I keep yanking on his arm. "No, you're not."

"I'm scared and I'm ready to run. That's a coward."

"But you're not scared for you. You're scared for me."

"What's the difference?"

"A lot."

I try a different tactic—one I've never used before. One I don't even know how to use.

I stand in front of him, taking his face in my hands and pressing my body to his. His eyes turn wary. He knows what I'm doing, but he's not about to stop me. He breathes in deeply before weaving his arms around my waist and holding me to him.

"Please, Ryan," I whisper, my eyes begging his. "Please don't try to do this. You're not a murderer. It's not worth it."

He leans his head down until our foreheads are touching. "It is to me."

"Not to me. And if you die…" I can't finish that sentence. I can't even finish the thought.

"If anything happens to me, Trent will get you out of the city. He'll run with you."

"Why don't you run with me now?"

"Because it's not only about you. It's about every person in this building. It's about everyone in The Hive. All the women in the stables, the babies being traded to the Colonies."

"Crenshaw's daughter," I mumble.

"Yeah. With Marlow and the Colonies gone, things could be different."

"They could get worse."

"Or they could get better. We'll never know until we try. Which is why you need to go. Now."

He's right, but he's also wrong. We have to try. We have to get Marlow out of power, but what he's wrong about is me. I'm not going anywhere. Not without him.

"All right," I say quietly, pulling away. "I'll go."

He's not buying it. I don't have to look at him to know it; I can feel it in the way he doesn't answer me—and just as I'm planning on double-crossing him, I get the feeling he's going to double-cross me. It's all for the greater good and because everybody cares about everybody, but in the end isn't it all just lying? I don't care what color you paint it, it's still ugly.

I hear footsteps down the hall. People are filing into the doorway, nervous eyes scanning the room like they suspect they're being led to the slaughter. Like they're looking for more blood and bodies. More hungry cannibals licking their lips and gnashing their teeth.

Trent leads the way, jumping smoothly down into the drain. Ryan and the guards from outside start to lead people toward the hole, the first group being the Team Leaders that were captured and held inside the building, used to keep up communication with the other Colonies. It was Trent's idea to bring them out. He said we might need them again when we made our move against the stadiums. They could help us walk right through the front door.

I watch as they go one by one down into the darkness, a few familiar faces (Melissa included) passing me by slowly, and I start to wonder how long this is going to take. There are a lot of people here, and even if all of them aren't going, enough are. And they're making a lot of noise.

I bolt from the room. I don't bother using stealth or finesse; it doesn't matter. Ryan has his hands halfway to the center of the world helping to lower people down. He doesn't even see me leave.

When I'm halfway to the roof, I hear the first blast. It's far off, but not far enough. I'd say it came from somewhere within a five-block radius and it's not alone. It's followed quickly by another. Then another.

I weave through the now panicking crowd up the stairs, breaking into a run wherever I can find the space. Once I reach the fire stairs heading toward the roof, I'm completely alone. Right until I find him.

He's exactly where I expected him to be: right where he was last night as dawn was breaking and he was worrying about losing his castle. Beyond him on the horizon I can see plumes of smoke rolling into the sky. It's something I usually only see on this scale during market days when all the gangs meet, eat, drink, barter, and make me ache with loneliness.

"What was it?" I ask Vin.

"The barricades keeping the Risen up against the outer gate. He's blowing them. In the next twenty minutes the outside will be swarming with more zombies than it's seen in years."

"And Marlow will be inside."

"That's the plan." He glances over his shoulder at me. "Isn't it also the plan that you leave with everyone else?"

"That's Ryan's plan, not mine."

"He wants to keep you safe."

"And you're using that to your advantage."

He looks away again. "I use everything to my advantage."

"And everyone?" I ask hotly.

He ignores me.

"I'm not going."

"I'm not surprised. He'll kill Marlow whether you're here or not."

"Not if I kill Marlow first."

Vin shoots me a look so sharp it hurts. I feel it sting in my skin as my heart rate spikes painfully. "You will not," he snarls.

I narrow my eyes at him. "You don't get to tell me what to do any more than I can tell you what to do."

"Listen to me, Joss," he says harshly, taking my arm in his iron grip. "You will stay as far away from Marlow as possible, do you understand? If you go near him, you'll ruin everything. You'll not only get me killed, but your boy as well. Do you understand me?"

"No," I growl, trying in vain to pull away. "I don't understand your plans at all, which is why I don't trust them and it's why I won't listen to you. I think you're using Ryan. I think you're going to let him do your dirty work for you and then you'll betray him. You'll get him killed."

He lets go of my arm, nearly shoving me away as he does it. "You don't know that."

"I do, because I know what you're capable of."

"No one knows what I'm capable of. Least of all me."

"But you're not denying it, which is the scary thing. You're not even trying to lie to me."

"Would it make you feel better if I did?"

"I will kill you," I warn him, my voice laced with venom. "If Ryan dies in there, I will kill you myself. I will do it slowly with a smile on my face and I will dance in your blood as you die."

Vin smiles slowly. "I think you mean that, Kitten."

"I will live it if you make me. It's up to you."

His smile fades as another explosion erupts in the streets.

Captain Hook approaches.

"I don't know exactly what's going to happen today," he tells me seriously. "But I swear to you, if I can help it, I won't give you a reason to kill me."

I sigh, offering him my hand. "That's crap, but I'll take it. Only because I honestly believe that's the best I can expect from you."

He takes my hand in his, but instead of shaking it he squeezes it once firmly. Affectionately. "It's more than I've ever given anyone."

***

Vin called it: just over twenty minutes later and The Hive is outside the gates. They're smart and at least a little patient because they don't break the gates entirely, even though they've shown that they could have blown the old empty shipping containers to pieces the same way they did to the outer barriers. But they don't want this place swarming with zombies—not when they plan to take ownership of it.

Vin takes his six remaining Guard members with him to the gate. Ryan and I, one of us extremely sour-faced and annoyed at the other for not leaving when they were told to, stay inside and watch the arrival from the massive windows of the main sleeping area. Vin thought it was better

Marlow didn't see us right away, just in case he's angry with us—though I think if anyone should be angry, it should be us. And I am. I've clenched my hands so tightly my fingernails are leaving red crescents in my palms. If I press much harder I'll draw blood.

"You should have gone."

I roll my eyes. "Don't start."

"You'll never be safe if he's alive," Ryan continues, his voice tight. "You or any other woman in the wild. You can't tell me with what we know about him and his deal with the Colonies that you don't think he deserves to die."

"Who are you trying to convince, Ryan? Me or yourself?"

He doesn't answer and when I look over at him he refuses to meet my eyes.

"You don't have to do this," I tell him softly. "You'll hate yourself if you do."

"If I don't do it, who will?"

I look back to the gate as it swings open with a long, grating shriek. Men step through the container, moving into the open space inside the gates like they already own the place. Like it was theirs before it was even built. Like the world belongs to them, along with everything and anyone in it.

"I'm sure if you asked nicely you'd find a few takers," I mutter.

"Vincent!" a familiar voice cries, carrying across the gardens to the building.

When Marlow steps into the early morning light with his arms spread wide, I want to sprint to him. I want to leap into his arms and drive my knife so deep into his back it passes through his body and pierces me on the other side. I will gladly bleed with him if it means I can watch the light drain from his eyes up close and extremely personal. I will suck his last breath from his lungs and hold it in my mine until his life is burned out in the angry ash of my heart.

I don't like murder, I'm not a killer at heart, but this man is a now a threat to the only thing in the world I can even vaguely call mine, and if killing him with my bare hands keeps that safe, I'll gladly live with his ghost for the rest of my life.

Vin approaches Marlow without hesitation. They hug each other warmly, and that right there speaks volumes. There are no searches, no patting down to look for weapons. There's so much trust here, so much tried-and-true history that they don't consider each other the least bit of a threat. Not an immediate one anyway. It makes me more and more convinced that Vin plans to use Ryan. Even if he's given an "opening," I wonder if Ryan will be allowed to kill Marlow.

"Here they come," Ryan mumbles.

Marlow is walking with Vin across the gardens, happily surveying the area with a grin on his face. He points to plants as they pass them, gestures to the roof, asking Vin questions as they go. Vin looks like he's answering, a similar grin on his face, but as they get closer I can see a tightness around his eyes. Maybe it's the glare from the sun, but more than likely it's Marlow. It's too many cooks in the kitchen. *His* kitchen.

"It's impressive," Marlow says as they step inside, the doors being yanked open by a mix of Hive and Guard.

All six of Vin's men are with him, the only followers he has left in the building, while Marlow has brought eight of his army. The rest are outside in the gardens milling around, checking out the grounds. I can see a few wandering toward the water, some others looking at the animals. Slowly but surely they're circling the building. It's a not-so-subtle message to Vin that Daddy is here and he'd better not forget it.

"They did a great job setting it up, but that's what they do," Vin agrees.

"And where are they now? How many workers are there?"

"They're locked safely away," Vin lies. "I didn't want itchy trigger fingers to kick off a war. They're not a strong group, not when it comes to fighting."

"More farmers and bakers, eh? That was to be expected. We'll split them down the middle. Send half to The Hive, leave half here. We could use skilled farmers at home. Could cut our dependence on other resources."

I bristle at the vague reference to his deal with the Colonies.

"So what else is here? Are there many women? Have you started training?"

Vin shrugs carelessly. "Haven't had the time. We only just took control of the building."

"Good, good. We'll want to get on that quickly. A lot of our inventory is aging, looking tired. You could start fresh here. Get all new girls. Speaking of…" Marlow turns to face me, a wicked smile on his ugly face. "Hello, my dear."

"Fuck you," I tell him coolly.

Marlow throws his head back, laughing full from the gut. My knife hand itches.

"Oh, I do like you," he finally says, crossing the room slowly. Ryan moves closer as well. "I'm so glad you're still alive. I was worried about you."

"You sent me to die."

"I sent you on an errand. If you had died on that errand you would have showed me you're weak, but here you stand—alive and well and beautiful as ever. Vincent, what are your plans for this one?"

I glare at Vin over Marlow's shoulder, just waiting for one of them to give me a reason.

"I hadn't decided yet," he says simply.

Marlow nods thoughtfully, turning to head back toward Vin. "I think we'll keep her as a bargaining chip. She still a Benjy?"

"Far as I know."

"Good. If we're going to keep this place we'll either have to fight for it or pay for it. I'd rather not lose any men right now, not with things as tense as they are, and Westbrook has expensive tastes. She could be just what we need."

And there's my reason.

I take several quick steps toward Marlow's turned back, my lips curling up over my teeth in disgust. I'm almost to him, Vin shooting me a horrified look over his shoulder. I'm reaching out to take hold of him with one hand and unsheathe my knife with another. I'm going to kill him. I'm going to end this for everyone.

I'm swung off the ground and spun around in a circle. Shouting in anger, I thrash and claw at the arm around me. I know it's Ryan but my frustration is so deep I dig into his skin, drawing blood and snarling like an animal. The room spins in front of my eyes in a blur, and just before my feet are put back on solid ground I catch a familiar face in Marlow's guard.

Andy.

"Slow down," Ryan whispers brusquely in my ear, his arm still around my waist as he holds my back against his front. "Not yet."

"Tie her up," Marlow commands, sounding oddly disinterested. "Be careful not to mark her skin, but keep her contained. I'll take her with me when I leave. Now, Vincent, show me the rest of the building. I want to see what I'm buying."

Marlow and Vin leave without a look back, followed by four of each of their guards. Ryan and I are left alone with the remaining crew: two of Vin's men, four of Marlow's. I'm both relieved and annoyed when Andy steps toward me with a length of rope.

"Put her down by the door," Andy tells Ryan sternly.

He does as he's told, leading me to a vacant chair by the door and gently pushing me down until I'm glaring up at Andy.

"Tie it loosely," Ryan warns under his breath.

Andy shifts his eyes to the other men in the room. They're all watching us.

"So I don't mark her skin. Yeah, I heard him."

"So I can get loose and snap your neck," I tell him, leaning forward to get in his face as he leans down to tie my ankles. "I've missed you, Andy. Did you miss me?"

"Shut your stupid mouth," he whispers bitterly. "If they hear you—"

"They'll know all about you. That's the point."

He tugs harshly on the rope wrapping around my ankles. I fight the urge to wince as the rough fibers scrape across my skin.

"Go ahead, tell them. They'll kill me right here and you'll be next."

"You heard Marlow. I'm expensive. You guys aren't allowed to touch me."

"Not you. Him."

I sit back hard in the chair, my eyes going to Ryan. He's watching Andy's hands as they secure knots, each movement making me more and more Marlow's prisoner.

Andy cuts the rope with a small knife before sitting up on his knees to tie my wrists.

"If they hurt Ryan—" I begin, my teeth clenched tight.

Andy looks at me sharply. "They won't. Not if you keep it together. You're too emotional. Sit back, shut up, and let me do my job."

I lean my head back until it rests against the chair, my eyes open and vacant.

Emotional.

Not as bad a word as hope, but definitely not good. It's deadly. More deadly than Risen, zombie, Colonist, or gang. I've run from it for years—

hidden in the dark, scurrying like an animal—and now here it is, the thing that will get me killed: I've gotten emotional and it's made me stupid.

"Fine," I spit out. "I'll be quiet."

"Good. Keep your mouth shut and your ears open. Be patient. Be smart. Wait for the right moment."

I lower my eyes to his face, ready to ask him what he's talking about, when I feel the cold steel of a blade sliding against my wrist. He's finished tying my hands down, but he's done it loosely. There's just enough play for me to lift them slightly. Just enough room between my skin and the wood for the thin blade of his knife to hide.

Chapter Twelve

Ryan goes to stand with the other men in the room, siding with the two guys from Vin's Guard. I think he's a little relieved. I'm still here, where he doesn't want me to be, but I'm contained. Me being tied to a chair doesn't exactly bother him because he has no intention of Marlow leaving with me. He has no intention of Marlow leaving at all.

That worries me.

In my gut I know Ryan shouldn't do this. For one, Vin wants it. He pushed him toward it, practically putting the idea in his head. Vin's joy is a huge red flag for me. Secondly, it's an emotional decision, something I can say from experience is a bad idea. I'm regretting a lot right now as my butt goes numb in this uncomfortable chair and my fingers cramp from slowly working Andy's knife back and forth over the ropes holding me down. I don't know if he meant for me to cut myself loose with it or hold onto it to defend myself when things get ugly, but I'm not interested in being caged so

I'm putting it to use immediately. SOB could have sharpened it for me, though.

The third most obvious reason to me why Ryan shouldn't kill Marlow is that Ryan isn't a killer. It's not in him. Zombies are one thing; a man is another. Ryan's a diplomat, not a mercenary. He's done it before and I know it's still with him. I don't want more blood on his hands that he'll never be able to wash off.

"That's it."

Vin's voice drifts down from the rafters where he and Marlow are walking around the upper level. They make their way slowly down the large open staircase toward the main floor where we all wait patiently. Or anxiously. Or murderously.

"It's not as big as the aquarium," Marlow says critically. "But the grounds are bigger. There's more space for gardening. Farming. Could be worth it. It could definitely be worth it."

"It being me," I shout before remembering I'm supposed to shut up.

My hand on the knife freezes as all eyes shift to me.

Marlow chuckles as he and Vin clear the stairs and cross the room. "Don't flatter yourself. You'll definitely grease the wheels, but you won't cover the entire cost. We'll have to check the other inventory we get from this place. Where are they, by the way?"

"Where are who?" Vin asks innocently.

"The other people. The hundreds of people you claimed you have hidden away here. Did we not see the entire property? Where are they?"

"Basement."

"We saw the basement."

"Sub-basement."

"Vincent."

"They're around, don't worry, Marlow," Vin sings easily. He slowly paces around the room, subtly putting distance between himself and Marlow. "I said they were being kept safe. I didn't say they were being kept safe here."

"Don't double speak with me," Marlow warns.

"It was a misunderstanding."

Marlow watches Vin closely, his eyes narrowing to sharp slits. "Maybe we need to be more clear with each other. Bring me the girl!"

Two of Marlow's men take hold of my chair and drag me backwards to the center of the room. Vin's eyes follow me with interest, but he never stops moving. Never stops circling Marlow so very slowly.

I'm parked beside Marlow, the chair slammed forward so hard I worry for a second it will tip over and my face will meet the beaten hardwood floors. I also worry I'll lose hold of my knife. I grip it so hard it turns slightly, the blade digging into my skin.

"Take it easy, Marlow," Vin warns casually. "Westbrook won't want her with a broken face."

"What good is she as payment for an empty building?"

"I don't know what you mean."

"I want the people, Vincent. This place is useless to me without the people to run it."

"Bodies," Vin says thoughtfully, still turning.

Still pacing. He drags every eye in the room with him, Marlow's men tensing as he steps behind them, between them, swoops in slowly near Marlow before gliding away again. "Hands, legs, feet, arms, backs to break. This world is worthless without people, isn't it? No one to work the fields. No one to cook and clean. No one to create the law, to break the law, enforce the law. No one for the zombies to eat. No one to watch over you while you sleep. No one to warm your bed."

"Get to it," Marlow snaps.

Vin suddenly stops moving and I'm almost dizzy because of it. It feels like the entire room jolts. He's standing to Marlow's left, the same side I'm sitting on. Ryan, I notice, is standing to Marlow's right, just outside his peripheral.

"I want the building," Vin tells him firmly, no longer whimsical. "I want the building and half the people in it. Men or women, I don't care."

"And what will you do with it?"

"I'll run it, same way you run The Hive. We'll do business, same as you do business with the Colonies, but I don't like the terms. Both those and the building will be entirely mine."

"Why would I ever allow that?"

"Because if you don't, you'll never see a single one of the people from this place. You can have half or nothing. Run the numbers on that and get back to me."

"You're an idiot. What's happened to you?"

Vin smirks at him. "Same thing that happens to every man who tastes power. I've grown hungry."

"You've gotten greedy."

"I've become wise," Vin counters in an eerie whisper. "I know you can't man this place. You wouldn't know how even if you did have the bodies to fill it—which you don't, by the way. Do you know how I know that? It's because I know everything about you."

Marlow examines Vin for a long time, neither of them moving. "So this is what it's come to? After all these years, after all I've done for you, you're going to turn on me? You're no better than your dad was."

"Oh I'm much better than my dad was, because I have his mistakes to learn from. I won't live under your thumb forever and I definitely won't let you put me in the bottom of the Sound."

"You're on the same course. He tried to shake me on, just like you're doing now."

Vin's responding grin is cold. "He wasn't holding all the cards."

Marlow grabs a fistful of my hair, yanking my head to the side violently. I bite my lip to keep from crying out in pain.

"Not all the cards," he sneers.

"Take her," Vin replies flippantly, waving his hand like he's brushing off the loss of a sock. "I'd hate for you to have made the trip for nothing."

Marlow shakes his head, his face contorted in anger. "I could take everything from you right now."

"And lose one hundred head. This building too. What would be the point of paying Westbrook for it if you can't manage it? Give the building to me, half the people will be yours, we'll work as partners, and you'll never have to do business with the Colonies again."

"I have a better idea," Marlow snarls. "You and your pathetic Guard will die here and now, but not until you watch me drain every last cent out of this girl. Then I'll burn this building with your bodies inside it and leave its charred remains as a reminder to anyone who ever thinks they can take what's mine!"

Vin pinches his lips together briefly, appearing to think it over. "Well, I mean, it's less appealing than my solution, but it's something to think about. Let me sleep on it?"

"You're not seeing another sunset."

"I'll bet you anything I see one more than you."

The room explodes into action around me. Marlow releases my hair as I frantically saw at the rope holding my left arm down. I feel like weeping at the end, my weak and sore muscles in my still-healing arm aching and crying out against the abusively odd angles I'm asking my hand to work at. I cut my skin again, deeply. Blood oozes over the ropes down onto the seat, seeping hot and sticky into the fabric of my jeans. Finally I cut the rope hard enough to get my arm free.

I look up to find Vin and his Guard fighting the men that came in with Marlow, Andy included. Andy has jumped in to fight Ryan, a fact I'm almost happy about because I think it's less likely he'll actually kill him. Andy might hurt him for show, and that pisses me off something awful—I'm not even promising I won't seek revenge for it—but at least I don't feel like he's going to die right this second.

It's when I feel Marlow's hand on my chin, forcing my head back roughly, that I realize I'm the one in real danger.

He doesn't say a word to me. He stares down at me gasping for breath and fighting to free myself, a cold glint in his eyes and a stone's grasp on my face. I only have a second to think about it, a moment to react, and even as I do I know it won't be enough.

I spin the knife in my hand, pointing the blade out and down. I want to go for his neck or his eye, do him like a zombie on the streets, but I don't have the time or the reach. His arms are blocking me and I have to make do with what I've got.

I slash my small blade across his stomach, sinking it as deep as I can. He gasps, his hand falling away from my face as he doubles over in pain and surprise. Both will wear off too soon.

He's stumbled back too far for me to be able to make another stab at him so I don't bother. I can't reach my bigger, sharper knife I strapped to my ankle, so I do the only thing I can: I start hacking at the other rope on my right hand and hope I can get free before he recovers.

I never stood a chance. Maybe not ever. Maybe not since the day my parents died and I ran and ran and ran. I've been running for years. Hiding from the monsters that want to destroy me, that won't quit until I'm lying on the ground in a pool of my own blood and the stars are going black in the night sky for the last time. Maybe I was never meant to be more than a memory in the mind of a bright, beautiful boy. Just some words on a wall. Hidden music echoing in the darkness.

As Marlow lifts his head, his eyes landing on mine and promising me the end I've always known was coming, I'm surprised to find myself calm. I'm not ready to die, not by a long shot, but if it has to happen at least I got to live—even if it was just for a little while, a brief flash of lightning in the eye of a terrible storm. It was still brilliant and it was mine.

Marlow disappears from view. He falls to the ground in a blur of color and slices of silver. He cries out in rage and pain, a terrible howl that echoes through the whole room. Men stop fighting, putting distance between each other to look at the madness still brewing at my feet.

It goes on forever, but when it's over, when the crazy finally stills and the room is deathly silent, we all stare in amazement.

Marlow is dead. More than dead, he's nearly disappeared. His body is riddled with stab wounds and bite marks, his blood running across the floor in wild, dark torrents as his vacant eyes stare up at the ceiling. His mouth still hangs open in an expression of shock and pain. It happened so fast. Too fast to follow and too fast to understand.

And there in the center of it, coated in blood, red tissue dripping from his chin like the juice of a watermelon from a starving man's maw, is Andy.

Chapter Thirteen

"The f—" Vin begins, his face a mask of shock and confusion.

Ryan is at my side immediately. He takes my borrowed, craptastic knife from my hand and uses it to quickly cut the ropes still holding me down. When I'm free, my eyes still fixated on the mess at my feet, he runs his hands over me. I hear him hiss when he finds the cuts on the inside of my wrist.

I shake my head weakly, dragging my eyes to his. "It's nothing. It happened while I was cutting myself free."

"What about your leg? It's wet with blood. How bad is it?"

"The blood's from my wrist, it's fine."

Ryan lifts my arm into the air, hovering my bleeding hand above my head as he rips the sleeve off his shirt to apply pressure to my cut.

"It's not fine for your wrist to be bleeding like this. You might have nicked the artery."

"I'm still doing better than he is," I mutter,

looking around Ryan at Marlow.

Andy is sitting on top of him. His eyes are closed and his hands are pressed into the open wounds he dug into the man's body. I can hear a hum coming from his motionless mouth—a mouth still dripping with blood and tissue. He's not even a little bit worried about the men surrounding him, staring at him, and he shouldn't be. No one is moving. So far, Ryan and I are the only ones who have really spoken since it happened.

That won't last.

"Vin!" I shout.

His eyes snap to mine for the briefest of seconds, but it's all he needs. He's back in control of himself. He scans the room, his eyes lingering on Andy for one long moment, then he's all action.

"You're leaving," Vin tells Marlow's men.

"Is he…" one of the men begins before becoming lost. "Is Andy…?"

"A cannibal, yes. And if you don't want to become the second course to his dinner, you'll get your ass out of here now. Let this be a warning to you all. The Hive is not welcome here. This is my house, aligned with the cannibals and run by my rules, and anyone who has a problem with that or thinks they have the balls to rip it from my cold dead hands is welcome to give it their best shot. Now get out!"

They run. They don't even hesitate, and I don't blame them one bit. Two of Marlow's closest men, his most trusted allies, just went biblical on his face. There is no loyalty anymore. Leadership is dead and when you find yourself on an every-man-for-himself-type basis in the middle of a room full of enemies, psychos, and traitors, running is the smart choice. I would applaud them if Ryan would let me lower my hand.

"I'm not going to die," I tell him irritably.

"Not if I can help it, no."

"Everyone out now," Vin says sharply, already ushering his Guard toward the back of the room. "We gotta move."

"Where are we going?" Ryan asks, helping me to my feet.

"The showers. We need to get in the tunnels now."

There's shouting from outside. Men come running from every corner of the property, all of them heading for the group of guys that just left.

Vin points out the window. "That is not going to end well for us. Marlow came here with at least thirty men. They won't be afraid of a traitor, a flesh eater, and a girl when it dawns on them that they have us seriously outnumbered. They're shaken but they're not idiots."

"Andy!" Ryan shouts.

Andy looks up calmly, his eyes creepy crystal clear. "I'm right behind you."

The swarm outside is growing. Several men are already running toward the door, about to make it inside.

"Then you're already dead," Vin replies darkly.

We run for the back of the building. I don't know if Andy is behind us, but I know Marlow's men are. I hear the door crash open, barked orders, the thunder of too many feet on the floor—too many to fight, too many to run from, but we do it anyway because every one of us is a child of the wild. We don't know how to quit.

Vin leads the way through the back halls, down the stairs and straight to the very familiar, very troubled shower room. It's seen a lot lately, but somehow I know I'll never see it again. I'll never come back here, no matter who is running the show. This place is tainted. It's dead to me, and when Vin throws open one of the cupboards and yanks out what I recognize as homemade explosives, I feel cotton candy light and sweet at the sight of it.

"What are you planning to do with that?" Ryan asks, scowling at the bundle in Vin's hand.

"Blow the exit behind us."

"You'll kill us."

"I know what I'm doing."

"Obviously not. That much clay will level half the building."

Vin is on the floor by the drain, circling it with brown lumps of explosives linked by a wiry black fuse. Most of his men are gone down the hole, running for their lives. If we're smart, we'll be right behind them, but it looks like the guys want to cat fight for a minute first.

"We don't have time for this," I warn them.

"Then get moving," Vin tells me.

Ryan shakes his head angrily. "The tunnels will collapse on us. We can't outrun what you're about to do."

"Get her out of here, Hyperion!"

"Don't kill her, Vincent!" Ryan shouts back.

Vin stops to glare up at Ryan, a rare moment

when the curtain is clearly raised on his emotions. He's livid. "I told you, I know wha—"

"That's too much clay," Andy says calmly, appearing in the doorway. "You'll kill us all."

Vin drops the explosives on the ground, making Ryan flinch. "Fine! You do it then. I'm getting out of here. Lower her down to me."

Vin smoothly drops himself down the hole before the guys can respond. I turn to look at them, to tell them to forget the explosives, but I hesitate when I see Andy.

"What's in your hand?"

"A heart."

"No."

"Marlow's?" Ryan asks, eyeing Andy warily.

"Yes."

"Why?" I demand.

"For the ceremony."

"What ceremony?"

"Do you really want to know?"

"No," I groan, feeling sick to my stomach.

"Kitten!" Vin cries from the darkness at our feet. "Now or never!"

He's not kidding. The building is filled with the sounds of footsteps and shouts. They don't know exactly where we are, but it won't be long until they find us. If we're leaving, we need to go now.

I look at Ryan. "You'll come down right behind me, right?"

"On your heels."

"Kitten!"

"Ryan."

"Go, Joss," he tells me firmly. "Go to

Crenshaw. I'll meet you there."

I lower my legs down into the hole. I do my best to not panic the second Vin grabs them. My first instinct is to kick the hell out of him until he lets go, maybe because he's kind of pissing me off lately, but also because I don't like being touched by someone I can't see. That's how zombies get you: in the dark when your guard is down.

Ryan takes hold of my right hand, my good one, and helps to lower me down into Vin's arms. It feels weird. It feels wrong. When he lets go of my hand, his face disappearing from the circle of light above me, it feels like goodbye.

"Come on."

Vin doesn't hesitate to grab my hand and yank me forward. Once we're running at a sprint he lets go so we can both run our hands along the walls of the tunnel for guidance. I want to yell at him that we need to wait for Ryan, but I know it's better to get out of the way. Back there I'm a liability. With me gone he can concentrate on the dangerous, stupid, necessary thing he's about to do.

"Do these tunnels branch out?" Vin asks me.

I nod even though he can't see it in the pitch black we've dropped into. "Yeah, they do. A lot."

"Do you remember how to get out?"

"Not really."

"Great. So somewhere down here your buddy Trent led all two hundred of my people into a maze he doesn't know how to get out of?"

"Trent can get out," I assure him, grunting as I stumble on something in the dark.

I can feel Vin backtrack, coming into my space.

"You okay?"

"Yeah, I'm fine."

"This is pointless," he says bitterly. "We'll never find our way out of here in the dark."

"Do you think we're far enough away from the blast they're about to set off?"

"No."

"Oh."

Vin curses under his breath. I hear his feet shuffle through the water as he feels around the tunnel, looking for God knows what. The cannibals keep torches in the tunnels they use but they said they'd never been this far north before, and if they left one from their visit, we passed it back at the drain. No way I'm going back looking for that.

"We should keep moving," Vin says, taking my hand again.

I pull it back. "And go where? Deeper into the tunnels with no clue where we're going? We could accidentally circle back and end up right under the MOHAI again."

"We're still under it now," he says impatiently. "We haven't run very far."

"We need to wait for Ryan and Andy."

"He told us to go. Besides, does your boy know how to get out of here? Can he see in the dark?"

"No, but Andy can. He's a cannibal. He knows the tunnels."

Vin chuckles darkly. "That son of a bitch. Don't think I'm taking him out the second I get the chance."

"Take him out how?"

"Not on a date, that's for sure."

"You're going to kill him?" I ask in amazement. "Why? He killed Marlow for you!"

"He didn't do it for me."

"It's still done."

"Not the way I planned."

"Oh no!" I cry sarcastically. "Vin didn't get his way. Poor baby."

"It makes a big difference how he did it. The difference between me taking over The Hive and The Hive chasing me into the sewers like a friggin' rat."

"How would you ever have taken hold of The Hive?"

"It doesn't matter," he replies with his signature composed calm. Whatever he's mad about, he's stowing it. For now. "It's done. It's all jacked, and now every member of my Pod is lost somewhere under the city."

"I told you, Trent can find his way out. You'll get your precious followers back. Which reminds me."

I take a swing at him. I'm not aiming for his face, but I'm not worried if I hit it. When my fist connects with something solid and slightly meaty, I'm pretty sure I've hit him in the chest.

"Ow!" he cries. "You punched me in the boob!"

"You were going to let Marlow have me, you ass!"

"Oh come on. No matter what, he wasn't making it out of that building alive."

"Ass."

"Whatever. Be mad, but while we're talking

about betrayal, how did you know Andy was a cannibal?"

"He ate Marlow, genius."

"Drop it. You knew before then, didn't you?"

I take a slow, silent step back from him. "Yes."

"How?"

"How do you think? I came here with the cannibals. I met him in the underground where they live and I'd seen him in The Hive when I went to Marlow with your ring. I put two and two together."

I take another step back.

"Where are you going?"

I freeze. "Away from you. I don't want to get punched in the boob."

His laugh fills the darkness with warmth that makes me realize I'm shivering. It's cold in here. My feet are wet and chilling my entire body, but more than anything I'm nervous. I'm worried about Ryan and part of me is just waiting for an explosion to rip through these tunnels until the sky collapses on us, smothering everyone.

"They're taking a long time."

Vin quiets, and just like that the warmth is gone. "I know."

"Should I be worried?"

"You should always be worried."

"Should I be scared?"

He doesn't answer right away, and when he does I wish he'd kept his mouth shut.

"Yeah."

"What if Marlow's guys got them?"

"Then they're dead."

It's amazing how fast my throat closes up. How

with those words, with the simple, ugly thought of it, my body wants to fold in two until I'm choking on the sobs rising in my chest.

I take a shaky step. I'm heading north.

Then I'm heading south—right onto my ass.

I feel like I'm underwater. My hearing is gone, my sight is destroyed from the sudden burst of bright firelight that flared up and burned out almost instantly. I have no idea which way is up or down, left or right. I try to call out to Vin but I don't know if I make any noise. Even if I do, he probably can't hear me.

I rise up my knees in the water, taking deep breaths that fill my lungs with smoke and dust that I can't see but I can definitely smell and taste. My hearing is coming back to me, but it's nearly worthless. It's a horrible ringing that I think is more painful than the *boom* from the blast was.

A hand brushes my arm. I'm shocked when my first reaction isn't to lash out in defense, to break every finger attached to it, or to run in the other direction. Instead I latch onto it with mine, immediately feeling the familiar hard circle of Vin's ring under my fingers.

"Are you okay?" I try to ask.

Whether he answers me or not, I don't hear it. His hand takes hold of mine, lacing our fingers together. He pulls me up, then we're running. We rush blindly through the tunnels, both of us tripping and stumbling over hidden obstacles or over our own feet. My balance feels off and when he falls to his knees, I know his is too. It's disorienting not being able to see, but with our hearing messed up too it feels like we're running in nothing. Like we're nowhere when we could be anywhere.

I don't know how long we run and I definitely don't know where we are, but when a light suddenly appears ahead, I yank Vin to a stop.

"Who do you think it is?" I whisper.

It's stupid and pointless, but I ask anyway.

The light is beginning to grow. It moves like firelight over the glistening, wet walls and part of me relaxes. It's a torch, one being carried by someone pretty tall. Someone like Trent.

The outline of the person is beginning to take shape as they close in on us. They're not just tall. The blackness of their shadow fills the tunnel behind them, making them look broad. Huge. Not like Trent at all.

More like Bryan.

Chapter Fourteen

The closer the torchlight comes, the more the tunnel fills with darkness. With shadow that's building behind the figure. Then it's not shadow. It's form, full and large. Too big to be friendly. Pale skin. Bright eyes. A malicious smile.

I look anxiously at Vin, desperate to warn him but lost over how to do it. How do you tell someone who can't hear you that the man cornering you both in a pre-dug grave is a killer? Worse yet—he's a cannibal.

I squeeze his hand hard, pulling his eyes from Bryan and down to me. His brow is pinched in confusion so I hurry to clear up our situation for him. I flip his hand over and scribble franticly with my finger. He's a smart guy. I'm hoping he can pick up what I'm saying.

Rebecca.

When I'm finished, I open my eyes emphatically and I write one more letter firmly across his dry palm.

X

He gets it. I can see it in the calm that comes over his face. The confusion clears and suddenly Vin is very, very sure of his world. He reaches slowly for my side. I want to ask what he's doing but when his fingers close around my ASP, I know. I shake my head, wanting to tell him I need it to fight, but he already has the weapon and he's pushing me behind him. I hate this and I want him to know it. I want to fight him on it, tell him I can help, but there's no time.

Bryan lunges at Vin. He wastes no time trying to get his hands on the smaller man's neck, but Vin is fast. Scary fast. I've never seen him fight before, there was never a reason, but seeing it now reminds me of something Nats said about him once. He's always lived like this. The end of the world, living in the wild—that's nothing new to Vin. He was an orphan on the streets when he was just a kid. He's always known how to fight. To survive.

But if he was an orphan as a kid, how does he have his dad's ring? His dad who was killed by Marlow for betraying him?

Bryan tosses aside the torch. The entire tunnel is instantly plunged into darkness and my heart leaps into my throat. I can hear my blood rushing in my ears and I wonder if that's my hearing coming back or my body going insane with terror. I'm scared for Vin because he's obviously Bryan's first concern, but I'm scared for me too because once Vin is dead, so am I.

I pull my blade out of my boot as I lower myself into a crouch. I doubt Bryan can see any better than we can, not immediately after using the torch. There's a very narrow window of opportunity here where he's just as blind as we are and if we're going to have any chance of surviving this, it has to happen when the playing field is nearly even.

I cautiously reach out with my free hand while keeping my knife steady in my right. I creep forward, feeling for legs. I'm hoping I'll know Vin's when I feel it—which means I'll probably know it when I don't feel it too. I need to find Bryan's leg. I need to take him out.

Water splashes against my face. I'm wound so tight I nearly cry out, but then I hear a shout. It's muffled and distant but it's there, which means my hearing is coming back—just in time to hear Bryan's teeth tear through my flesh.

I shake off the imagery steadily building against the blank canvas of my sight and I reach for the splash. I get hold of wet jeans just for a second before my left arm is kicked sharply. I eat the whimper of pain that shoots through my still healing arm, gagging on it as it lands bitter and salty in the back of my throat. Gritting my teeth, I reach out again and wrap my aching, angry fingers around ankle. It thrashes roughly to get rid of me, but I hang on. Quickly, I slide my hand up the leg to find the calf. It's huge. It's a hulking, rippling mass of muscle, and while Vin is an athletic guy, he's not built this way. At least I definitely hope he's not because if this is his leg, he's going to be seriously pissed at me in a second.

I slash my knife across the back of the leg. Just at the back of the ankle.

Right across the tendon.

The man goes down immediately, his right leg made useless by my blade. I feel the spray of water as he hits it along with a loud cry of pain and surprise. It echoes through the tunnel and deep into my ears.

There's a second spray, a second cry, a loud grunt, then a sharp crack. I know that last sound. That's my ASP doing what it does best: laying the dead down.

There's silence after that. I know I'm breathing harsh and rapid, but I can't hear it. Or else it's so loud and constant it's a white noise and it's all I hear. Either way, I'm waiting. I want him to speak, to tell me he's alive. To reassure me I didn't help kill the wrong man. That I'm not about to be next.

"Kitten."

I leap for the sound. I stow my knife so I don't slice him in my rush, but then I throw myself against him. His arms go around me and it's the hug I wanted to give him when I first saw him back inside the Colony. It's easier here in the dark with no one watching, no one wondering, no one assuming. When it's just Vin and I, and we know what we are and what we aren't. What we are right now is alive. Alive and very, very lucky.

"You okay?" he asks, his voice close to my ear.

I nod. "Yeah."

"You're shaking."

He's right—I'm trembling from head to toe and it's not from the cold. It's from reality. It comes from knowing Vin and I just killed again. We didn't put a Risen down. We killed a person. Yeah, it was in self-defense, but you can tell yourself that all day long but in the end it is what it is: murder.

Vin insists I'll get used to it. Ryan says I never will. Based on how I feel right now, I'm starting to side with Ryan.

"I'm fine," I lie. "You?"

"I'll be all right."

I pull back to try to look at him. His voice is getting clearer, but also rougher. I can hear him better now and what I hear is pain.

"What did he do to you?"

Vin clears his throat. "He got ahold of me. Nearly choked me out. That boy was strong."

"I'm sorry."

"Why? I'm counting myself lucky he didn't take a bite out of me."

"I'm really sorry."

"What the hell are you sorry for?"

"I don't know. I never should have let him get his hands on you."

Vin chuckles, his voice sounding strained. "I was thinking the same thing about you, Kitten. Don't be sorry, you did plenty. How did you manage to take him down?"

"I cut his Achilles heel."

"Damn," he coughs.

"Yeah."

"Wait, he and I were wrestling blind. How did you know you weren't cutting my leg?"

I step away from him slowly.

He grabs my hand. "Kitten."

"I was pretty sure I had his leg," I admit.

"*Pretty sure?*"

I shake my hand free of his grasp. "Are you still standing? Did I cut your leg?"

"No. But—"

"Then calm down! We have to get out of here. He's not the only wolf in these woods."

I hear Vin's feet splashing away from me in the water.

"Where are you going?" I cry, anxious and annoyed that he's leaving me behind.

"I'm looking for the torch he had."

"He tossed it in the water. It's useless."

"I doubt it." I can hear him sloshing around, his hands probably dragging through the water. "These tunnels are full of moisture. They have to be burning something that can stand up to that."

"What are you going to light it with if you find it?"

"I just found it. And we're going to use whatever he has on him."

"I'm not searching him," I say immediately. "What if he isn't dead?"

Vin chuckles again. "Oh, he's dead. Here's your ASP back, by the way. You might want to clean it while it's still dark."

I reach out, my fingers immediately connecting with his arm. I trace it down to my ASP which I snap out to length and swish around in the water at my feet.

"I'm not going anywhere near him."

"One of us has to."

"Be my guest," I mutter, stowing my weapon.

"I just did all the work," he snaps at me.

"Did you? Really? All of it?"

"Search him."

"I have flint," I snap back, reaching into my back pocket.

"Are you kidding me?"

"No. Who goes anywhere these days without it?"

"It's everywhere you want to be," Vin grumbles, pulling the flint from my hand.

"What?"

"Nothing. Before your time."

"You're not that much older than I am."

The flint sparks, the torch instantly catching fire in a sputtering blaze between us. The light ignites Vin's face, casting shadows over his skin, under his eyes, at the corners of his mouth. He looks it then—older than me. His skin has seen more sun, his mouth has formed more frowns. But it's his eyes that show it the most. They're hard like glass.

It makes me wonder what mine look like.

"I've got ten years and a lot of lives on you," Vin tells me quietly, his voice still gruff from his fight with Bryan. "Even if we were the same age, I'd still be older than you."

"That doesn't make any sense."

He smiles wryly. "Just because you don't get it doesn't mean it doesn't make sense. Now come on. I want to get out of these tunnels."

I follow closely behind him as he takes us back the way Bryan came. I hope it's the way out. For all we know it could be leading us deeper inside this underground maze, maybe guiding us into Bryan's secret lair where he kept snacks locked up just in case. I'm worried every time we round a bend that we'll run smack into another cannibal or a cave of horrors, but I'm equally anxious to run into Ryan. I know he told me to run to Crenshaw, to leave him behind, but I don't know if I can. He has to be down here. I refuse to believe he was taken by Marlow's men. The explosion went off, he and Andy got the job done. But did they do it in time or was it a last resort—an effort made to save the rest of us that cost them both their lives?

It's exactly the kind of self-sacrificial, heroic bullshit Ryan would pull.

"We're out," Vin says.

Up ahead there's light shining down from a manhole. It's faint—just a few pinpoints coming through the holes in the steel disc—but it means the outside world.

"Hopefully we can open it."

Vin nods in the growing light. "They seal some of them."

"It's to keep people like you out."

"You mean people like us."

"No, I mean you," I correct him. "People like you and everyone in The Hive."

"Sounding kind of judgmental there, Kitten. You got something you want to say?"

"Babies."

Vin stops, taking my arm to stop me as well. When I meet his stare, it's angry but controlled. "Do you know what it's like for a kid to grow up in The Hive? Any clue?"

"No. But I know what it's like to grow up without a mom," I reply hotly.

He releases my arm, his face disgusted. "Oh

boo hoo. We all know what that's like. Trust me, it's better to grow up without a mom in a Colony than it is to grow up with one in The Hive. If it's a girl, she'll end up right where her mom is. If it's a boy, he'll probably end up dead by the time he's nine and either one of them could end up hooked on Honey, tweekin' and itching for a fix all day every day. It's an ugly place to live if you don't know how to do it right so, yeah, I think those kids are better off getting out."

"But no one is given a choice. You can't take that from people like you own them."

"Marlow does own them," he replies coldly. "Or he did. Whoever takes his place will own them now and they like it that way. You know what comes with being given choices? You make bad ones. You make ones that get you killed. A lot of people can't handle that pressure anymore. The stakes are too high. It used to be you made a bad choice and you ended up driving a Honda for six years wondering why you didn't grow a pair and go for the Camaro. Screw the gas mileage, it made you feel alive! But now making bad choices gets you killed or worse—it could get your kid killed right in front of your eyes. People can't handle that. They gladly hand over their rights and their choices so nothing is ever their fault." He laughs harshly before it turns into a cough. "I wish you could be in the room when those babies are taken from their mothers."

"I'd rather not," I mumble, feeling sick.

"No, if you're going to judge it you need to see it. Those women, they cry and they moan for a day or two but then they never talk about it again."

"Maybe it's too painful. Maybe they know it wouldn't do any good."

Vin nods grimly in agreement. "Because they know how to survive. Hold the torch. I'm going up to see if I can open this thing and get us out of here."

I take the torch silently. Vin climbs the metal ladder to the top before pressing his neck and shoulder up into it. I hear him grunt, curse, then grunt again.

"Are any of them yours?" I blurt out.

I expect him to ignore me. Maybe even yell at me. He surprises me when he laughs.

"No," he replies, taking a step down to look at me. "I can guarantee you that none of them are mine."

"How can you know for sure?"

"Because I don't dip my pen in the company ink."

I frown. "What does that mean?"

"It means I'm not dumb. Look, can we talk about my sex life another time? I need help with this."

"How am I supposed to help you?"

"Climb up here with me and help push."

I look around for a dry spot on the ground. Of course, there is none. "What about the torch?"

"Drop it. We don't need it."

I don't like the idea of going into the dark again, but he's right—if we can get out through this hole, we don't need the torch anymore. I take hold of the ladder before dropping our only light source.

We're instantly plunged into darkness and even the light from the holes in the cover seems faint for a minute. When I climb up the ladder I'm careful not to take hold of anything but steel. I don't want to go grabbing anything and give Vin the wrong idea.

"You ready?" he asks when my face is level with his.

"Ready."

"Push!"

We both grunt, curse, then grunt again, but this time we get results. The cover screeches loudly as we push it up out of its home to slide it over the pavement above. This has got to be one of the holes the cannibals use on a fairly regular basis. Otherwise it probably would have been rusted shut. The thought that they use it gives me hope that we're close to home, though where exactly 'home' is for either of us at this point is pretty open to debate. For Vin I imagine it's wherever his people from the Pod are. For me, I know *who* my home is. Now I just need to know where he is.

We both squint into the bright light of the afternoon sun. It's painful compared to the darkness we've been living in for the last couple hours.

I stare back at the hole. I feel like a traitor leaving it.

"He'd want you to keep going," Vin tells me quietly.

I nod my head numbly, knowing he's right but unwilling to move from this spot. It feels like leaving Ryan. It feels like I'm giving up.

"Where are we?" I ask hoarsely before clearing my throat. I will not cry, not over nothing. I don't know anything for sure yet so what's the use in crying about it?

"We're near the Elevens," Vin whispers.

It surprises me that he bothers with the hushed tones. He's the Stable Boy of The Hive. He's a big deal in any territory.

"Why are you whispering?" I ask him at full volume.

He pulls me into an alley before clamping a hand down firmly over my mouth. I try to twist my head to get free but he holds me tightly.

"First of all," he breathes harshly, "if I whisper, you do the same. If you have to question me, do it quietly. You got it?"

I glare at him, but I nod my head.

He releases my mouth. "Second, the reason I'm whispering is because some of these guys owe me money."

"They owe you money," I whisper obediently, "and you're hiding from them?"

"I'm not exactly in the enforcing mood at the moment. If they see me, they'll expect me to collect. I don't have time for that right now."

"What do they owe you for?"

"Gambling."

"The Arena?"

"No. Poker."

"I'm terrible at poker," I mutter, glancing up and down the street.

"It's because you're a bad liar."

My shoulders slump. "Why does everyone keep saying that?"

"Because it's true. Lie to me right now."

"No, that's stupid. Whatever I say you'll know I'm lying."

"Doesn't matter. I want to see you do it. Lie about something. Anything. Your age, color of the sky, whatever."

I stare at him, my mind going blank. I open my mouth but nothing comes out.

He smiles with satisfaction. "Told you. You're a terrible liar."

"Some people might think that's a good thing."

"People like your Hyperion? Yeah, I'm sure that Boy Scout likes it."

"Do you have a problem with Ryan?"

"Nope, but he has a problem with me."

"It's because you suck."

Vin turns his smile to me, his eyes bright with amusement. "Story of my life."

I don't want to talk about Ryan with him anymore. I don't want to keep saying his name. It feels like it gets weaker every time I use it.

"Shouldn't we get out of here?"

"Yeah. Where would Trent have taken my people? The Hyperion?"

I shake my head firmly. "No, no way."

"Your place?"

"No. He knows better."

"Where then, Kitten? Where are we going?"

It's a bad idea. I'm not even sure it's where Trent would have taken them, but I know it's where I want to go. It's where he told me to go to find him.

"The woods," I whisper. "We're going to see the wizard."

Chapter Fifteen

Who knew Vin the violent, usurping pimp was a *Wizard of Oz* fan?

I do. Now.

Ever since I whispered the word "wizard" twenty minutes ago the guy has been singing *We're Off to See the Wizard* nonstop, over and over again. The real pain? He's actually really talented.

"Are you done yet?" I ask irritably.

He grins. "Is it stuck in your head yet?"

"On repeat. Full volume."

"Then yes, I'm done."

"You're the worst."

"So I hear. Z at two o'clock."

He's right—there's a shambling, moaning zombie heading our way just off to my right. I slip out my ASP, knowing it's my turn. This has been constant since we came up out of that hole. I was surprised at first that we didn't hear or see a sign of the Elevens this deep in their territory, but now that I see how many zombies are in this area it makes sense. Marlow killed the barriers holding in a swarm of easily a hundred zombies. Now they're everywhere. Every gang is probably on lockdown waiting to find out how bad things get. I remember Bray telling Ryan they were doing this exact thing when the northern Colony fell for the first time. "This is just as bad as that day—if not worse. Those of us in the wild haven't had time to clean house completely from that accident. Now there's a new swarm on top of everything else. The world is slipping back into chaos. It's reverting back to the first days.

I approach the Z quickly and swing my ASP wide. It comes around to connect solidly with the side of the zombie's skull where it makes a disgusting *thunk* sound. Not a crack like it should, but the soft tissue noise of the metal sinking into the rotted out mush that is this guy's face. I've probably damaged his brain, but I definitely haven't destroyed it.

"Need help?" Vin asks, sounding bored.

He doesn't sound like he'll actually give help if I need it. It sounds more like a taunt than anything else. I ignore it and him.

I take a step back as the zombie stumbles toward me, then I bring the ASP toward him on a backhand. It hits him in the face, right in the eye, and the force of the blow snaps his head back. I take the opening to put my foot in his gut. He lands on his back on the ground, his broken, grappling fingers clawing at the air to find me. I quickly circle around to his head and bring my ASP down hard on his face twice, using the hard ground under him to solidify my blows.

"How did you ever survive out here alone with skills like that?" he asks.

"Shut up. I'm good."

"You're slow."

I stow my weapon before casting him a smirk. "Am I?"

Before he can answer, I'm gone. I'm running.

Vin is good at a lot of things: overthrowing a dictatorship, taking out zombies, wooing women, getting stabbed, singing show tunes. But what Vin is not good at, what he's gotten soft on, is cardio. He's lived too long and too cushy inside The Hive. He hasn't had to run for his life on a regular basis for years, and while he's still in great shape, he's not in as good of shape as me. Not even close.

The second my foot hits the grass of the park, though, I throw on the brakes. I barely maintain my balance, and when Vin slams into my back we both stumble forward. His arms go around me to keep me standing but instead of feeling closed in or freaked out, I'm amazed. I'm too shocked to notice anything but what I see in front of me.

The woods are full. There are tents peppered in with the trees, sections of tall grass have been trampled down to make what looks like a small road, but most importantly is this: there are people. Lots of people.

"What's happening?" I breathe.

"I don't know," Vin replies, his voice low and tight near my ear. "But we're about to find out."

"Hold it right there!" a man shouts, jogging toward us.

We've been noticed. How could we not be? We came barreling toward this place at full speed right out in the open, and as stupid as it sounds, I thought it was safe. I never thought in a million years that the Colonists would take the woods. Why would they want it? It's out in the open, it's vulnerable, it's dangerous. What are they doing here?!

"Are they the cannibals you sided with?" Vin asks me.

I shake my head. "No. There are too many and they wouldn't come out in the open like this."

"Colonists," he growls.

"I think so."

"Who are you?" the man asks, slowing as he approaches us.

I look him over quickly, checking for weapons. So far his hands are empty but I recognize the matte black shell of a gun on his hip. When I glance at Vin I see him eyeing it too.

"No one," Vin tells him calmly.

The guy frowns at Vin, his eyes on his neck. On the tattoo openly displayed. "You're Hive."

"What of it?"

"You should leave. This isn't your fight." The guy sneers at Vin. "Nothing ever has been."

Vin takes a menacing step toward him, ignoring the gun. "You think you know something about me?"

"I know about your kind. You're as good as Colony which means you're an enemy and you should leave before I put you down."

The guy's hand is resting on the gun now. I don't know if Vin believes he has bullets for it, but as the man's words sink in, I realize I believe it. 100 percent. As though that very gun were pressed against my forehead.

"You're a Vashon," I say quickly.

The guy's eyes flicker to me. "Yeah. I'm from the island. Who are you? A Hive whore?"

I narrow my eyes at him. "No. I'm Joss."

"What's a joss?"

"The girl about to kick your ass if you call me a whore again."

I can't see his face, but I hear Vin snicker.

"Sure," the guy replies sarcastically. "Why don't you and your man pack it up? No one here is shopping for what you're selling."

"Where's Crenshaw?" I demand.

That gets his attention. He steps back from Vin, looking at me with interest.

"How do you know Crenshaw?"

"How do *you* know Crenshaw?" I fire back.

"He was one of the founders of the island. Every Vashon knows about Berny Crenshaw."

"Berny?" I nearly choke on the sheer normalcy of it.

"How do you know him?" he repeats.

"He's a friend." I shrug, feeling weird using the word.

The guy looks doubtful but he hollers over his shoulder for someone to get Berny and bring him to the perimeter. When he looks back at me his hand is still on his gun and his eyes are narrowed.

"We'll see how your story shakes out in a minute, won't we?"

"You're way less fun than the other Vashons

I've met."

"When have you ever met a Vashon before?"

"I was on your island."

"We don't allow Hive on our island. Ever."

"I told you, I'm not Hive. And I was there to meet with your council."

His eyes harden. "You're one of the three. The ones who sold us out to the Colony."

"No, that was…"

Oops.

"Who then?"

I glance nervously at Vin. "No one."

"It was Marlow," Vin tells him plainly. "He sold everyone out. It's why The Hive has fallen."

"That's not the story we're hearing here."

"What story is that?"

"That The Hive tried to take a Colony. That the Pod cleared out before they could get their claws in it. That the Colonies are marching on that Pod right now."

"The Colonists are attacking the Pod in the north?" I ask incredulously. "How did they kn—"

"Athena!"

I look past the guy to the tents of roughspun cotton in raw colors. To the clean, easy moving people around them. To the break in the crowd that has formed around a great, white wizard. He has his staff, his robe with the little blue sailboats, and the biggest smile I've ever seen on his face. He looks at home here with these people. Like Merlin at Camelot.

"Crenshaw," I say with relief.

"Come, child! Come," he calls, beckoning me

forward.

I glare up at the guy who held us back, tempted to flip him off as I pass. Vin follows slowly behind me as I make my way into the forest I don't recognize anymore. The air feels different. There's so much more movement in it. It's so much more alive. There are smells I don't know and some I thought I'd never know again. And there are so many people. The park is swarming with them but they don't feel like insects. They don't make me cringe like Risen or Colonists or cannibals lurking in the dark. It feels... I don't know. Almost good.

Crenshaw hugs me for the second time this year and I'm worried I'll get used to it. I might even like it a little. When he releases me I can't get over how happy he looks. The man is literally glowing.

"You have done well, Athena," he tells me in a hushed tone. "I did not believe it possible, but you have proven me wrong. You have made me a believer. Perhaps I always should have been."

"Cren, what's going on? That guy—"

"Ah, yes," he interrupts, nodding to the jerk who called me a whore. "The soldiers at the perimeter. They are imperative. The gates to Hell have been flung open. Wraiths are again a danger. But these soldiers, they have made my home a safer place than it has ever been. I owe them a great debt."

"Not that one," I mutter. "That one gets nothing."

"Did he treat you poorly?"

"Sort of."

Crenshaw's face falls into a scowl. "Well that

simply will not do."

"What's going on here?" Vin asks bluntly. "He started to say something about the Colonies marching on the northern Pod where The Hive attacked."

I suddenly realize who I'm standing with: Crenshaw and a Hive member. I would tell Vin to cover his tattoo if there were even a millisecond of time to do it, but there's not.

"Who is this?!" Crenshaw demands, his voice bellowing and angry. Heads turn to see what's happening. "Who have you brought here, Athena? What devils have you consorted with?"

"Calm down, Cren. He's not a devil."

"He is a hornet of The Hive. In my house!"

I put my hand on Vin's arm, pushing him back gently. "You should step back."

Vin looks down at me, disbelieving. "Are you for real?"

"He doesn't like The Hive. I wasn't even supposed to go to them for help."

"You went to Marlow for help?!" Crenshaw bursts.

I literally growl in frustration. "I didn't have a choice!"

"There is always a better choice. Defeat is a better choice than dirty dealings with the devil."

"Crenshaw, I'm sorry. I tried everything else, but there was no other way. And he isn't Hive anymore. He helped me escape the Colony!"

"Where is Helios?" Cren demands, searching the woods and road behind me. "He would never—"

"He's not here?" I ask, the fight leaching out of me.

I hate the sound of my own voice. It's weak and afraid.

Crenshaw's eyes sharpen at my tone. "No. He is not with you?"

I shake my head mutely.

"When were you separated? You cannot be separated, Athena. To succeed you must remain together. It is how I have seen it."

"Seen what?"

"The End."

I nod slowly, acting as though I understand. "The end of…"

"The End of Nothing. The Beginning of Everything."

"Okay," I tell him calmly. "Okay. I'll find him. I promise. Has anyone else shown up here recently?"

"The Vashons."

And my annoyance is back. I sigh tightly, reining it in. "Yes, I see the Vashons. Anyone else?"

"Who else should I expect?" he asks suspiciously.

"No one."

"Athena."

"Cren, I hate when you take that tone with me," I complain.

"It's because it's fatherly," Vin says.

I shoot him a warning glance, one reminding him to keep his mouth shut. So far the fact that I've lost Ryan has bought him a chance at being forgotten for a moment. He should capitalize on that.

"Do you know who Trent is?" I ask Crenshaw. "He's a member of Helios' family. Tall, thin, blond hair, creepy as balls blue eyes that see right through you into your soul."

Crenshaw leans on his staff, nodding sagely. "I have seen the boy, yes. Excellent hunter."

"He really is, yeah. He hasn't been here, has he?"

"Maybe with about two hundred people running for their lives?" Vin adds.

Crenshaw eyes Vin with open disdain, then shakes his head. "There has been no such visit. Should I be expecting one?"

"Maybe," I reply reluctantly.

"And who are these people the boy has with him?"

"Refugees," Vin says solemnly. "Former prisoners of the Colony to the north. We have released them from the bonds put on them by the Colony. They are now free men and women of the wild, although they will need shelter and guidance in order to survive."

I stare at Vin in amazement. He sounds exactly like Ryan when he's talking to Crenshaw. Did I miss something in my meager childhood? Was there a book I was supposed to have read? *The Complete Idiot's Guide to King Arthur's Court*? It seems like silly me has been reading any survival manual or How To book I could get my hands on while all these Lost Boys were reading *Lunacy: A Visitor's Guide*.

"I see," Cren replies softly. His eyes are still wary, but they're not as sharp. He's not quite ready to crack Vin over the head with his staff anymore, though, and that's a plus. "You helped to free these people?"

"He led them to freedom," I correct in my best imitation of crazy speak.

Cren's eyes widen. "For truth?"

"Yeah."

"And he has returned you to me unharmed."

"*I* returned me to you unharmed, but he was there. He didn't hurt me."

"I saved your life, Kitten," Vin protests, dropping the act.

"Don't oversell it. You helped a little, and so did I. We're even." I turn back to Crenshaw. "How did—"

"Saved your life," Vin mutters under his breath.

I take a steadying breath. "How did this happen, Cren? How are the Vashons here?"

The old man beams at me. "Persephone."

My heart skips a beat. "Seriously? Ali is here?"

"Persephone is here."

"Yes, yes, Persephone. She's here? She brought the Vashons here?"

"Yes. She was moved by your visit. There are those who believe you to be a traitor, but Persephone is not one of them. She convinced a large number of the Vashons to travel with her across the waters. They came here to me to find shelter." Crenshaw chuckles as he looks around. "I must say, it is lovely to have visitors."

"How large of a number?" Vin asks.

Cren turns to him, his eyes narrowing slightly. "How large of a number of what, Hornet?"

"How many people came across the water?"

"Over three hundred."

My knees go weak. Three hundred. Three hundred people!

I want to dance. I want to sing. I want to kiss Vin soundly on the mouth in front of everyone here. I can hardly breathe as my mind does the math.

I don't know if we can win this thing, but we have a snowball's chance in hell now and that's a lot better than we were doing ten minutes ago.

"I need to find Ryan," I say urgently.

"Yes," Crenshaw agrees. "Helios is imperative."

"Assuming he's still alive."

Crenshaw and I both glare at Vin. He stares back at us unflinching.

"I'm being realistic," he tells us.

"Why would Helios be dead?" Crenshaw asks me.

I bury my face in my hands for a second, unwilling to look at either of them. Unwilling to let the terror in my heart show.

When I lower my hands, I look Cren in the eye. "When we ran from the northern Colony we left through the tunnels. Ryan stayed behind to help blow the entrance to make sure none of The Hive could follow us. Vin and I were running in the dark. We couldn't go back for them and we couldn't wait. We were lost. So we ran."

Crenshaw presses his warm, dry hand to my arm, squeezing it gently. "He is alive. Of this I am sure."

"How?" I whisper pathetically. Hopefully.

He smiles at me like I'm a child—one asking how he knows the sky is blue. "Because I can feel him. Can you not feel him, Athena?"

I shake my head.

"Well," he replies, clucking his tongue and removing his hand from my arm. "You will. When you are ready to admit it, you will."

"Admit what?"

"Incoming!"

We all turn to look at the perimeter of the forest where Crenshaw's soldiers have gathered. They're standing tense and ready, facing off with a herd of people running straight toward us. Past the pounding of their footsteps and the occasional panicked cry, I can hear the low constant moan of another herd.

"Is this your friend, my dear?" Crenshaw asks me bitingly. "The one leading a horde of wraiths to my front door."

I nod stiffly, my eyes easily finding Trent in the crowd. "Yeah, Cren. He's one of mine."

Chapter Sixteen

The Vashon soldiers are good. They collapse on the weak side of the park in a heartbeat, forming a line of defense so thick I wonder how Trent and the Colonists will get through. Then they split, just before the crowd mows them over, and they let the panicked mass spill into the makeshift village. It fills quickly. I'm bumped from side to side, my shoulders brushing with others, and my body stiffens in annoyance. The old fear begins to build. I can feel the tightness in my gut and in my limbs that warns me to get away. It's telling me that if one of these people turns, we'll all be dead.

I turn to tell Crenshaw we should move out of the crowd, but when I look for him he's gone. Vanished silently into thin air.

"Wiley old SOB," I mutter.

"Joss."

I spin around to find Trent effortlessly jogging through the crowd toward me.

"Trent, where did you go? What's happening?"

Before he can answer me, Trent spots Vin. He holds out his hand to him, surprising both of us. It's such a human move for my robot.

"I hereby happily return your people to you," he tells Vin. "Good luck."

Vin smiles as he shakes his hand. "Not a fan of leadership, huh?"

"People are whiners."

"I won't argue with you there."

"Trent," I nag.

"What?"

"Where did you go?!"

"To the cannibals. I led them through the tunnels to the cannibals' home, but none of the Colonists wanted to be there and I don't think the cannibals were very happy about it either. I released the prisoners, then—"

"You did what?" Vin snaps.

Trent looks at him with utter calm before repeating, "The Colonist Leaders you had locked up. I let them go."

"They'll go straight back to the Colonies and tell them what's happening!" I cry.

"I certainly hope so."

"Why would you want that?"

"Because they don't know what's happening."

I look to Vin, completely confused. He looks back at me with an expression that clearly says, *Fix it before I kill it.*

"All right, all right," I mutter. "Trent, what's your plan? Please tell me you have a plan. Please tell me there's a reason why you just completely screwed us."

"The Leaders only know that a Hive member," he points to Vin, "took over the Colony, held them hostage, and that The Hive came to the Pod to take it over but the people were evacuated. That's all they know. That's exactly what they'll tell the Leaders in the stadiums."

"They'll immediately send an army up there to take back the Pod before The Hive can get too comfortable," Vin says, understanding much more than I do.

Trent nods. "Yes."

"We'll have to move fast."

"We should already be moving."

"What are we talking about?" I demand.

Vin grins at Trent. "Your creepy friend here is smarter than I gave him credit for. He's diverted Colony forces away from the stadiums to fight The Hive for the northern Pod. They'll be weakened because they think the only threat is in the north. They don't know anything about us down here right outside their door."

"What about all these people, though? They have to have seen the Vashons crossing the water to get here."

"Not if the Vashons did it right," Trent disagrees.

"Judging by the way they're handling that Risen crowd," Vin says, glancing over his shoulder to watch the soldiers systematically mow down the advancing horde, "they did it right. They know what they're doing."

"So wait, we have a Vashon army of three hundred people, plus two hundred Colonist refugees?" I ask.

Trent shakes his head. "More than that. Sixty or so cannibals are here too."

"The cannibals came with you?"

"After we heard the blast they got nervous. They came out of the tunnels."

I glance around, noticing some whiter-than-white skin in the huge crowd. "Okay, but they aren't all fighters."

"No, but twenty or so are."

"Twenty of them, maybe fifty fighters from my people, three hundred Vashons, and a weakened Colony defensive line," Vin surmises before whistling happily. "We might be able to pull this off."

"Oh, you're in this now?" I ask him, disbelieving. "Since when?"

He frowns at me, feigning hurt. "Kitten, it's for the greater good."

"It's for *your* good is what it is. You lost your Pod, now you want a shot at another one."

"A bigger one," he amends.

"You'll get nothing if we don't move on this right now," Trent reminds us.

"You're right. Where's the head of these Vashons? We need to talk to him."

"Her," I correct.

Vin scowls. "A woman?"

"Not just any woman," I tell him with a satisfied smile. "Persephone."

It's not easy to find her. The place is packed with confused, scared people milling around and looking suspiciously at one another. Getting them to fight together is going to be a nightmare—one we'll need a miracle to make it out of—and I'm wishing for Ryan more than ever even as my stomach fills with dread every second I don't see him.

But Cren promised me he's alive, and even if it's stupid and superstitious, I'm putting faith in that.

We finally find her back at Crenshaw's hut, the wise old wizard standing beside her. She looks different than I remember. Her hair is pulled back fiercely in a tight, dark ponytail and her serious face has devolved into an angry scowl. I know we parted on decent terms, but as I look at her speaking to other Vashons, her hand resting comfortably on the gun at her hip, I'm suddenly worried.

"Is that your friend?" Vin asks.

I swallow hard before shaking my head. "Not a friend exactly."

"That one is," Trent says, waving.

Sam waves back from behind Alissa, his face breaking out into a broad smile when he sees us. He nudges Ali then points in our direction. Her eyes scan the crowd and when they fall on me, they narrow.

My hands start to sweat.

"About time you showed up."

I look around me, unsure she's talking to me.

"Yes, you," she clarifies. "Where have you been? We show up to fight this war with you and you're nowhere to be found."

"Fight this war with me? You kicked us off the island!"

"Because we had to fight off the Colonist

attack that you brought down on our heads," she fires back.

I purse my lips, wanting to fight, but I don't have a leg to stand on.

"So, where have you been?" she insists.

"We were getting more help."

She points back the way we came. "You mean the shaking, terrified group of Colonists out there? Perfect. They'll be a huge help."

"There are others," I insist, getting angry. "Fighters."

"Really? Where?"

"They're out there, mixed in with the Colonists."

"And where did you scrounge them up from?"

"The sewers," Trent tells her.

Her eyes go wide. "Cannibals?"

"Where else was I supposed to go?!" I shout.

"You've mixed flesh eaters in with our people? Unbelievable. Sam, go tell Alvarez now. We need to separate them immediately."

"Wait, where will they go?"

Sam ignores me, taking off at a sprint.

"Not here," Ali says firmly.

"You can't kick them out. The outside is swarming with zombies."

"Yeah, speaking of, what the hell? Do you people ever kill them?"

"All the time," I reply defensively.

"Yeah, it shows."

I don't think I like her tone.

"We had them down to nearly nothing before a Colony collapsed and swarmed us again. And this new wave we're seeing? You can thank Marlow for that mess."

Ali grins darkly. "If I see Marlow, I won't be thanking him. I'll kill him."

"Too late," Vin deadpans.

Her eyebrows shoot high. "Really? He's gone?"

Vin nods once.

"Well, one down. One to go." She looks from Vin to Trent, her expression darkening. "Where's the other guy?"

I cringe inwardly, looking away to hide it. "He's missing."

"You should find him. I like him better than this one. This one is trouble."

I don't have to look up to know she's talking about Vin. Or to know he's grinning at her.

"Come with me," she says briskly.

She walks away without waiting to see if we follow.

Turns out Ali isn't in charge. I don't know why I'm surprised by that. She's a nurse or a doctor—I'm not sure which—but she's not a soldier. Not like most of these guys wandering around the forest are. They've contained the swarm of zombies that followed Trent, the Colonists, and the cannibals here. They're already making piles of the bodies and lighting fires. It's a method of mass disposal I haven't seen in years—not since I was a kid and it seemed like the entire world was always on fire. The sky was constantly choked with black and gray smoke, the sun peeking through to find the ground scorched black from the constant pyres. We burned most of the living that way too, partially to be safe and partially because no one had time for burials. As the acrid smoke hits my lungs, I'm reminded of an important fact - while the fires burn the same whether the fuel is human or zombie, the smell is very, very different.

We pass Crenshaw at a workbench surrounded by bowls, powders, and what looks like wire or twine. Ali asks him if he wants to join us, but he stays behind to 'work,' whatever that means. Ali takes us deeper into the forest to a massive tent swarming with people. They're running in and out of it, disappearing inside or into the trees. I feel anxious just seeing that level of activity. It throws me when Ali walks us casually inside.

There are tables set up around the room with one massive one in the middle. Guns rest on the outer tables, but on the inside are a bunch of maps and papers and I wonder if that's what everyone else gathered when the world fell: maps and Old English novels.

"Alvarez," Ali calls out.

An older man with tan skin, wrinkles around his mouth and eyes, and dark, graying hair looks up sharply. "Bishop," he replies, his voice deep and calm.

"Who is Bishop?" I ask Ali.

"Me. It's my last name," she mumbles quietly. "He calls my husband Bishop too. Confusing as hell."

"Only to you," Alvarez replies with a smirk. "I know exactly who I'm talking to. Who have you brought me?"

"These are the people who came to our island. The ones who decided to overthrow the Colonies."

Alvarez looks us over, his eyes lingering momentarily on Vin and his neck. "A Hive member was on our island? I'll have words with Taylor about that."

"No, he wasn't with us. It was someone else," I tell him.

"And where is he?"

I sigh, wishing I could just wear a sign that says 'I lost Ryan. I'm sorry.'

"He's missing," Ali says gently.

I can feel her looking at me. Feeling sorry for me.

I hate it.

"Maybe he's in the throng of people that just flooded my camp," Alvarez suggests gruffly.

"We need to talk about that. There are cannibals mixed in that group."

He stands tall, glaring at all of us. Even Ali. "So Sam said."

"What do you want to do about them?"

"Advise them to not to eat anyone."

"Seriously."

"I am serious. I don't have time to deal with them and their dalliances. Tell 'em to keep their hands and mouths to themselves. We have bigger fish to fry. Night will be coming soon."

"What happens tonight?" Vin asks the older man.

He eyes him again, more thoroughly this time, before answering. "Tonight we attack."

"The stadiums?" I ask.

"No, Tokyo."

I frown. "Where is Tokyo?"

"He's joking," Ali tells me quietly. "Yes, the stadiums."

"You don't know where Tokyo is?" Trent asks me.

My cheeks burn with embarrassment. "Shut up! I was eight years old, okay? I didn't make it through a lot of school."

"I'll teach you."

"Wonderful. I can't wait."

"Can anyone you brought us be of any use?" Alvarez asks Trent.

Trent points to Vin. "He's your man. I don't have anything to do with them."

"They belong to The Hive?"

"No," Vin says firmly. "They belong to me."

"They belong to themselves," I mutter.

"You're splitting hairs. They follow me."

Alvarez nods. "Then I'll need you to calm them down. They're creating chaos in my camp. We'll find them all shelter. Maybe in a building nearby. We'll protect them, but those who can fight will need to join us tonight."

"Agreed."

"Good. Now if you two," Alvarez says, pointing to me and Trent, "don't have anything else to do, I'm putting you to work. I assume you know Crenshaw?"

I nod. "Yeah, of course."

"Good. You'll be working with him and his assistant. We need all the hands over there that we can get."

Alissa takes us back to Crenshaw's hut where we last saw him hunched over a table full of random. Vin goes with Alvarez, looking oddly at ease striding into the crowd next to the obvious head of the Vashons. It's probably because of his ego, or maybe it's because he was simply born to lead, but I've never seen Vin look so… right. This is bigger than The Hive. It's bigger than the stables and being someone else's servant, and as I watch him go I wonder if this isn't where Vin was always meant to be.

He could be a great leader if he could stop stabbing everyone in the back.

"Bray!" Trent calls out happily, startling me.

A face I vaguely recognize looks up then smiles. "Trent!"

The guy runs to Trent but stops short. I think he was going to hug him before he remembered who he was dealing with. In the end, they awkwardly bump knuckles.

"Where's Ryan?"

Where's my sign?

"Taking care of some things," Trent lies easily. "What are you doing here?"

"I was looking for you guys! You and Ryan straight up disappeared. No one knew where you were and no one was looking."

"You're not supposed to."

"I know," Bray says, not sounding the least bit sorry. "But I wandered in here, just to see. This park was where I found Ryan last time so I gave it a shot. I ended up hanging by my ankle from a tree."

I grin. "Crenshaw's traps?"

"Yeah," he chuckles, looking embarrassed. "He caught me. I don't know what he was going to do with me but I told him I was sorry for trespassing on his turf and that I was looking for Ryan. He said he knew where he was but that I couldn't go there. Not right now. I asked him if I could wait here and he said no, but I could learn. So this is where I've been for the last few days."

"What's he teaching you?" Trent asks.

Bray's eyes light up with excitement. "Everything."

What he's been teaching him is explosives, which to a bored fifteen-year-old boy probably feels like everything.

"How does Crenshaw know how to do this stuff?" I whisper to Ali.

We're standing at a table of our own where I'm helping her roll bandages. She's set up shop beside Crenshaw for two reasons. One, she loves him; and two, with all kinds of bubbling, boiling concoctions, open flames, and sharp utensils in newbie hands, there are a lot of injuries at the explosives table.

"He's not a real wizard, don't ever tell him I said that, but he is kind of a magician. He's into all things nature and if you mix the right combination, nature knows how to go 'boom.' Big time."

"He must have taught Ryan," I muse, thinking of the fight he had with Vin about the size of the clay.

"He taught Jordan too."

"Your husband?"

Ali nods.

"Is that how he lost his hand?"

She freezes. In fact, everyone in earshot does too, and when I stop to think about why we're all ice sculptures, it dawns on me that that was stupid. It was thoughtless, tactless, and rude. But here's the problem with me—I never know that until the damage is already done.

"I'm sorry, I shou—"

"He lost his hand to a zombie bite," Ali answers, cutting off my apology. "He was bitten while fighting one and he didn't even think about it. He wanted to live more than anything so he cut his hand off to stop the spread of the virus."

"Wow."

"Yeah. So we took him to a town, one that had put up fences and locked out the zombies. They let us in but they almost killed him because he'd been bitten. A nurse helped me save him, but a doctor tried to kill him."

"Westbrook?"

Ali nods, flexing her jaw once quickly as though relieving tension. "Westbrook. Jordan survived but that guy wouldn't let it go. When I got pregnant he couldn't take it anymore. He called my baby a half-demon. Then he started sending people in to kill anyone who didn't agree with him, so we ran. That was the last we heard from him and his Colonies for years, but the threat was always there. We always wondered if he'd run out of room and come after us again. And what do you know? He did."

"I'm sorry," I say grudgingly, unable to look at her. "We screwed up. Because of us they think you were making a deal with Marlow to come at them.

We didn't know."

She surprises me when she smiles at me faintly. She shocks me when she reaches out and tucks my hair behind my ear in a gesture so motherly it makes me cringe. "You gave us a reason to finish this, once and for all. To put an end to the wondering and worrying of when he'll come after us again. It's a relief," she laughs. "Thank you for that."

I look away, pulling my hair out of her reach. "I don't think anyone should be thanking me for anything."

"Too late."

I open my mouth to reply, but I never get the chance. The sun is fading, evening is coming, and suddenly in the peaceful green glen where Crenshaw has made his home, a cry rings out.

"Incoming!"

I look around anxiously, trying to find the source of the shout.

"What's happening?"

Ali's face is tight, her hands clamping down on the rolled gauze in her hand so hard it dissolves into a mad mess of lazy loops through her fingers.

"Zombies," she tells me tensely, her eyes on the makeshift road. Men and women are running down it. They're heading for the entrance to the park. "Probably people too. They made the same announcement when Trent and the herd showed up."

Something in me aches. It clenches hard and holds that way. It hurts and I hate it, but it's good. I know what it is.

It's hope.

I move to fall in line with the people running down the road. Ali grabs my arm hard.

"No. We don't go."

"Why not?"

"Medics and explosives experts—we're too valuable to risk losing. It's why we're hidden away in the middle of the woods."

"Not me." I pull my arm away, shaking my head. "I'm a fighter. It's the only thing I'm good at."

I run for the road. If Ali calls after me, I don't hear it. All I hear is the pound of feet on packed dirt. It's a steady rhythm that loosens the tightness in my chest. It's a song I know in my veins. One beating in my blood louder and louder with every step. I'm running toward something I don't understand, but still it's familiar. Still I know it.

When we reach the clearing barricaded by fire still pouring black smoke into the air, I don't slow. The rest do, but I don't. I run. I run toward the fire and the haze. I run into the darkness blotting out the sun. To the rancid air stinging in my lungs, the smoke burning my eyes. I can barely breathe, I can barely see, and all I can hear is the persistent pounding that's beating against my body, begging to come in.

I search the ugly gray world until I find it. Silhouettes of black against the darkness. There are so many of them. So many that I don't know.

And there's one I'd know anywhere.

When I see him, it's in me: the beat of his heart – the one I'd follow to the ends of the earth – it's in my blood. It's not calling me, it's pushing me. It's willing me to him until I leap into his open arms and feel his warmth, his strength.

His relentless life.

Chapter Seventeen

"I thought you were dead," I whisper against his skin, my mouth pressed to his. "I thought I lost you."

He doesn't answer me. He holds onto me, his mouth over mine and his hands in my hair. I don't need words from him. I don't even know what ones I'm saying to him, they simply spill out in an avalanche of everything I avoid and bury too deep to find. I don't need to know where he was or what happened. It doesn't matter. What matters is that I lost him, just like I always knew I would, but by some strange, insane, otherworldly twist of fate and luck, I have him back.

All around us the pyres still burn as more bodies are thrown on them. I hear people shouting, fighting, struggling. We should help them. We should stand and fight against the onslaught of zombies that will never end. But if they'll always be there, then they can wait. We can take one moment in this stupid, thieving world and make it ours. Just his and mine, alone in the crowd and the chaos.

"Ryan!"

With Trent.

I groan, letting my head drop back until I'm staring up at the distorted sky.

"Hey, man," Ryan chuckles. He squeezes me to him tightly one last time before letting me go.

I've never been so annoyed with him. Or Trent. Or the world.

"Good to see you're still alive."

I nearly die when Trent hugs him. Trent, my Robo-Boy, my unfeeling machine of a strange, bizarro man, hugs another human being. And he does it like he means it.

"I wouldn't be if it weren't for Andy," Ryan admits when Trent lets him go.

"Did you come out through the tunnels?"

"No, we didn't have time. We had to light a short fuse and if we'd gone into the tunnels, they'd have collapsed on us before we got far enough away. We snuck out of the showers just after we lit it and headed for the back. When the explosion happened it shook everyone up. The lights went out, the walls started crumbling. No one knew where it was coming from or if the building was going down. It was nuts. Andy hid us in a dark corner until the coast was clear, then we ran out the back toward the water."

"But you can't swim," I protest.

Ryan blushes, embarrassed. "Yeah, I know. Andy was mad. He had to swim us both out. I laid there like a log and let him float me away." He chuckles nervously. "I was panicking the whole time."

He's trying to play it off like it's nothing, but I can tell from his body language that it was hard for him. Maybe even a little horrifying. But he hates that weakness and I get that so I let it go unnoticed.

"Once we were out, we headed for The Hive," he continues. "Andy knew it'd be nearly deserted with most of Marlow's men still up at the Colony. He said we had some recruiting to do."

"People were willing to defect?" Trent asks.

"Oh yeah. Andy wasn't kidding when he said there were some angry people over there. Seventeen people left with us."

"Can they fight?"

"A good portion, yeah." Ryan searches the people around us. The crowd is thinning as the fight dies down. Not nearly as many zombies followed Ryan and the others here as followed Trent. I know part of that is the fires; they don't like the scent of their own. "Where's Vin?" Ryan asks suddenly.

I blink, surprised he cares. "He's here somewhere. Probably with his flock."

"I need to talk to him."

"Why?"

"Because we have a few to add to that flock."

Ryan gathers together the newly arrived Hive members. Including Andy, looking cleaner than the last time I saw him, he's right—there are seventeen. A lot of them are women and I realize when I see Freedom and a put-out-looking Elise, the girl who tried to mount Ryan the last time I saw her, that these women are from the stables. It makes me nervous whether they'll really be happy to see Vin or not. If they're angry enough at The Hive to run away given the chance, then I think they're probably angry at Vin too.

"Vin!" Freedom shouts happily when she sees him.

Then again, what the hell do I know?

"You crazy bitch, who let you out?" Vin shouts back, opening up his arms.

Freedom runs into them, followed by Elise and four other women. They take him to the ground, all of them giggling and laughing, Vin being the loudest.

"I do not understand this at all," I mutter.

"Really?" Trent asks, sounding genuinely surprised. "You just did this to Ryan."

"Not like this."

"No, you're right. It was way more intimate what you did."

"Why were you watching?" I groan, turning red.

He grins. "Because it was beautiful."

***

An hour later I'm back in the central tent with Ryan, Vin, Trent, Ali, Sam, Alvarez, and a few other Vashons that I don't know or recognize. I ask Sam why Taylor isn't here and he looks at me like I'm crazy.

"Someone has to stay behind and watch the fort," he replies.

I notice that Sam sticks close to Ali. He's always with her and I wonder what that's all about.

I wonder if Taylor put him on guard duty—but if she's so valuable, why is she here?

"We'll attack at the gates, but we'll go in over the walls," Alvarez tells the room. "Crenshaw and the Hyperion boys will detonate the flash grenades at each gate of both stadiums, causing a distraction and panic. While they run to the gates to defend them, Teams One through Eight will go over the fences. Remember," he says sternly, catching everyone's eye, "we are going for containment. Use lethal force only if you absolutely have to."

"You won't have to," Vin says clearly from his corner. He's standing with his back against a support post, his eyes on the room, but his body language is clearly removed from the group. "It's easier than you think to overthrow one of these things. Most of the people inside don't want to be there."

"Even so, they don't know why we're there. They will defend themselves, so be prepared. And capture who you can. We want their Leaders. We need information."

"We want Westbrook," Ali says.

Her voice is quiet but it carries through the tent to every corner. I watch each Vashon nod in agreement.

I hate the Colonies as a whole, as an idea and a threat, but the Vashons are obviously working on a whole other level.

The group is disbanded after that. We all have our orders of where we're supposed to be. It's hard to believe that this is really happening. We've made an attempt on a Colony once already, but it was waiting for us. The work was done. This is different. This will be a true fight.

"Sam," I call as I see him passing through the room. He hesitates for a second, his eyes going to Ali then back to me. She stops to talk one of the other Vashons and I get the feeling it's for Sam's sake to give him time.

"Hey, Joss," he says easily, stepping toward Ryan, Trent, and I. He does that weird handshake/embrace thing guys do before stepping back. "What's up?"

"Are you Ali's bodyguard or something?"

His face goes immediately blank. "Yeah. Why?"

"Why does she need one?"

"For protection."

"From who? The Colonists?"

"Westbrook?" Ryan guesses.

Sam shakes his head. "Nah, nothing like that. They should be scared of her." He chuckles. "Them I won't protect."

"Then who are you protecting her from?"

"From herself," he says plainly.

I frown. "You're protecting her from herself?"

"Kind of all of us. Look, she's moving so I need to go. Stay safe out there, all right? Watch each other's backs."

Sam takes off after Ali, no other words of explanation given. I'm more confused now than I was before I talked to him.

"What is a sixteen-year-old kid protecting a grown woman from?" Ryan muses.

"I don't know, but your crew is about to leave

without you."

Ryan and Trent follow my eyes to the growing crowd around Crenshaw. They all have backpacks, dark clothing, and the most cautiously excited expressions on their faces I've ever seen. This team is purely for distraction. All these guys have to do is follow Crenshaw's instructions to the letter to light off a series of highly visual, nearly powerless explosions around the gates. They're giving the illusion of a breach. It's the truest magic I've ever seen Crenshaw wield.

I turn to Ryan, feeling anxiety in every fiber of my body. He's going to leave me again. He'll go with Crenshaw, I'm going over the fence, and it's too much too soon but I'll never say it.

"How many fingers you got?" I ask him curtly.

He grins as he holds them all up and wiggles them at me. "Ten. Five on each hand."

"Two hands, two arms, two eyes."

"Two legs, two feet, ten toes."

"One liver, two kidneys," Trent lists off. "One appendix, but you could lose it and be fine. Two lungs, one heart, one gall bladder—"

"Yes, okay," I snap. "You know organs. Thank you."

He smiles at my annoyance. "You're welcome."

"Two hearts," Ryan corrects, tapping my chest lightly.

I roll my eyes at the sweetness of the gesture, unable to handle it the way a normal person with real feelings that they can understand would.

"Just bring it all back with you," I tell him.

"Leave no appendage behind."

"You got it. Be careful in there, Joss."

I grin. "It'll be easy."

He kisses me. It's quick and firm and right in front of everyone. The most amazing part about it—I like it. Out in the open and everything. I really, really like it.

"Trent."

Trent nods distractedly, securing his backpack. "Bring him back in one piece. I know."

"No. Well, yeah, please do that, but I was going to say 'take care of yourself.'"

He blinks at me, a system error crashing his processor. Finally he blinks again, his eyes clearing. "You too," he says quietly.

"Thanks."

And just like that, my Lost Boys are gone again.

***

"Line up," our commander whispers harshly.

Eight other people and I in Team Three are in position on the outside of the baseball stadium. We line up quickly with our backs against the wall. Then we wait.

I shift the fake gun they gave me around in my hands, unsure how to hold it. It's carved from wood and stained black, an illusion that will hopefully fool people in the dark chaos we're about to create inside this Pod. I got a quick rundown on handguns from a Vashon named Todd before we left the forest. Basically I was told I wasn't trusted to have a real one and I do not blame them one bit. I wouldn't know what to do with the thing.

As Todd showed me how to use it as a melee weapon, he explained that since their island was founded by a group that was mostly military, the Vashons still have guns and a decent supply of ammo. In fact, he was military once, back before the big collapse and the cure that kicked it off. He was stationed just outside the gates of Ali's old home, Warm Springs.

Apparently when they helped the farmers of the original Vashon Island clear it of zombies, they mostly used brute force or through 'strategic strikes,' whatever that means. I think it boils down to cracking skulls. Bullets, they decided, were better saved for humans. And they were right. With the near extinction of guns these days, the sight of one is pretty horrifying—like seeing a dragon or Bigfoot.

An explosion rips through the night. It flares up, black smoke billowing around it as a sound like thunder cracks through the still air. As quickly as it appeared, it's gone, leaving my eyes momentarily stunned. Another explosion follows that one, then another. There's shouting from inside the stadium. I hear cries of terror, some sounding like children. The foreign sound of a baby crying wafts over the walls and blends with the cracks and bangs of Crenshaw's magic.

Men and women shout muffled commands. We hear them in the momentary return to silence as Crenshaw and his crew wait. They're drawing the Colonists to them, then they'll give the sig—

Boom!

There it is. Our commander doesn't say a word. With the sound of the second round of explosions, he and another member of our team climb like monkeys up the tall fence. We hand up a heavy roll of the thickest fabric I've ever seen, which they toss across the layers of razor wire at the top of the fence. The heavy material weighs the metal coils down to make it easier for us to clear them while also keeping us relatively safe from the sharp edges just dying to slice us open.

More explosions are going off in the distance at the other gates, at the other stadium. We're attacking all at once in a mad rush to confuse and panic them. From the sounds of it, it's working.

I wait my turn anxiously, then climb over the fence. As I swing my legs over, I get one stuck on a stray piece of metal and take a slice down my leg. I hiss in surprise but quickly pull my leg free and scurry down the other side to the ground. Our commander is waiting there, a man from Vashon Island who I've seen only once before in the large tent with Alvarez. He doesn't ask me if I'm okay. He doesn't offer me a helping hand because I'm a girl. As I hit the ground he shoves me forward to catch up with the others and get out of the way of the next climber. I was pretty neutral to him before, but I think I'm in love with him now.

I run quickly behind the others as we sprint across the neglected, dusty ground between the outer chain-link fence and the interior concrete walls. According to the plan, these inner walls have doors in them—ones that will lead us into tunnels inside the stadium under the open-air seating. I hope the plan is right, because when I glance up at the dark gray mass beside me, I'm thinking there's no way of climbing that thing. Without an entrance, we'd have to fly to get in—and I'm all out of fairy dust.

The line I'm following comes to a sudden halt. Our commander goes rushing past me to the front and disappears into the shadows at the base of the wall. I wait anxiously, uncomfortable with the bodies pressed so close at my front and back, not to mention the sound of explosions still going off and shouts echoing from nearby.

Finally the line moves again and we're racing forward. I follow blindly until I'm passing through a thick doorway into a dark tunnel that makes me cringe. It's dry in here. There are really low wattage lights spaced out across the ceiling, but it has that boxed-in feeling of the tunnels—the ones where Vin and I fought for our lives and took one in return. The one where I was sure I'd lost Ryan forever.

I take a breath, shake it off, and suck it up. If there's one thing in this world I can count on, it's the fact that it's haunted. Everything has a memory. Everything will remind me of something horrible if I let it.

The tunnel is curving and rising, taking us up and around. We follow them until we see light pouring in from the center of their world: the heart of the Colony.

My first impression when we exit the tunnel and I can see it clearly?

Place is a shit-hole.

I'm stunned by it. It's nothing like the Pod in the north. Nothing. What used to be a sports field covered in unnaturally green grass is all brown earth farmed to within an inch of its life. There are pens filled nearly to bursting with animals of all different kinds, all mixed in together. Tents and badly constructed, tiny buildings are built into the stairs and seats. Hundreds of them. Small fires burn at regular intervals around the base of the seating, just outside the reach of the overused fields. They have power but it looks like none of it is being used on the inside. All of it is being spent on the huge, barely working spotlights that were meant to light night games but have now been redirected to watch the perimeter. If a large portion of their guard wasn't up north fighting the cannibals, we never would have made it as far as we have tonight—they would have seen us coming a mile away—but as I look around I wonder what they would have done about it. The Vashons had trebuchets and God knows what else to defend themselves. As far as I can tell, these people have chickens. Mangy ones.

"Fan out!" our commander shouts. "Weapons up! Form a line around the field!"

Other teams have shown up through the tunnel entrances around the field. They start to spread out just like we do until we all link together, forming a circle around the field. Every weapon, even fake ones like mine, are drawn and pointed up at the seating where the Colonists are scurrying to hide inside their shacks. Not a single one is putting up a fight. They're all too terrified.

Somewhere down in the street, Alvarez and a few other teams will take the Colony guards down. If they're anything like these people here on the inside, they won't fight them too hard.

This all feels too easy. Almost unfair. I want to lower my 'gun' because I'm starting to feel guilty lying to them with it.

"Hold steady!" Todd, my gun coach, shouts.

So that's what we do: we point our mix of real and fake weapons at the cowering, hiding Colonists and we wait.

Somewhere from the utter silence behind me, a cow moos mournfully.

Chapter Eighteen

"What do you mean you're staying here?!"

Vin pretends to wince at my shouting. "Kitten, please. My ears. You're shrieking."

"You're being a coward!"

"I'm being an opportunist."

"Selfish."

"A little, yeah."

I collapse in a chair across from him inside the large tent.

We're early to our next strategy meeting with the Vashons. I don't know why we're meeting again so soon—everyone knows what we're going to do: move on to the next Colony, the one in the south against the water. The people we've taken in so far have been eager to talk. Once Alvarez showed up in the middle of that field and announced what his intentions were, the people began to slowly come out of their hiding places. Turns out not all of them live in the tents and shacks out in the open. A big portion of the Pod lives inside the structure where there are offices turned into dorm rooms, kitchens, showers, bathrooms, even nurseries and play areas. It's not at as bad down there as it is up top, but they're so overcrowded they've spilled out to live with the animals and crops. Word from the other teams is that the football stadium is just as bad. It's no wonder the Colonists rushed up north to save the MOHAI from the Hive—they can't afford to lose all that space.

Now Vin is telling me he isn't leaving. His flock isn't leaving, either, and I'm thinking the crowded Colonies are about to get worse before we can make them better.

"Where will you put your people? There's no room in the stadiums," I protest.

"We're not staying in the stadiums."

"Then where?"

"The MOHAI."

I sigh in annoyance. "In case you forgot, The Hive has the MOHAI."

"In case *you* forgot, the Colonists went up there to take it back. Whoever won that fight has the MOHAI—and no matter who the winner is, they don't have a leader at the moment. The Colonists have lost their home and The Hive has lost their boss." He spreads his hands with a smile. "Easy pickings for a man with an army."

"What army?"

"The small army of Vashons that Alvarez is giving me to squash whoever is in power."

I narrow my eyes suspiciously. "He's giving you an army to take over the MOHAI for yourself?"

"He's giving me what I need to take the

MOHAI back."

"For all of us. For the greater good and all that crap."

He shrugs. "That was never specified."

"Don't do this, Vin," I tell him seriously. "Don't double-cross this guy. It's not smart. He's too powerful."

"I'm not double-crossing anyone."

"It's shady at best."

He leans forward, catching my eye. "You afraid for me, Kitten?"

"Always. I'm always afraid you're going to get yourself killed, and probably me along with you."

"Have I gotten you killed yet?"

"So close, so many times."

He sits back. "Take it easy. Alvarez is going to have all the problems he can handle with the two stadiums and all those people on his hands, not to mention whatever you all find down south. Once I show I can be trusted with his people to take over the MOHAI, he'll gladly hand it back over to me. I'll even agree to take on more people. Make his life a little easier. He'll be thrilled."

"No double-cross?" I ask warily, afraid of the fact that I actually kind of see his point. Either I've been around him too long and he's rubbing off on me, or Vin is turning into a vaguely decent human being—something that seems as likely ice cream.

He draws an X over his heart, grinning. "Cross my heart and hope to die."

"Careful what you wish for," I mutter.

The tent door flips open. People begin to pour in, one by one taking their seats around the room. I wait patiently.

When Trent and Ryan step in, I smile.

"Ten fingers?" I ask Ryan.

He grins. "And ten toes."

"Yes!"

I raise my hand for him to give me five of his fingers. Trent goes to step past me to sit down, but I raise my leg to block him.

"You too, buddy," I tell him. "Ten fingers? Ten toes? Six eyes? Seven brains?"

"I'll add anatomy to the list of classes you'll be taking from me."

I drop my leg with a *thud*. "Sit down," I grumble.

He does, but not before he covertly gives me his knuckles to bump. I don't look at him when I do it, but I know he's smiling. It's then that I realize his smile doesn't creep me out like it used to. I've seen it enough to make it normal, and the fact that anything about Trent seems 'normal' to me is a very disturbing fact.

"Is everyone here?" Alvarez asks, taking his position behind the central table. He glances around the room, looking annoyed. "Where are Bishop and Haskins?"

"Who's Haskins?" Ryan whispers.

I shrug.

"Ali is…" a woman begins before faltering.

We all stare at her expectantly. My gut is clenching with nerves. Was she hurt? There wasn't any real fighting and she didn't even go to the Colony.

"She's…" the woman tries again, glancing

around at each of us nervously.

Alvarez nods curtly. "Got it. We'll move forward without them."

"Is Haskins Sam?" I whisper to Ryan.

He nods, his brow creased. "I think so, yeah."

"The operation went well. Better than expected," Alvarez says, but he doesn't sound happy. "Conditions inside were worse than we thought and a depressed population is an easy one to overtake. They're passive. Any change in their government seems like a ray of hope. The southern Pod won't be as easy."

"Do they live differently?" my commander asks. I think his name is Roberts, and I'm beginning to wonder if I shouldn't have known his name before following him into a fight. I'm getting complacent. Comfortable.

It makes my skin itch.

"The living situation in the south is vastly different from the one we've just seen. I sent scouts to eyeball it before we made camp here. They've come back with reports of electricity, lots of it, and more than one building. They've taken over a park on a peninsula in Lake Washington as their main hub of operation. They've built a small warehouse along with a few other buildings, but most of the people are living in homes farther out on the peninsula, surrounded by the water."

"Homes as in shacks?"

"Homes as in homes. Mobile homes and manufactured homes."

Someone chuckles. "They took a page from our book."

"They've taken a lot of things from us," Alvarez agrees darkly. "There are fields there, but not many. Hardly any farming, very few animals. A lot of it is green open spaces. The standard of living in the south is light years beyond what's going on in the stadiums, and that's a problem for us."

"They're comfortable," Trent agrees quietly. "And they're happy."

"Dead on. We can't surround them and take them peacefully like we did here. They'll fight back because they have somewhere to hide and they have something worth defending. Crenshaw," he says, catching the old man's eye, "we'll need more than just a light show this time around."

Cren nods slowly. "I shall summon the whole of my powers. They are at your disposal."

I'm surprised when Alvarez bows slightly. "Thank you." He stands to face the rest of us as like nothing weird just happened. "They have boats that regularly cross the channel, but we aren't sure exactly where they're going yet. My guess is that this Pod is acting as a hub in the supply chain coming from the stadiums and the MOHAI. It's taking a cut and sending the rest to another location across the water. We haven't been to see it yet, but we're assuming it's on Mercer Island. We think Westbrook has built himself a mini-Vashon."

"One he's not sharing," someone says bitterly.

"No."

"He really is following in your footsteps, then, isn't he?"

Everyone turns to the open tent door. What we find there shocks only a few of us, but that's only because the others don't know enough yet. They will. And when they do, they will not be happy.

Andy stands next to Elijah, both of them looking completely unhappy. When I glance at Alvarez, he looks the same.

"Uh oh," I mumble.

"Everyone," Alvarez says tightly, "this is Elijah and Andy. They're going to be joining us on our next operation."

"Twist!" Trent whispers to me.

I scowl at him. "What?"

"This just got interesting. Shhh."

"Don't start that again."

"Shhh."

"I will cut you."

Trent reaches for his belt. "Here's my knife. Shhh."

"Who are they?" Todd asks.

I'm impressed when Alvarez answers without hesitation. "Cannibals."

Cue chaos.

People are so angry. It's ugly. They don't riot or throw chairs—they have too much respect for their leader for that—but they do shout out protests that leave my ears ringing for a minute.

I'm impressed again when Alvarez calls for silence and they almost immediately give it. It reminds me of Vin and his Colony, and when I look over at him I'm not surprised to see him staring blankly at Andy.

Vin shooting you daggers—that's a slip in his calm. It's a rare moment of mistake that he'll quickly correct.

Vin watching you with silent calm—that's deadly death danger. That's a lion biding its time and planning its attack. Get your affairs in order, 'cause you're already dead.

"If we go in by boat, they'll see us coming," Alvarez says sternly. "If we go in on land, they'll see us coming. We'll never break through their narrow gate out onto the peninsula. Elijah and his people have offered to help us with a different strategy."

"More tunnels," I groan.

"That peninsula used to be a city park," Elijah tells the room. "There are water lines. Sewer lines. Drainage lines. There are ways into their compound that they won't see coming."

"What's the price?" Vin asks.

Elijah looks at him with tired eyes. "The price?"

"Yeah. There's always a price. What do you want in return for this guided tour of the underworld?"

"They want the MOHAI once it's retaken," Alvarez says.

Vin's nostrils flare slightly, but he holds perfectly still. "Is that all?" he asks, his voice low. Deep. Dangerous. "And we're giving it to them?"

"That's the plan, yes."

"I have a better one. Kill them."

"That doesn't exactly help us."

"All right, then just kill this one," he says, nodding toward Andy. "He's a traitor. He's Hive."

Andy snorts. "As much as you are, *brother*."

"Do you have him fooled?" Vin asks coolly,

pointing to Elijah. "Does this guy trust you the way Marlow did? Until the bloody end?"

"I would never betray—"

"Let me stop you there because you're a liar, plain and simple. To be a member of Marlow's inner circle means you swore an oath, and if you lied to him you'll lie to these people too."

"You openly betray everyone who has ever trusted you and you have the nerve to throw stones at me?" Andy growls through clenched teeth.

"I'm open about it. You're a lying coward."

"You're a selfish prick. You're worse than a traitor because you never had the balls to belong to anyone or anything in the first place. You're nothing but a cocky little boy playing at being a man when what he really should be doing, what would benefit us all a little more, is if he'd disappear. And that's what you'll do someday. You'll die, you'll vanish, and no one will care that you're gone."

His words sting me, but I'm not sure why. I doubt they've even scratched the surface with Vin, but for some reason they hurt in my heart. Maybe because I wonder if they're true. I sneak a peek at Vin to find him watching Andy with a familiar wry smile on his lips. He watches him for a long time before calmly and clearly telling him:

"Eat me."

It's a trigger for Andy. I know firsthand how much he hates judgment on their lifestyle, and somehow Vin must know it too.

The room erupts around me. Andy makes a lunge at Vin. Elijah goes to grab him. Ryan steps between them. Trent easily gets ahold of Andy from behind. Andy slips from his grasp only to be grabbed again, this time by both Elijah and Trent.

Vin never moves. The rest of the room bursts with people shouting for calm, grabbing at angry hands, but he and I both stand perfectly still inside the madness. With the entrance of the cannibals, this was already a powder keg waiting to blow and Vin just lit the match. This was a union that was destined to die violently, but what choice do we have? How many choices do we ever have? None. Or at best we get two and they're never good. The sum of the life we live is the lesser of two evils. You dance with the Devil you know because he'll leave you broken and bleeding, but at least you have a chance in hell at making it home to recover. It's the unknown that will kill you, and even though I know that, even though I've lived it every single day for the last nine years, I'm still foolishly hoping that this time it will be different.

Maybe this time it will set me free.

"Are we going to have to separate you two?" I ask, shouting over the noise of aggression and rage, staring straight at Vin. He locks eyes with me, his face impassive. "Or can you play nicely?"

He smiles broad and easy. "I'm sugar-sweet, Kitten. You know that."

"Can you tone it down a bit?"

"You want me to be less me?"

"I want you to shut your mouth a little more."

His eyebrows raise in surprise. "You giving me orders now?"

"I'm giving you advice. If you can't say

something nice—"

"Say something painfully honest?"

"Shut your trap."

He grins again. "That's not how it goes."

I gesture to Ryan, Trent, and Elijah forming a barrier between him and a still seething, though quieting, Andy. "Neither is this. If you can't play nice, you need to get out of the sandbox. I'm getting past the fact that we're all meals on wheels to them and if I can do it, anyone can. Even you." I look around to the rest of the room. "All of you can. And you will or we're boned. We may as well just go home now."

Vin waves my words away. "I don't care what they eat. Or who. Live and let live, I always say."

I shake my head, feeling exhausted. "I really doubt you've ever said those words before."

"Maybe not, but it's true. The cannibalism thing, that's never bothered me."

"Then why are you pushing his buttons like this?" Ryan asks, turning to face Vin. I don't care for his back being to Andy. The only thing keeping me sane is that Trent is there too.

"Because he's a liar," Vin says simply. "He's betraying The Hive after how many years under their roof? At their table? In their beds?"

"So you don't trust him. Fine," I say, letting my exasperation show. "We all know it. Bottom line— can you work with him or not? Can you all get past your issues and work with them to get this thing done?"

Eyes hit the floor or shoot to the sky. People avoid looking at each other and I don't know if it's because they're ashamed for hating someone they don't know just because they... well, because they eat people and that's jacked up, or if it's because they don't want to face the fact that they can't get over it. I understand either way.

Vin looks Andy up and down slowly. I know why he's doing it. He's dragging the moment out to stress every last person in the room—everyone but him and probably Trent, because Trent doesn't stress. I don't like it one bit. I feel like Vin is trying to make Andy slip up so he has a reason. The same reason he had with Breanne.

"Yeah, I can work with him," he says finally. But then his eyes swing to Alvarez. "But they don't get the MOHAI. Not a chance."

"Who would you suggest inherits it, then?" Alvarez asks, but he already knows.

Vin stares at him long and hard without answering.

I see Alvarez's jaw clench once tightly, but then he nods. "It's yours if you can get it back. Elijah, the same goes for you and your people. If you get us into the southern Pod like you promised, then it's yours. Deal?"

Elijah nods, his eyes still on Vin. "Deal."

"Great," Alvarez says sarcastically. "Now can you all stop acting like children and get back to business? We still have a lot of work to do."

***

Three hours later finds me eating my last meal in the forest. We're having a late breakfast, then it's off to war. I'm noticing that this overthrowing business is exhausting. I keep accidentally looking off in the direction of my loft, dreaming of my bed and my bathroom. After the tense meeting we just had with the cannibals, I'm even having thoughts about my bottle of vodka.

"It took you long enough to come back," Lexy tells me bitingly.

The girl is ruining my meal. Ever since the stable girls showed up, she's been attached like glue to Vin's side. I recognize it for what it is—infatuation. No way Vin is leading her on. He barely tolerates her, which isn't to say he isn't sleeping with her, but he definitely isn't putting pretty pictures in her head. She's doing that all on her own.

"That's what he said," I grumble around a large bite of bread, gesturing to Vin.

"We were sure you'd left us to die."

"Sorry to disappoint."

"Don't be. We wouldn't have been sorry to see you go."

I look up from my plate to eye her carefully. I do it for too long. She twitches under my stare, making me grin.

"'We,' huh? You're a 'we' now?"

Vin looks up sharply. "What? No."

"Vin," Lexy protests.

"Are you sure?" I ask him.

"Yes," he tells me angrily. He stares Lexy down. "And, no, we're not a 'we.' We're nothing."

"I'm sure he doesn't mean it, Lex," I tell her consolingly. "Never give up hope."

"Kitten," Vin growls in warning.

Lexy shoots me an icy stare from across the table. It's cute how hard she tries. "Be sure to watch your back out there, *Kitten*," she spits sarcastically. "I'd hate to see you get hurt."

I put up my finger in her face, getting serious. "Watch yourself. You're toeing a dangerous line with me right now and I don't want to have to remind you what happened to the last girl who threatened me. Forget Vin, I'll put you to bed with Caroline. You get me?"

Lexy pales. She glances once at Vin, then Ryan and Trent. All of them keep their heads down, carefully pretending they have no idea what's happening. Finally she stands slowly, turns, and leaves without a word.

"Well, that's handy," I mumble, picking up my bread.

"Kinda harsh," Ryan comments.

I hate that I immediately feel a twinge of guilt just from those two words from him. "I did him a favor," I say defensively. "That girl was one kiss away from collecting his hair. I don't have time for that kind of crazy."

"Amen to that," Vin says heartily, raising his glass to me.

"Calm down, Romeo. You're the idiot who keeps getting us into these situations."

"'Us'?" he asks with a sly grin. "Are we an 'us' now?"

"No," Ryan replies darkly.

I roll my eyes. "Can we talk about something else?"

"I think there are almonds in this bread," Trent states affably.

"What happened to your dad?" I ask Vin.

"Maybe pecans?"

He doesn't have to say anything—I can feel Ryan's annoyance rolling off him in waves that crash over me again and again. But I don't care if I'm being too blunt. Vin is the rudest person I know. I don't owe him any attempt at etiquette.

Vin eyes me shrewdly. "He died."

"No kidding. How, though? Marlow did it, didn't he?"

"Yeah."

"Why?"

"Because he lied to him."

"About what?"

"About everything."

"Nats said you were an orphan before the fall. How did your mom die?"

Ryan nudges my arm. I scoot away from him.

Vin shrugs. "I don't know. I never knew her. She ran when I was born."

"Why didn't your dad raise you?"

"He did. He was a drunk and a druggie. As soon as I was old enough to run away, I did." Vin sets his food down and leans across the table, giving me his full attention. When he speaks, his voice is flat. Dead. "I lived on the streets and I took care of myself. When the illness came and everyone started dying, I thought it was great. I thought that finally all of the worthless, lazy deadbeats out there would be gone and all that would be left were people like me. Smart and fast. Tough. So I went back to my dad's house a few months after it started. I wanted to see his fat corpse banging around inside his tiny, filthy apartment. I wanted to be the one to bash his head in. But you know what I found instead of a zombie? That SOB was still alive. He'd stolen food and drugs, probably killed living people to get it, and he was still alive. He attached himself to me after that. I couldn't shake him and for some stupid reason, I couldn't kill him. I prayed for him to get bitten, but it never happened. Eventually we took up with Marlow when he was just getting started. Dad sold Honey for him, but he took more of the drug than he sold. He got into trouble and Marlow put him down. Tossed his body in the Sound while I watched. He let me keep his ring, though."

"Why do you keep it if you hated him so much?" I ask quietly, stunned by this amount of information from Vin.

He holds his hand up, showing me the ring. "Marlow said to wear it and remember what happens to traitors. It kept me in line. Now I wear it so I'll always remember not to be stupid like my dad was. Stupid and weak won't get you anywhere but dead. It's the only thing that loser was ever able to teach me."

He slams his hand down on the table, the ring making a sharp sound against the metal of his battered plate.

"Anything else you want to ask me, Kitten?" he asks calmly.

I shake my head stiffly. "No, I'm good."

"Great. I gotta hit the head."

Vin stands abruptly, his legs knocking the table

and spilling my cup of water. The liquid runs over the uneven surface, chasing the path of least resistance until it finds the edge and begins to drip down onto my leg.

"Maybe don't go digging around in people's pasts anymore," Trent recommends before taking a bite of apple.

"Trent, I don't say this as often as I should," I reply, feeling exhausted and stupid, "but I think you're absolutely right."

Chapter Nineteen

I don't see Vin again after that. He leaves to go get his castle and he doesn't find me to say goodbye. I don't know much about people, but I know I messed up. I know he's mad at me and fair enough. I would rage out on him if he did the same thing to me. Especially in front of other people. I thought I was being blunt and calloused the way he always is, but now I'm not so sure. I think I might have just been a jerk again.

Not long after Vin leaves with his small army, we head south in the largest gathering of human beings I've seen in years. Once you take everyone out of their tents and away from the trees, you can see how many there really are—a buttload. We picked up more people willing to fight from the stadiums. I think the count I heard was around one hundred, but when you consider the number we lost to Vin heading north, we're about where we were before. He even took the girls from the stables with him. I'm not surprised in the least that Freedom knows how to fight. Her temporary pimp Dante even came out of The Hive with them, leaving me amazed at the amount of loyalty that's built into that place. Their sense of family is a lot like the cannibals': it's everything to them.

I'm already nervous about marching across the city to an area I've never been to before, but what makes it worse is that we have company.

There's a horde of zombies following us. A big one. The Vashons actually gathered it together! They hunted these things down from all over the city and drew them to the park. I thought it was insane, but they weren't worried. I guess this is part of what they did when clearing their island. You get as many together as you can in a contained area and destroy them as a group with fire, explosives, whatever. I guess it uses less physical effort and lowers your level of one-on-one contact with them. It makes you far less likely to be bitten because you never get that close. The only real danger is the herding—you have to give them something to follow, and once you do, you better hope it knows how to run.

And what are we leading these zombies toward? What's our endgame?

They're a gift for the southern Colony.

"A guest should never arrive empty-handed," Alvarez had explained with a wink.

The majority of us left camp well ahead of the herd to make sure we had a buffer, but we still come across random strays on the way. There's a circling group of Vashon soldiers constantly jogging by, up and down our caravan, keeping up a patrol. Even if a Z does show up, none of us has to deal with it. I feel weird about that. About being taken care of. It's something I don't think I'll ever get used to.

"Good to see you found him again," Ali says, showing up beside me out of nowhere. I jolt, wondering if she's been taking shadow lessons from Cren.

"Good to see you with us again. Were you sick?"

Ali falls silent. It drags out for a long time, making me worry. And wonder.

"Yeah," she finally says, her voice low.

"Are you feeling better?"

"Almost."

"What's wrong with you?"

Ryan subtly nudges my arm with his. I look up to find him shaking his head at me faintly.

"What?" I ask.

"Just leave it."

"Leave what?"

On the other side of me Ali chuckles.

"She doesn't know she's being rude," Ryan tells her. "Sorry."

"I'm not being rude!" I protest. "And don't talk about me like I'm not here. I was trying to be nice asking how she's feeling."

"I'm fine now," she assures me, still grinning.

"Good," I grumble, feeling stupid and annoyed with the whole conversation. And yet for some stupid reason, I keep talking. "I grew up alone. I haven't spent time with people in years. I'm not good at it."

"Yeah, me either," she says lightly.

"You're better than me."

"I have more practice. It'll come to you."

"If everyone doesn't run screaming from me first."

She looks at me sideways, her eyes flitting to Trent and Ryan next to me. "Certain people never will."

"I don't know about that."

"I do. My moods are pretty touch and go. I have good days and I have bad days."

"And you have really bad days," Sam chimes in.

I look behind us to find him walking a few paces back. Always close to Ali.

She gives him a severe look that's ruined by the grin tugging at her lips. He smiles sweetly at her.

"I do," she admits. "I have really bad days. But people like Sam are still with me."

"And Jordan."

Ali nods, pursing her lips thoughtfully. "Yup, Jordan has never run screaming. Not even when I told him to."

"Why would you tell him to?" I ask.

"Because I love him and I feel like he deserves better than me."

Yeah, I know the feeling.

I want to know what's making Ali sick even though I'll never ask about it again. I told Ryan he's my social compass and if he tells me to leave it, I'm going to leave it. No matter how much it haunts me. I have a couple of theories, but none of them really make sense. Leading contender based on bad moods that make her dangerous?

She's the Incredible Hulk.

***

Alvarez wasn't kidding—this Pod is completely different.

The Colony up north is nice compared to how I live, how Ryan lives, and definitely how the stadiums live: it's clean, there's power, it's not overly crowded. But this... this is different.

I can't say I like it more, even though I get why a lot of people would. Especially the people living in the stadiums. Show this place to them and they won't be cowering anymore. They'll be ready to fight. Some would probably be ready to kill.

I can see it through Trent's binoculars where it sits across the water. The peninsula reaches out and juts north to run parallel with the shore road we took to get here. We did it so openly it makes me nervous. I'm still getting used to being seen by a few people in the same room as me. Parading around for hundreds of people to see? That's disturbing.

We rolled down the street right up against the bay, showing them that we were coming. They can see the majority of us, they can see the trebuchet. They're watching us set up shop dangerously close to their gates at the entrance to their Pod and I take a little satisfaction in watching them scurry and scramble. They're freaked and it shows.

There's an outer fence beside the gate—one nearly identical to the fence I climbed to get into the stadiums, razor wire and all. After that there's a gate that connects to a wall. They've built a decent perimeter around the island. Alvarez said there are houses all over the place along with a warehouse, but I can't see much other than trees and the odd patch of roof peeking through.

"Why don't the Vashons have a wall like that?" I muse.

"They're in deeper water. It's a natural barrier against the zombies," Trent replies instantly. "They're also on an island. This is a peninsula. There's land access to block."

"That makes sense."

"Also they're paranoid nutjobs."

I chuckle, sneaking a glance at him. He's smiling.

"How long do you think we have before our shadows get here?" I ask, gesturing over my shoulder.

Trent studies the crowd of monsters making their way steadily toward us. I imagine he's using the feel of the wind, the direction of the sun, the height of the building—all of it together in his massive brain to come to a scary accurate prediction.

He shrugs. "Eventually."

"That's it?" I asked, surprised by the simplicity.

"Assuming they don't get distracted, yeah. They'll be here when they get here."

"Distracted as in get ahold of the Vashons leading them and stop to eat?"

"Yes. Meaning that."

"That's pretty vague."

"If you want a more accurate ETA, you'll have

to go ask the zombies."

I scrunch my up my nose with distaste. "Pass."

Instead of running to my doom, I lean over the edge of the building to see around two hundred worker bees moving in the streets below me. Alvarez has ordered almost everyone to build barricades in the streets near our camp. Old cars, old furniture scrounged from inside homes, random debris from the streets—it's nothing like the barricades the MOHAI had built up to keep the zombies in, but it should be enough to keep any stragglers from getting lost along the way to the Colony's gate.

None of us will be going anywhere near it. Well, no one but the unlucky few who have to guide the zombies there. The rest of us are either coming in underground with the cannibals, creating diversions to confuse and distract, or hanging back with the trebuchet to help Crenshaw cast his spells. The cannibal crew will come up inside the walls, place more explosives to weaken them from the inside, then run like hell back to the tunnels and back to base. From there, we'll sit back and let the zombies do the dirty work, flushing people out of the bombed-out Colony and running panicked into the night. Then it's ours. Easy.

It sounds like a brilliant plan on paper, but something about it doesn't sit right in my gut. I have an anxious, sick feeling that just won't go away.

"Do you see the docks?"

"No," I mumble, searching the shoreline.

"That's because there aren't any on this side.

They must have their docks on the other side, the one closest to Mercer Island."

I lower the binoculars sharply. "Then why did you ask me if I saw them from here?"

"I was testing you."

"Testing me on what? Whether or not I know what a dock is?"

"You didn't know where Tokyo was."

I roll my eyes, lifting the binoculars again. "Let it go."

"I'm looking for a baseline on your knowledge. I'll know from there where to start with your education."

"Dude, that was a joke. You're not actually teaching me."

"Why don't you want to know things?" he asks, sounding disappointed.

"I do know things," I snap.

"Why don't you want to know more things? You should always be looking to learn. That's why I read."

"He is right, Athena."

Crenshaw. He snuck up behind us with his crazy light tread, but I wonder if Trent didn't hear him coming.

I lower the binoculars again but stow the sigh building in my throat. "He's always right."

Cren comes to stand beside me and take in the sights. The view is actually really pretty with the setting sun glistening off the water that's rolling gently in and out against the sandy shore. It'd be beautiful, maybe even peaceful, if you only removed the slavers shouting from inside their walls.

"Are there inconsistencies in your education?"

"Glaring ones," Trent confirms.

I smack his arm. "Not glaring ones. I'm not dumb."

"A lack of knowledge does not indicate meager intelligence," Crenshaw scolds. "I have no doubt of your capacity to absorb knowledge, child. You need only to be presented with it. If the boy has offered it to you freely, you'd be a fool to deny it."

"You just told me I'm not dumb but then you called me a fool in the same breath. You see that, right?"

"I said you would *be* a fool to deny it." Crenshaw looks over my head at Trent. "Perhaps English should be your first lesson."

"I speak English!"

"Yet you do not always comprehend it."

"Did you come up here to be mean to me?"

Cren looks perplexed. "Who is being mean to you?"

"She's very sensitive," Trent comments, jumping up to sit on the wall going around the edge of the roof.

He's precise as a cat on Ritalin, but the move still makes me sweat.

"I'm sensitive because you guys are mean to me. I'm too fat, I'm too skinny, I'm rude, I'm a fool. Lay off me."

"I did not seek you out to be cruel to you," Crenshaw says, his tone softening. "I came to speak to you about something very important. Something regarding the Hornet. I wish—"

"Cren, you don't have to worry about him," I say quickly, knowing where this is going. I'm headed toward a lecture about the company I keep. "He's not Hive anymore. He was, he was very deep in it, but he's not now. He's not a good guy, but he's not a devil. I promise."

He doesn't answer me. When I turn to look up at him, he's looking at me heavily.

"Perhaps your first lesson should not be English, but rather social etiquette."

Uh oh.

"That's probably a good idea," I reply slowly. Cautiously.

"You have a very bad habit of interrupting. And assuming. You would do well to listen a little more and speak a little less."

"Okay," I mumble, looking away. I have been sufficiently shamed.

Again, he doesn't respond. Seconds slip by and I begin to understand that we're all waiting on me. Reluctantly, I look up at him.

He quirks a waiting eyebrow.

No, I think glumly, *this is the shaming.*

"I'm sorry, Crenshaw."

"Thank you."

"What would you like to discuss about the Hornet?"

"I wish to speak to him." He takes a deep breath. I watch his hands clench on his staff, the knuckles going momentarily white. "I would ask after my daughter."

He's right, I assume too much. I did not see that coming. This conversation just got a whole lot of awkward and I'm suddenly wondering where Ryan is. Trent and I are not the right people for this.

"Um, okay. Yeah," I stumble. "He's gone now. He went to the northern Colony to take it back."

"I know that."

"Oh."

"I should have spoken to him before he left, but I was hesitant. I waited too long. Now I worry."

"About your daughter?"

"About time." He pauses to take another slow breath. When he speaks again, he doesn't sound exactly like Crazy Crenshaw. He's that weird mix I get now and then when reality creeps in and you can see the hairline cracks in his world. "I'm an old man. I have seen so many things in my life. I've had the great honor to be loved by a beautiful creature of grace and brilliance. She gave her life to give me the greatest gift a man can receive from a woman: a child. But then I lost her too. She was taken from me or she went, it doesn't matter. She's gone. Now with the world as it is, with the fighting and the upheaval, who knows if I will ever find her again? I should not have waited. I should have found her ages ago. I should have spoken to the Hornet when I had the chance."

"Cren, it's not too late. Vin will still be there when this is done. Trust me, he's too terrible to die. The devil doesn't want him."

He turns to face me. When I see his eyes, I take a step back. They're hard. Fierce. I've only seen him like this once before and that time he pulled a weapon on me. I may not be well educated, but I am a fast learner. I'm not getting stabbed today.

"If you remember anything I've ever told you, child, make it this: there is never enough time. You may have years, you may have days. You may have a matter of seconds. No one knows, but no matter how much time you have, you'll always wish it was more. Do not put off what needs doing." He grabs my hand and squeezes it urgently. "Leave tomorrow for the cowards. Today you must be fearless."

Chapter Twenty

My favorite part about the plan for taking the southern Colony is that I'm not in it. Not really. We have over three hundred people here ready and willing to fight to the death to overthrow these pompous, pampered zealots, and we don't need more than twenty-five of them to lift a finger. The rest of us are here only to make them sweat.

Ryan, Trent, Bray, and Crenshaw are our explosives experts. They'll work the trebuchet with a team of three other guys from the island who know how to use it. Give them a spot to hit and if it's in the machine's range, they'll nail it. First try. The Vashons don't play.

Elijah, Andy, and seventeen of their people are going underground. They'll get inside from the tunnels, somewhere I hope I never have to go again. Each one of them will be packing a bag full of explosives compliments of Cren and his apprentices, and I'm sure every one of them will be sweating bullets the whole way there wondering if they're jostling that Bag-O-Boom too much. One false move, just a little too much pressure on the wrong spot, and *BAM!* We'll remember you fondly. I'm sure you'll make a wonderful BBQ for your cannibal buddies to doggy bag home.

As the sun begins to set, we light torches up and down the shore. Trent says it's sort of a filter. Even if we have more light behind the torches, it'll be hard for the Colonists to see what we're doing through the glare and smoke of the line of fire near the water. And what we're doing is nothing. We're wandering around, we shout to each other now and then. Sometimes a group will be sent running and yelling for no reason, going nowhere. It's all meant to confuse the Colonists and keep their attention on us. They need to be frantic, on edge, always wondering what we'll do next or how many of us there are. We don't want them aware of the moles creeping into their home through their floor or the housewarming gift we've brought them that's slowly making its way down the barricaded street toward the gate. That'll be a fun surprise for them.

"Athena!" Crenshaw shouts to me from across the camp. "It is time!"

I jog toward him, making sure to keep up my routine of looking busy.

"Time for what?"

Crenshaw's eyes are bright and wild with excitement. His face is flushed, his mouth pulled taught in a manic grin. He looks the maddest I've ever seen him and for some reason, I love it. Crazy suits him.

"Magic," he whispers dramatically, his eyes

going wide.

I chuckle, shaking my head. "I'm not in the magic show, Cren. Alvarez told me it was tunnels or crowd. I chose crowd."

"A wise choice. The tunnels are fraught with danger. Men will die in there tonight."

"That's chilling."

"I wish you to join me," he says, falling serious. His smile is gone but the light is still wild in his eyes.

"Why?"

"For protection."

I fight the urge to sigh. To roll my eyes and tell him I can take care of myself, that I don't need protection from anyone or anything. It's Vin pushing me behind him at the first sign of danger. It's Ryan sleeping between me and doors. How does everyone so easily forget that I lived alone and survived for years without any help from anyone?

No one but Crenshaw.

And that's how I manage to keep my eyes steady and my breathing even. I remind myself that Crenshaw has always been there for me. He took care of me when I was sick, he gave me medicine when I was hurt, he kept me company when I craved it and let me walk away when I couldn't handle it anymore. And I didn't realize it until now, but he let me take care of him too. He took meats from me, he listened when I warned him about outside dangers creeping close. He kept me talking when there was no one to hear me. He saw me when no one else could.

Cren kept me from being a ghost.

He kept me alive.

"All right," I agree with a smile, trying to bring his smile back. "I'll stick with you. Thank you for protecting me."

I don't understand it when he doesn't smile like I hoped. In fact, he frowns, his face looking suddenly so long and tired that I worry I've made some serious social error. If I have, I have no clue what it was.

"Come," he says, turning to go and repeating softly, "it is time."

He leads me through the camp until we stand at its edge underneath the long shadow of the trebuchet. It dances over us as the fire from the torches flickers in the wind. It's cold here by the water. I pull my coat tighter around myself, my hand accidentally slipping through the rip in the sleeve—the one I got when a wolf nearly took a chunk out of my arm thanks to Ryan.

He's there on the other side of the machine. He, Trent, Bray, and the Vashons helping them work the thing are standing patiently, watching Crenshaw and I approach. They're waiting on orders from the wizard.

My wizard.

"Gentleman," Crenshaw greets them heavily. "Are we ready?"

Ryan bows slightly. "We wait on your signal, Master Crenshaw."

Cren nods slowly, looking at each of them. I expect him to give a speech or offer some words of wisdom or encouragement—something about courage, bravery, honor, intelligence, peanut butter.

Anything. But they get nothing.

"Load it."

I watch as the guys snap into action. I lock eyes with Ryan for a small second, and while he smiles at me confidently, I feel cold inside. The sick feeling that's haunted me all day is back with a vengeance, slipping under my skin and chasing away the warm fuzzies I was just feeling a second ago. I don't know what's changed. Maybe the wind shifted or I'm registering the magnitude of what's happening. I don't know. All I know for sure is that I'm grateful Crenshaw asked me to come here with him.

You cannot be separated, Athena. To succeed you must remain together. It is how I have seen it.

Seen what?

The End.

Do I believe Crenshaw can see the future? No. I'm not nuts. But do his ominous words sink into my brain and make me nervous? Maybe even paranoid?

I wish you to join me.

Why?

For protection.

Yeah, they sure as shit do.

I watch Ryan closely as he works with the other men to prep the weapon. His hands move quick and strong as they bring the arm down to the ground, a large net of bulky stones rising into the air across from it. He's slow and gentle as he helps load a small, dark ball of deadly into a basket at the opposite end of the arm. As I watch him handle the explosives my sight goes fuzzy at the edges and I can see my pulse vibrating my vision. I realize I'm holding my breath.

I let it out in a loud burst of air, gasping a little after.

"Are you okay?" Trent asks, looking genuinely concerned.

I nod. "I forgot to breathe."

"Maybe biology will be our first lesson?"

"It's beginning to sound like I'll be going to school for the rest of my life."

"It's not unlikely." He gestures to the trebuchet standing between us. "Do you want to know how it works?"

"I'll wait and see."

"Seeing something is one thing. Knowing the mechanics of how and why it does what it does is completely different."

I shrug. "I don't know why it rains but it still does. The world is doing fine without me poking around in its underwear drawer."

"Ready!" a Vashon cries loudly.

I take a few steps back from the machine. Trent is right—I don't know how it works and I'm suddenly worried I'm about to get my head snapped off.

"Fire!"

There's a sharp *snap!* followed by a groan. I watch the net of stones drop rapidly, forcing the arm to shoot up into the air. It drags a long rope behind it, arcing it up and over the machine. At the end of the rope is the bag of explosives. It swings out high above us. At the tip of the arc, I watch in amazement as a small, round shadow flies out of the bag and soars far down the shore. It's headed straight for the gates.

I lose sight of it in the dark. I'm worried it missed its mark and hit the water, but then I find it again. I catch it for just a split second as it's haloed against the lights around the Colony gate. I don't even have time to process that I've seen it when it explodes.

It's immediately very clear that these are not flash grenades.

The night lights up in a blaze of angry red and orange, but it doesn't fade out immediately the way the grenades did. This is meant to burn. It's meant to destroy and it does its job. They haven't hit the gate. We're waiting on that. We're drawing them out and bringing them running the way we did with the stadiums to make it easier for the cannibals to do their job on the inside. This was their signal. Right now they should be running around like the phantom ninjas they are, slipping through shadows and leaving behind lit fuses at every corner of the Colony. They'll destroy a lot of buildings, but the important thing is that they'll send people running into the open. Then they'll disappear back into the tunnels, blowing the exit behind them and heading home.

That's when the boys will hit the gates.

"How long do we give Elijah and his people?" I ask.

Ryan's brow shoots up in surprise. "They're people now, huh?"

"People who eat people, but yeah."

"They have thirty minutes," a Vashon guy tells

me. He's probably in his forties, short and stocky. He reminds me of Taylor. "We'll launch two volleys while we wait. Hopefully they remember to stay away from where we're firing."

"What's a volley?"

"It's like buckshot," Trent says.

I stare at him, waiting.

He stares back.

"Buckshot," Ryan begins mercifully, "is scattered fire. Comes from one source, smaller ammunition. It's less precise but it can be more damaging. We're gonna do a mix of small explosives along with stones. We don't want to blow the whole place up right now, but we want to keep them scared."

"What if we hit someone with a stone?"

"It will kill them," Trent answers plainly.

"Aim!" Crenshaw shouts to his team.

They move quickly to their places, each of the men taking position around the trebuchet. They roll it over the uneven ground on its large wheels until it's facing farther inland. They're aiming closer to the heart of the Colony.

"Load!"

More stones and dark globes are carefully lowered into the waiting bag.

"Fire!"

The trebuchet launches the mix of ammunition toward the center of the peninsula in another high, sweeping arc. I don't see any of it fly this time. It feels like we wait forever for the impact, but finally it comes. Several small flashes of light explode on the other side of the wall. I can't see the fires on the ground, but their light flickers against the underside of tree branches, desperate to climb the tall, dry trunks.

The watching crowd of Vashons cheers and shouts across the camp. They're so loud I can barely hear Crenshaw speak.

"The Page is approaching."

It's a girl a few years younger than I am with long, light hair and a very serious expression. She's panting for breath when she reaches us.

"Master Crenshaw, they've given the order!" Her words fly excitedly out of her mouth in one quick rush. She takes a deep breath. "They're here. The zombies are here. He says to blow the damn gate."

Cren stares at her, his face pinched with annoyance. "Did he say that word in front of you?"

"Zombies?"

"No, the swear. Did he use that word in front of you?"

"Yeah."

"Yes."

"What?"

I smile. This is funny from the outside.

"'Yes,' not 'yeah.' And I will blow the cursed gate. Please tell him that exactly as I have said it. Do not swear again, young lady. Not until you are older and have a stronger understanding of the weight of the words you use."

"Yes, sir," she says meekly.

"Very good. You wil—"

"Return fire!"

I look across the water to see a comet blazing

into the sky. It's a big ball of burning that's been hurtled into the air, and it's heading straight for us.

I go to run back, desperate to get out of its way, but suddenly Trent is there. I run smack into him.

"Move!" I shout, struggling with him. "Run!"

"Joss, no!"

"Run toward it!"

Everyone is yelling at once. I can't understand all of it and I definitely can't understand why they'd want me to run toward the fireball. I don't have time to ask or fight about it because Trent easily lifts me up and runs us forward—right into the danger. As he swept me up into his arms I saw Cren take hold of the Page girl. He's running her right behind us.

The fireball blazes closer to us. It looks large enough to blot out the sky—definitely large enough to crush us all into ash. But just when I think it's going to drop right on top of us, it soars over our heads and touches down somewhere far behind us. Trent drops to his knees, curling his body over mine to cocoon me between him and the ground. There are screams when it lands, our intentional chaos in the camps suddenly turning very real. I wait, listening to Trent's breathing against my chest and the sound of dirt and rock raining down around us.

When it stops, I hear fire burning strong and angry. My pulse quickens.

The trebuchet.

"Trent, are you okay?" I whisper.

He nods his head, uncurling from around me. He leaves me sitting on the ground in front of him as he sits up straight on his knees. The fire is burning behind him but I can see the arm of the machine standing up straight into the sky.

"Do you know why you couldn't run backwards?" he asks seriously.

"Because I'd get smashed by burning death?"

"Because you would have been racing on a path to meet it."

"It didn't make sense to run toward danger. I've kinda lived my life doing the opposite."

"We didn't run toward it. We ran under it."

"I get that now."

"Remember it." He stands, offering me his hand. "The night's not over."

I let him help me up. I was right, the machine is still standing, but the fire is dangerously close to it. Crenshaw is watching the Page girl run to the roaring crowd of worried Vashons, shouting for her to get to safety, while the rest of the group is already back at the trebuchet to make sure it doesn't catch on fire.

"Is it okay?" I ask Ryan.

He looks up from where he's checking one of the wheels. "I don't know. Are you okay?"

"Yeah. You?"

"Yeah. Thanks, man," he says to Trent with a jut of his chin. "I'm glad you were there to stop her."

"No problem."

"He's fine, too, by the way," I snap, annoyed they're talking about me like I'm not even here. Let's move past the fact that I wouldn't be here if Trent hadn't stopped me.

Ryan chuckles. "I know he is."

"We've got a problem!" Bray shouts.

Ryan and Trent run around the trebuchet to where Bray is crouched by a rear wheel.

"What is it?" Ryan asks.

"It's cracked."

Ryan swears, his hands diving into his hair and rubbing it roughly.

"We can't reposition it," Taylor's stocky twin tells us. "If we move it, that wheel will split in half and it'll never shoot straight. We'll have no aim."

Trent steps up, touching the crack in the wheel. "It's deep. Almost all the way through. If we fire it at all it'll snap, most likely while the arm is in motion."

"Which means our aim is gone anyway," Ryan says, sounding resigned. Then he swears again and I think he's lucky Crenshaw is too far away to hear him.

"What do we do?" I ask. No one answers me and I realize that's my answer. "There's nothing we can do, is there?"

"No. It's dead," Ryan admits.

"But the gate."

"I know."

"Maybe the Risen will take it down on their own," Bray suggests. "There are a lot of them."

"It'll take too much time," Trent tells him.

Ryan nods. "We needed them cruising right through that gate to flush the people out. We can't give them a chance to defend against the herd."

"We need to tell Alvarez. He'll have to send in more people."

"The tunnels?" I groan.

"Or the water," one of the Vashons replies. "The cannibals are blowing the sewer tunnel entrance once they're out. There's no way to tell them to stop. Tunnels aren't an option anymore."

"How long until they do it?"

"Soon," Bray says.

Ryan looks around urgently. "Where's the Page? We need to tell Alvarez we can't blow the gate."

"She's gone. Crenshaw told her to go so she ran..." My words taper off as I look around, spinning to search the area. "Where's Crenshaw?"

"I don't know," Ryan answers.

"I don't see him," Trent says.

And that's when I get scared.

"Crenshaw!" I shout, spinning around again.

"Guys," Bray calls from the explosives table.

"Crenshaw!" Ryan yells.

"Guys."

"Crenshaw!"

I can't say exactly why I'm so worried, but something inside me is terrified. It's the same cold feeling I had when I looked at Ryan and he smiled back at me. It's that ominous sickness in my gut I've had all day. It's some part of me that knows the world better than I ever could that's screaming at me to pay attention. To see the signs.

"Crenshaw!"

"Guys!"

"What is it, Bray?" Ryan snaps.

"We're missing explosives. A lot of them."

I lock eyes with Ryan.

"He wouldn't," I whisper.

"Wouldn't he?" he challenges.

I wait two beats—two measures in my heart that scream in my ears loud and clear.

Go! Now!

Ryan is half a step behind me when I take off at a sprint toward the gate. He's fast, faster than Vin is, but he's not as fast as me. Nothing is as fast as me.

Nothing but fate.

Once we're away from the camp, I can't see anything. The lights ahead at the gate are burning bright but they're not focused out this far. I'm running in a dead zone of darkness where the sound of the crowd behind me is fading and the chorus of zombies rolling down the road right beside us is deafening. We're stupid if we think the Colonists can't hear this. They know what's coming.

But it will never get there if that gate stays standing.

Not far ahead, where the water meets the fence line, I see a spark—once, then twice, in the familiar motion of someone striking flint.

I want to shout again to tell him to stop, to wait, to see how dangerous it is to be this close to the gate, this close to the zombies barreling down on it. Cren isn't a fighter; he never has been. He doesn't even like killing animals to eat them. If this herd of Risen reaches him, he's done for. Ryan and I probably are too. Who knows? We might already be dead.

Another spark and then something catches. It buzzes with orange life in the darkness and I can see the outline of Crenshaw and his bathrobe billowing in the wind.

Before he can throw it, the night erupts in a series of explosions from inside the Pod. The ground shakes underneath me, making me feel unsteady on my sprinting feet. I try not to stumble just as flames blow into the sky in pillars that devour trees as they climb. There's screaming drowned out by a few smaller explosions.

The cannibals have done their job, which means we're late doing ours.

"Throw it!" I scream to Crenshaw.

He's hesitated, the burning fuse still eating its way down to the explosives in his hand. He's running out of time.

Luckily he hears me. He reaches back then launches the bomb forward, straight at the gate. It lands just shy of it, bouncing and rolling over the ground until it comes to a stop a few feet away.

"Get down!" Ryan shouts at me.

I throw myself to the ground just as it explodes. There's more fire, more dirt and debris falling from the sky, along with the very satisfying sound of metal groaning in angry protest.

When I look up, I find Ryan on the ground next to me and an inferno burning at the gate. It's still standing, but it's taken a good hit.

Before I can catch my breath or stand, there's another spark. I bury my head in my arms, preparing for another blast.

When it happens, it's big.

Too big.

There's the initial burst that sounds exactly like the first: boom, rain, groan. But then almost immediately there's another one. And another. And another. They keep coming in rapid fire until I stop counting them and the sky feels like it's falling down on top of me. Large chunks of dirt and rock pelt my back and legs. I feel like I'm deaf or underwater, the way I was in the tunnel. It's too loud and disorienting. It also doesn't make any sense.

When the rain finally stops, I hesitantly look up. The gate is gone. It is completely and utterly destroyed, and just in time too. The zombie herd, not even the least bit worried about the explosions ahead of them, are wandering directly toward it. They'll walk right in, make themselves at home, sleep in their beds. Snack on their brains.

The part that's crazy, though, is how it happened. I'm not an expert on explosives. I actually don't know jack-all about them, but I know it's weird that one bomb did minor damage while one just like it threatened to crack the earth in half.

I sit up, glancing at Ryan to find him on his knees, staring in amazement at the devastation surrounding the Pod.

"Ryan."

He looks back at me with his face still intact, not a drop of blood to be seen, and I sigh with relief.

Then I nearly scream when I see his expression.

"Joss, it—" He chokes on his words.

I die a little when I hear his voice. It's off. It's the wrong key played in the middle of your favorite song. It's someone changing the lyrics on you and it all stumbles to an awkward halt as you look around dizzily, wondering what went wrong. But when I see his eyes, I know what it is. It's fresh pine and twinkle lights. It's *Jingle Bells* played backwards. It's blood on the stockings and lower intestines on the hardwood.

It's a bloody bathrobe bobbing in the water.

Chapter Twenty One

Ali has the body. What's left of it. The explosion tore through everything. Metal. Stone. Flesh and bone. I don't want to see it. I already did. I saw enough. I'm not sure why Ryan takes me to see it again, but I don't ask and I don't fight.

I don't care.

I follow him and I watch him. I look at him the way Trent told me to—trying to understand how he works. Not simply accepting that he does, but wondering why. How. I'm looking at the complicated mechanics of his muscles moving his bones and his lungs filling with air and his blood somehow staying inside his body, warming his skin from the inside out. It's impressive how he does it when everyone else keeps springing leaks.

It was the Colonists. Not directly, but it was their explosives that killed Crenshaw. He launched a second bomb at the gate, one that did the job and sent pieces of it flying everywhere. Right into the field of landmines they had set up against their wall.

The falling debris triggered them all, setting off a daisy chain of explosions that tore through the earth, heading straight toward us—right through Crenshaw. It was the shrapnel that did him in. The blast kicked him back into the water, but not before shards of cement and steel ripped through his flesh. According to Ryan, he was dead before he landed. The only reason Ryan and I are still alive is because we were already on the ground when it happened.

"Ali has him in this tent by the water," Ryan explains, though I don't know why. I didn't ask. "She said Crenshaw used to love the water, back before the gangs and the Colonies took over the bay."

I can see the tent just ahead of us. The sun is rising behind it, the first rays of light scorching the city, setting the tent on fire and making it glow with an eerie light.

He holds open the flap for me. I go in without hesitation and I walk directly to the tables where the body is laid. Blankets have been pulled over it to hide the mess, but blood is seeping through. It's destroyed. It's nothing. It may as well be a zombie for how alive it is. Some would say that he's better off because he died as himself. He was never a mindless meatsuit for some unthinkable freak show.

I say that's bullshit. Dead is dead.

"Where's Ali?" I ask Ryan.

"Sam took her away. She needed to sleep."

"Why am I here?"

He pauses. "I don't know. To say goodbye?"

"Is that why you're here?"

"Yeah."

"Do you need me for that?"

More silence.

"No," he says quietly, but his voice is hard.

I turn on my heel, carefully avoiding his eyes as I leave. "I'll see you at dinner."

I burst out of the tent into the sunlight, leaving him behind, feeling like I'll vomit.

And I know. No one needs to tell me, because I already know: I'm being awful. I'm pushing him away, I'm acting like a coward, I'm ruining everything. I see it crystal clear. Don't think for a second I'm not aware of it. Don't think it doesn't kill me to do it.

Here's what it boils down to—instinct. This is my survival. Being alone is what I know and I tried something different and that's great—yea, me!—but it didn't work out because as nice as the ride is, the destination is always the same. Simple truth is everybody dies. I can't stop that and neither can they. I also can't handle it. My instincts are telling me to run away from Ryan as fast as I can, the same way they told me to run away from the fireball. It doesn't matter that I understand running away from it will get me killed. If it happened again, I'd still go the wrong way. Just like I'm running the wrong way right now.

I spend the rest of the day sleeping. It's my only chance to get clear of everyone. People know me now. They all knew Crenshaw and they've heard we were close, so now everyone wants to console the wild girl suffering a loss. It's a miracle I'm still here. I don't know how many times I look longingly through the throng of people surrounding me and dream of running through the streets. I want to go home, lock my door, and never think about this day again. I want to stow the crazy old man in the vault with the rest of them—the others, whose names I've managed to forget. The faces that are a blur, then a scream, then nothing.

So I sleep. I hibernate through the day and come out long after dinnertime. Long after I was supposed to meet up with Ryan.

"It's time."

I jerk my head up, surprised to find Alvarez standing in front of me. I hadn't realized I was parked on a cot in a tent, staring into nothing. I stretch my aching back, shaking my head to clear it.

"Time for what?" I ask groggily. How am I still tired after sleeping all day long?

"The burial."

I stand abruptly. "Nope."

His eyebrows form a deep V of disapproval. "Excuse me?"

"No," I tell him, swaying slightly. I feel lightheaded. Dizzy. "I'm not doing that."

"No, but the rest of us are and you're attending."

"No, I'm not."

"When did it sound like I was asking?"

"You can't bully me into saying goodbye to him."

"I don't intend to."

"Then what's the point?"

He steps in close, crowding me. "The point is we're honoring a man's life. I don't care how sad you are—"

"I'm not sad."

"Or how unaffected you're pretending to be. He was a great man, he treated you kindly, and you will show the proper respect for his passing. Now you will walk out of this tent tall, proud, and strong like the warrior he swore to me you were, or so help me God, I will send you on to meet him."

I believe him. There's a fire in his eyes that has never gone out, no matter what this world has shown him, and he's directing it straight at me. Right into my skin until it burns with anger and embarrassment. And shame.

I step around him because he doesn't give me an inch, then I walk slowly out of the tent. I do it tall, I do it proudly, but I feel anything but strong.

He follows me out, then leads me forward. We walk silently toward the shore where the sun is setting and the Colony is still burning and the zombies are still dining. And the sickness in my stomach gets worse.

Across the water is a madhouse. After the gate was blown and the Zs made their way inside to do their business and ours, the Vashons sealed it. They moved the street barricades and locked the survivors in with the infected. It's part of the plan that was never openly talked about before. It's a brutal move that I didn't see coming and I'm still working out how I feel about it. I can't tell if the horror and the hallow I feel inside is all from losing Crenshaw or if some of it has to do with the situation going on across the water.

I want to hate them. I want to think they're getting what they deserve for all the years of slavery, sitting in their comfy compounds while the rest of us struggled and died trying to clear the world of the plague they preach about cleansing. But then I have to hate the Vashons a little for that too. For cleaning their own house and leaving the rest of us to die outside. They were hiding from the Colonies like the rest of us, sure, but they still closed their doors in people's desperate faces.

Either way, I don't think anyone is a hero here.

Standing near the water I spot Ali and Sam. Ryan and Trent are not far away from them. I see several familiar faces, several people I could easily go stand beside and wait out this ceremony that I don't understand. That I feel too raw and scared to be part of.

I hang back, staying on the outside of the gathering.

"We're ready," Alvarez announces.

There's a raft on the shore that's covered in oily dark cloth. The body is there. The empty shell of nothing with Crenshaw's beard and staff. Several Vashons, men and women both, wade into the water with it. Guiding it. They go up to their waists before letting it go. Then they cast it off, shoving it out toward the wide mouth of Lake Washington just outside the peninsula.

No one says anything. There's not a sound aside from the water and the fire burning nearby.

When the raft is far out into the lake, Ali moves. She takes a bow from Sam, who lights the tip of an arrow for her. I watch her launch it, watch as it flies over the darkening sky before finding its home on the raft where it ignites immediately, the

279

entire vessel going up in brilliant flames.

That's it. That's the end. Most people leave after that. What else is there to be done? These days you're lucky if anyone remembers you, let alone buries you in any way. As far as the apocalypse goes, this was a very moving service.

Ryan and the boys leave eventually, all of them carefully pretending not to see me. It's not long before everyone is gone.

Everyone but Ali and I.

I want to go but I can't. I can't take my eyes off the fire on the water. My feet are rooted to the ground, the same ground where miles from here rests a forest. A quiet place with a small earthen hut kept hidden from the wild like a mirage in the desert. I never realized how beautiful that spot really was until now. I never knew how truly magical Crenshaw had been, not until he was gone and he took his magic with him. He took his words and his wisdom and I'll have to make it through this world without them. I'll have to make do with what he taught me, with all the things he gave me. Things like my name.

Persephone and I stand by the shore together but separate. We wait until the night comes in completely, until the last ember slips silently under the surface.

We stay with him and we send him on the wind and the water to the next world because it's our job.

We're his warriors. His Valkyries.

His family.

Chapter Twenty Two

We're back in the big tent. It's the center of our circus and we're coming to the last act. It's the Grand Finale. The moment we've all been waiting for.

"Westbrook is across the lake. He's in a mansion with several of his followers. It's isolated. It's not heavily guarded. They prepared for zombie attacks. Never an uprising."

"What's the plan?"

"We're going to kill him."

"Good plan."

I watch blankly as Alvarez and Todd hash out the details. We'll go in by boat, the same one the Vashons came over on that they've stored up north, out of sight. Only fifty of us will go. We'll storm the building in teams. We'll take it by force. No magic, no illusions, no lies.

We leave at dawn.

The room clears out. I stay behind, staring at the walls flapping lightly in the breeze. I don't know how long I'm there alone, but I don't have any desire to leave. I don't have anywhere to go. Eventually it starts to rain.

"Do you live here now?"

I turn to see Trent standing in the doorway, his hair laying flat and wet against his head. It makes him look different. More human.

"Maybe," I mutter, turning away.

He stays in the doorway behind me but I know he's there. I can feel him because he wants me to feel him. He wants me to know he's waiting.

"What?" I ask irritably.

"You tell me."

"Tell you what, Trent?"

"What's on your mind."

I chuckle dryly. "Shouldn't Ryan be doing this? He's our ambassador, right?"

"He already tried. You shut him down."

My stomach clenches with guilt.

"He says you need space," Trent continues.

"He's right. Bye."

"I told him he's wrong. I told him you need to talk to someone."

"And you thought the right person for the job would be you?"

"I killed my dad."

I spin around in my seat, my mouth falling open. "Why would you just blurt that out like that?!"

"To get your attention," he replies calmly. He grins slightly. "Did it work?"

"You're sick."

"But you're listening now, aren't you?"

I face forward, leaning back in my seat. "Come sit down. I'll strain my neck trying to look at you like that."

He moves silently through the room, sitting down next to me like a ghost. We both face forward, staring at the wall of the tent. The ceiling is dripping a little in the corners where the water has managed to pool, but otherwise we're safe and sound from the rain and wind outside.

"Did you really kill your dad?" I ask, my voice hushed.

"Yes."

"Why?"

"Because he was a zombie," Trent answers as a matter-of-fact. "I saw him be bitten, I saw him die, then I saw him rise again, so I put a bullet between his eyes."

"Whoa."

He looks over at me curiously. "Did you kill your dad?"

"N-no," I stutter, shocked by how easily he asks the question. "I didn't. I was eight and they were eaten. And I didn't have a gun. You know...because I was eight."

He nods in understanding, looking away. "Ryan's parents were eaten too. Kevin killed them for him. He didn't think Ryan could handle it."

"That was... thoughtful."

"He was a good guy."

We fall into a very strange silence. I'm digesting the conversation we just had, trying to follow the breadcrumbs back to the beginning to figure out how we got here while Trent waits patiently next to me. Finally I give up and break down.

"What am I supposed to talk about?"

"Whatever's bugging you," he answers vaguely.

"I hate that people die."

"Okay."

"That's it. I hate that people die. That's what's bugging me."

"No it's not."

I press my fingers against my eyes to keep my brain from exploding out my face. "Really, Trent? You came in here hassling me about this and now you're going to tell me how I feel?"

"I'm not telling you how you feel. I'm telling you that that's not what's making you act like this."

"Like what?"

"Do you really want me to say it, or will I get hit for saying it even though you asked me to?"

I drop my hands. "You'll get hit. Don't say it."

"So you do realize it?"

"Of course I realize it. I hate it, but I can't help it."

"It's how you deal with things. No one is surprised."

I look at him skeptically. "So people expect me to be awful and that makes it okay?"

"No, but no one expects you to change overnight, either. Definitely not Ryan. He's hurting too. He understands."

"Are you hurting?" I ask, genuinely curious if this odd bird's feathers can be ruffled. I can't picture it. He just told me he killed his dad as though he were telling me about retiring his favorite shoes. After that it's hard to imagine him torn up about anything.

"He was a nice man," he says noncommittally. "I'm sorry to see him die. I wasn't close to him, though—not like you and Ryan were—and that's what's making you act like this. It's not that you hate that people die. You hate that people close to you die."

I stare at him as he stares back at me, waiting for me to do something—cry, admit he's right, knit him a sweat. I don't know what he's waiting for but he's better at it than I am.

Finally I sigh, looking away. "You're right."

"A little louder please. My hearing is terrible."

I shake my head. "Your hearing is ungodly good and don't push it. I said it once, you heard me."

"What are you going to do about it?"

I groan. "Ah come on! I owned up to it, now I have to do something about it?"

"If you want to keep being around people and not act like a B-I-T—"

I reach over to clamp my hand over his mouth. "Nah nah nah," I warn him. "I can spell just fine so stow it. That will not be one of our lessons, thank you."

He smiles against my hand. I lower it so I can see it and when I do, I smile back.

"You're different than I thought you were," I tell him.

"How so?"

"I used to think you were a sociopath."

He laughs lightly, not looking the least bit offended. "You're exactly what I thought you were."

"A stone cold bi—"

"A perfect fit for Ryan."

I blink, surprised. "That's shockingly romantic to hear from you."

"Even sociopaths have feelings. You're rough around the edges but you're what he needs."

"What does he need?"

"I have no idea," he says emphatically. "But whatever it is, you have it. I don't know why he loves you because I obviously don't see it. I don't feel it. I don't get it. But there's something about you that Ryan does see. It's something he understands that no one else can. Not the way he does. You're not special, Joss."

"Awesome. Hurtful. Thank you."

"Neither is Ryan. But the two of you together, that's different. You guys make something unique, something you'd never be able to have with anyone else." He looks at me sideways. "So maybe don't run away from it just because you're scared."

"I'm scared he's going to die," I whisper nervously, afraid to say it out loud.

"He is going to die. That's a stupid thing to be afraid of."

"Jeez, Trent," I complain.

"What? It's true. He'll die, I'll die, you'll die. You pointed that out to me not too long ago, remember? No one lives forever. You're an idiot if you think otherwise. If you're so convinced he's going to die tomorrow, shouldn't you enjoy the time you have with him today?"

That hits home so hard I feel tears sting my eyes. I don't understand it right away. I have no idea why I react so violently to what he said—not until it sinks in for a second. Then it hits me like a freight train.

Crenshaw.

Leave tomorrow for the cowards. Today you must be fearless.

The last lesson he forced on me. His last, most desperate effort to change my world.

"Dammit!" I shout, standing reluctantly.

Stupid Crenshaw. Stupid Trent!

"Where is he?" I ask him.

"In one of the houses two blocks from here. Back toward town."

"Do you know the address?"

"2220 Sandy Drive."

"Thank you!" I shout, already heading for the door.

"What are you going to do?" he calls after me.

"I'm gonna be a man and tell a guy I love him!"

When I come out of the tent, I'm instantly drenched. The rain is coming down harder now. The ground is wet under my feet as it quickly turns to mud, and when I start to run, I worry I'll slip and fall on my face.

I run so hard it hurts. I want to tear my muscles. I want to claw my way out of this skin, out of this world, out of my mind until I find a bigger and better place where I'm not so scared all the time. So scared and so angry I can hardly see straight. And

I'm not when I'm with him. At least not as much. He's that place, that solace. The hideaway I need where I'm not alone for the first time in forever, and maybe that's the thing about Ryan that makes me love him like I do. The thing not everyone else can see. There's a place just for me with him. One that makes me better. A place where I want to be for the rest of my life, no matter how long that is.

So I run. I run and I fall, but I get up and I run again.

I burst through the door of the small, dark house, and I fall headlong into everything that's haunted me for months. That's terrorized me. That's made me doubt and wonder. I run straight into its depths, my breath on my lips as I gag on the words. It's not as scary as I thought it would be.

It's so much worse.

Ryan stands when I come crashing through the door. Bray is there with him and they look at me with sad, worried faces that make me cringe inside: it's more emotion, more feelings I don't know what to do with—and now the one that sent me running here is screaming in my veins so loud my head hurts.

I breathe heavily, trying to calm myself down.

"Bray," I say sternly, my eyes on Ryan, "find somewhere else to sleep tonight."

"Seriously? It's pouring out there," he complains.

"Bray," Ryan says firmly. "Get out."

He's angry, but he goes. He walks right past me out the door without a word or glance. He closes the door silently behind him, but I still know it when he's gone. I can feel it, like the air is moving around me differently. It's burning my skin and giving me goose bumps. I feel like I'm vibrating but I'm standing stock still, my eyes still glued on Ryan's. His face—his golden, glowing face—is shadowed by pain. I'm not good at reading people, but this feeling I know. It's this feeling I've avoided for so many years, but now it's caught up with me and it's brought so much more with it. So many things that I don't know how to handle.

"Are you okay?" I whisper.

His lips tighten until they're white and I worry for a second that he'll cry. I'm worried I won't be able to handle it.

"I'm okay," he finally replies softly, his voice steady. "Are you okay?"

"I talked to Trent."

His eyes widen. "How'd that go?"

I grin weakly. "I'm here. I'm going to try very hard to be nice."

He chuckles softly before sitting down in a chair behind him. I don't know why but I wish he'd stay standing. I don't feel like I can sit. I don't feel like I can be still or silent or at ease. I have an overwhelming feeling that there's so much to do and no time to do it. My head and my heart and my body are all talking at once and I can't make out a word of it. I don't even know if I speak the language.

"I'm going to miss him," I say, trying to purge this squirming thing inside of me.

Ryan nods. "Yeah, me too."

"He wasn't really crazy, was he?"

"I don't know." He smiles sadly. "I think he was when he wanted to be."

"I think he was hiding, like me."

"Whoa."

"What? You don't think so?"

"No," he says, his face still covered in surprise. "I think you're dead on. It's just a really insightful thing to say."

"I'm going to try to not be insulted by that reaction."

"Well, you're not exactly—"

"Insightful, I know. I didn't say you were wrong."

We fall into a silence that doesn't feel as awkward as it is. Maybe it's because he doesn't know. It's a one-sided feeling of anxiety and dread that he's blissfully unaware of. One that's tearing through me like acid in my gut, eating me from the inside out. How he doesn't see it on my face is beyond me. Maybe he's too spent. Maybe now isn't the time after all.

"You seem all right," he says suddenly.

It's surprising how wrong he is.

"I am," I lie.

"When you kicked Bray out I was ready for anything. You being all right wasn't what I expected."

"What did you expect?"

"Crying."

"Ha," I chuckle nervously. "Not if I can help it."

"Why then?"

"Why what?"

"Why did you kick Bray out?"

I look away, unable to face him. My heart is racing in my chest so hard it hurts. It's so loud he has to hear it. He has to know. If only he could know it and I wouldn't have to say it. I wouldn't have to be afraid of him. Of us.

"Joss?"

I ignore him, focusing on my breathing. I can do this. I *want* to do this. I need to do it because I need him and it doesn't make me weak or stupid. It makes me human. It makes me alive.

"Joss, look at me."

I shake my head faintly, closing my eyes tightly. I hear him stand up. I feel it in the air the way I felt Bray leave, my skin hypersensitive and wild. He comes to stand in front of me and I'm so grateful when he doesn't touch me. I'm tense from top to bottom. I'm trembling, shivering, shaking: a convulsing mess as though I'm having a seizure. Maybe I am. Maybe my body is going into shock from the crushing weight of this moment. From the heavy heft of his eyes settled on me.

My hands move on their own, guiding themselves smoothly over his body because my eyes have tapped out—they've taken themselves out of the equation. And this thing that I'm doing—that I'm trying to work through—it's going to have to happen in the dark—in the unknown and the unseen—and it's sick that I'm steady there. I'm best where the nightmares live. I'm comfortable here.

"No way," he says deeply, his hands stopping mine. He holds them in his own firmly. "We're not doing this. You can't even look at me. There's no way that's happening like this."

"Don't you want to?" I rasp, my eyes still closed.

He takes a tight, deep breath. I lean forward to lay my head against his chest. I follow it when he blows the breath out, resting my head against him in the safety of his heartbeat. I can feel it pounding against my skin through his thin T-shirt. Erratic. Uncontrolled.

I know how it feels.

"Yeah," he admits roughly. "More than you know. But not like this. Not with you upset."

"I told you I'm all right."

"Joss, you can't even look at me."

A hot tear escapes my eye and slides down my cheek. I shake my head back and forth as I try to open my eyes. I try to look at him and see him and know it's all right. That this is Ryan. That this is right. I know I want this, I want him, but I'm a hot mess and I'm screwing it up. I don't know how to do this. I can't do any of this, not like a normal girl. I've never been normal and I never will be and I'm so much baggage and crazy that I can't believe there's enough room in this house for all of me to be in here at once. I'm shocked by every second that passes when my emotions don't blow the walls of this place.

My tear drips off my cheek. I manage to open my eyes in time to see it land below me. It drops right onto Ryan's naked foot.

Immediately he knows.

"And it's definitely not going to happen when you're crying," he says softly.

His arms release my hands and go to wrap around me. He's going to pull me into an embrace, tell me everything is all right, and he'll fall asleep chastely beside me, snuggling in next to me and all my issues. It will go on night after night until infinity or we die and he'll never say a word. He'll never ask for more. But if I ever want the chance to let him in and watch him chase away my demons the way his laugh lights up a room, I need to man the hell up and offer what he'll never demand.

I push back from him before he can embrace me, my eyes finding his. He looks so worried it hurts. It almost lets me chicken out and bail on this entirely. It could be an awkward moment we both remember forever but never talk about. It could be the setting of the status quo. The beginning of our ending, riding this even plane until the end of our existence. Never more, never less.

Or it could be what Crenshaw said. The Beginning of Everything.

"I'm not crying because I'm sad," I say shakily. "I'm crying because I love you and I'm going to give you all of me."

He stares at me, stunned. I've seen Ryan in a lot of dire situations, facing a lot of overwhelming odds and obstacles, but I have never seen him so at a loss before. As the silence drags out between us, I worry I've broken him.

"Joss," he says gruffly, pausing to clear his throat.

Terrified of what he'll say, words begin to spill rapidly from my mouth. "I know it won't be your first time, but it is for me so don't ever tell me.

Never let me know for sure. I never want to know a name or a hint or hair color. Warn Trent, too, because he'll spill it and I'll kill him and I'll get mad at you an—"

"I love you," he cuts in quietly. My mouth clamps shut, making him grin slightly. He lifts his hand to run it along the side of my neck, back into my hair. "I've never said that before. You're my first time."

I can't handle this feeling. It's too full, too big, too much. It's him, it's Ryan, and it's everything in me until I'm bursting at the seams, and while I couldn't look at him before, now I can't look away. Not to save my life. Not even to save his. I don't know what happens to me. It's nothing I expected and I can tell from his reaction that he wasn't expecting it either. But when autopilot engages, when my survival kicks in, it's best to just stay out of its way and enjoy the ride.

I grab onto his shirt, fisting it in my hands and pulling him toward me. The last thing I see is his grin spreading into a smile before his mouth is on mine. Then I'm gone. Lost. All I know from that point is the cold of the room on my rapidly exposed skin, the heat of his body close to mine, the sound of his breath always so close, so desperate, echoing mine. I know fear, joy, want, a pinch of pain and a world of heat that starts in my stomach and burns through my veins until I can hardly breathe and I'm clinging to him as he clings to me, his heartbeat racing against my chest and sending me soaring over the night sky into nothing. I gasp his name, hear him whisper mine, then it's silence and stillness.

It's dark in the room. Nearly pitch black. Pure shadow and nothing, but it's all around me, surrounding me on all sides while I lay there with Ryan—with Helios. Burned by the sun, igniting the dark like a star on the velvet black. Unreachable. Untouchable. He's done this to me. For me. The dark, the empty, the lonely has been pushed from me until it's enveloped this room and left me nothing but a bright ball of energy, life, and light.

Shaking.

Afraid.

Awake.

Chapter Twenty Three

The Garden Gate.

That's what Westbrook calls his mansion. His fortress. His castle on the water.

It's a reference to the Pearly Gates and the Garden of Heaven, but it's also a nod to the guy who designed and built the place. Apparently he's taken over the home of a man who was once an electronics and computer expert—Bill Gates. The name means nothing to me, but the older crowd recognizes it: Ali, Alvarez, Todd. It makes me a little happy that Trent didn't know who he was either. We learned something together, and isn't that a fresh and new experience?

We got information on the building and the security around it from a few people that survived the destruction of the southern Colony. The Vashons watched last night as people spilled over the walls, desperate to get out and away from the zombies. I listened with Ryan as a lot of them landed on their own mines spread out along the shore, and we didn't sleep a wink. The few Colonists that survived were very eager to talk. Whatever it took to be kept safe from the absolute hell we unleashed on them.

"I feel like this has gotten away from us," I confessed as we laid together staring up at the ceiling of the dark, decaying house. "I thought we were freeing people, but what happened with this Colony... It's not how I saw it going down."

"It's more brutal than I expected," he admitted.

"Why did they do it like that? Why leave everyone alive in the stadiums but murder the entire southern Colony?"

"They weren't slaves here. Plus, we're getting closer to this Westbrook guy. You know how the Vashons feel about him. The closer we get, the angrier they get."

"Remind me not to piss off the Vashons," I muttered.

"Hmmm," he grumbled in agreement. I could feel his voice vibrating deep against my cheek where it lay on his chest, making me grin. "Once this is over we'll get some distance from them."

My grin vanished as I felt a strange panic set in. "Where will we go?"

"Where do you want to go?"

"Home."

"Your loft?"

"The city. Seattle. It's home. I don't want to leave it."

I felt his fingers thread slowly through my hair, stroking it gently. My eyes rolled closed with the relaxing feeling. If I were a cat, I'd have been purring.

"What about the woods?"

"Crenshaw's woods?"

"Yeah. We can add on to his house. Make it big enough for the two of us. I can keep up his gardens."

"Do you know how?"

"He was teaching me for years. I can run that place exactly the way he did."

"Will you wear a bathrobe and cook me smoked rabbit?"

He chuckled. "I'll even talk down to you and call you Athena if you want me to."

"No," I said, wrapping my arm around him and hugging him tightly. "You'll call me Joss. Always Joss."

"Tinkerbell?"

"No."

"Peter Pan?"

"No!"

"You sure you don't want me to call you Kitten?"

I pinched his side, making him yelp. "No."

"All right," he conceded. His breath brushed hot across my head. His lips landed lightly in my hair. "I love you, Joss," he whispered.

"I love you, Ryan."

I will never in my life get tired of saying that.

Now we stand on the deck of the Vashon boat guiding us across Lake Washington toward Mercer Island. Garden Gate is there in the gray morning mist that hovers over the water. It looks like a freak show against its perfect black backdrop. There are no lights anywhere on that island except for this one house—this one weird glass-walled house that's blazing with unnatural light.

"It's totally self-sufficient," Sam tells us as we stare at it in amazement. "It's built into the side of a hill and uses the earth for a lot of its walls to keep it cool in the summer and warm in the winter. It's covered in solar panels, it's using the water in the lake to generate power, there's a row of wind turbines up on the hill it's built into. Totally gated in on the back to keep the zombies out, but it sounds like they cleared them off the island same as we did."

"How do you know all of this?" Ryan asks him.

"Alvarez."

"How does he know?"

Sam grimaces slightly. "Interrogations."

"I don't want to hear about that," I warn him.

He shrugs. "I don't want to think about it."

"An interrogation is a formal line of questioning," Trent informs us. "It doesn't necessarily mean violence."

"Based on what happened to the southern Colony, I'm assuming this interrogation was violent."

"Safe assumption."

I shiver against the thought and the cold.

"Is Ali on the boat?" I ask Sam, surprised he's not with her.

Sam suddenly won't meet my eyes.

"Yeah," he says quietly, "she's here."

"Are you not guarding her anymore?" Ryan asks.

"No, I am. I'm on a break. She's with Alvarez." He shifts on his feet before muttering, "She shouldn't be here."

"Why not?"

"Because she's sick?" I ask, wondering if that's rude. Ryan doesn't nudge me so I figure I'm okay.

"Yeah. She's kind of on the edge right now," Sam says with irritating vagueness. "She…" He sighs heavily. He looks over his shoulder and stares at the back of the ship where I can see Alvarez and a long mass of dark hair whipping in the wind.

"Sam?"

His eyes snap to mine. He looks worried.

"Docking in five!" someone shouts.

We're coming up on the shore outside Garden Gate. My heart begins to pound in my chest.

"Just watch out for her, okay?" Sam says urgently.

"Everyone to their stations!"

Ryan nods as he turns to leave, going to our assigned post. "Yeah, we'll help you keep an eye on her."

"No, I mean *watch out for her*," he says emphatically.

The deck is swarming with people. A line runs between Sam and I, blocking him from sight.

"You mean like 'watch your back'?" I shout to him.

He doesn't answer and when the line of people is gone, so is he. Trent and Ryan have already moved on so I get my butt in gear and head to my post, but Sam's words are still swimming in my head, confusing me. Worrying me.

We break the mist and there it is, clear and glowing against the hillside. Somewhere inside, Westbrook is milling around in his pajamas. He's probably munching a donut and sipping tea. Maybe listening to music. He might be watching a movie. Or cartoons like a Saturday morning when we were kids and had homes and parents. And Saturdays.

"Hold!" Alvarez cries.

We all wait, dying to jump off this boat and head inside. It's going to be brutal, and I remind myself to be ready for that. I don't plan on killing anyone and I haven't asked, but I doubt Ryan does either. I'm not afraid to break an arm or deal out concussions with my ASP, but I'd rather not have any more living, human blood on my hands than I already do. I wonder for a second if anyone should clarify that to Trent, but before I can there's an explosion on the shore.

Several go off, dirt flying into the air and then raining down, pelting the side of the house and the water around us. Some lands on the boat but we all hold steady, waiting.

Alvarez's team launches two more volleys of stones against the shore until he's convinced every last one of the land mines waiting for us is dead. We learned our lesson back at the southern Colony; no one is falling for that trick again.

I wait anxiously in the silence that follows the last piece of dirt falling to the ground. It's creepy quiet. No one is moving inside the house and there are no guards or soldiers rushing out to meet us. It's completely calm and still. Almost like no one is home.

"Now!"

People spill off the boat, our feet pounding down the small ramp and onto the dock. We run in teams, each of us with our own orders of where to go. We're fanning out over each floor of this place, going into the guest houses, the massive garage.

Everyone's goal—find Westbrook.

We burst into the house and I do my best to not be distracted by it, but damn. It's ridiculous. It's unholy. It's so freaking normal that it's stupid.

Nicely upholstered chairs and couches, undented, unscratched tables, glass that hasn't been shattered, lights that are glowing warm and strong. It's completely ignorant to the world across the water. It's everything that annoyed me about the MOHAI and so, so, so much more. It's not just clean or nice—it's luxurious.

It makes me sick.

I snap out my ASP. I clench my knife in my left hand. I breathe in steady, I breathe out even, I swallow back the angry bile, and I calm my heart.

"Joss!" Ryan calls over his shoulder.

I nod, quickening my steps to follow him. "I'm right behind you."

We're the team searching the lowest level. Trent and Ryan move cautiously through the hallways, trying to find us a door that will take us down. Trent guides us through a huge, gleaming kitchen, past pristine bathrooms, some kind of game room. Finally he comes to a stop in front of a glass enclosure with a sturdy metal frame.

"No way," I mumble, staring at it like it's a unicorn in a tuxedo.

Trent pushes a circular button beside it. It lights up, followed by a polite *ding!*

"Yes way," he says in equal awe.

The doors to the elevator slide open silently in front of us. Soft classical music pours out into the hallway.

Ryan shocks me when he barks out a short, loud laugh.

"What's funny?" I ask incredulously.

"I don't know. When was the last time you rode an elevator?"

I shrug. "Not since I was kid. Are we taking this thing down?"

"Why wouldn't we?" he asks me like I'm crazy.

"How do we know we can trust it?"

Trent steps inside and jumps up and down fearlessly. When he doesn't plummet to his death, I sigh with relief.

"What if we get trapped in it?" I ask.

Trent shrugs. "Then we know it doesn't work."

Ryan steps inside, offering me his hand. "Are you coming?"

I don't hesitate to take his hand, but when he pulls me inside I feel like I'm going to hyperventilate. I don't trust this thing at all, but I trust Ryan and Trent so when the doors close behind me, I do my best not to scream and claw at the walls.

Trent pushes another button, a *B* this time, and we start to drop down smoothly.

"This is weird," I whisper.

"But also kind of fun," Ryan whispers back.

"We're here to take down the evil head of a totalitarian regime. We're not supposed to have fun."

Trent leans forward to look at me around Ryan. His face is shocked.

"Totalitarian regime?" I ask him.

He nods.

"I heard Todd say it. It sounds better than oppressive dickbag."

Trent smiles proudly at me.

Ding!

Seriously so very weird.

We pile out of the elevator and step into another hallway. Down here we find a massive swimming pool, a gym, a smaller kitchen, more bathrooms, and absolutely no people. By the end of it we aren't creeping cautiously anymore. We're walking around tossing open doors and shouting out what we find.

"Another play room!" Trent calls out.

"Showers!" Ryan shouts.

"I don't know what this is," I tell them, staring at the smallish room with all wood walls. "But there's no one in here."

The boys come to stand behind me.

"Sauna," Trent tells me. "You sit in there and sweat your cares away."

"Down in Fraggle Rock?"

Ryan claps twice.

"Well, that's it for down here. This place is empty."

"It can't be," Ryan argues, not sounding convinced by his own argument. "The survivors from the last Colony said he was here. They said he had a small group with him."

"Maybe they're hiding," Trent suggests as we head back to the elevator. "It's a big place. There could be secret areas."

"They definitely saw us coming," I agree glumly.

We load back into the potential deathtrap, this time Ryan getting to push the buttons. I want to punch him when he hits all of them.

"We'll check the other floors," he says defensively when I glare at him. "Maybe another team found something."

"Shouldn't we go ba—"

There's a loud crash from somewhere in the house. It sounds like an explosion tearing through the walls and my knuckles go white around my ASP and knife as I picture the elevator giving out under us.

"Where'd it come from?" Ryan asks urgently.

"How do we know?! We're in an elevator!" I shout.

He looks to Trent. "Up or down? Was it below or above us?"

"I'd say above," Trent replies calmly, though his eyes are narrowed. He's listening. "Someone's shouting. Do you hear that?"

"Who can hear anything over this stupid music in this stupid elevator?"

Ryan frowns at me. "Joss, calm down."

"You calm down! If there's another explosion this thing could kill us all!"

Ding!

I run sideways through the doors before they finish opening, desperate to get out of there.

"Left!" Trent shouts to me.

I turn to the left and sprint down the hallway. We're back on the floor we started on, but it looks completely different. There's smoke in the air, meaning I was right—it was an explosion. I don't know who set it off but it could have been any one of the ten or so men fighting against Vashons in the living room and entryway of the house.

Looks like someone did find something.

There are at least three bodies on the floor, none of them Vashons as far as I can tell, and when I see how the Vashons fight against the Colonists, I'm not surprised by the body count. In fact, I'm surprised it's not higher. There's a savage anger in the air that I haven't felt since the day I watched Ryan fight in the Arena. It's a nearly tangible thing, the bloodthirst.

A Colonist lunges toward me with a knife. I dodge it easily, bringing my ASP down on his arm with a hard crack that breaks his bone and leaves his knife useless on the ground. I kick it away, bring my ASP back up, then hit him in the shin. He goes down hard, alive but useless.

"Joss!" Ryan shouts.

"I see it!" I shout back. I swing my ASP around to hit a guy in the knee. He screams, falling to the ground in pain. "I've got it."

"Joss," he croaks.

I spin around, put on alert by his fading voice. He's up against a wall with a Colonist pinning him there. Ryan is fighting him, but the guy is putting his body weight into the attack. I see red, literally.

He's slowly sinking a knife into Ryan's stomach.

I run toward them, raising my weapon high. I don't hesitate and I definitely don't hold back. I come down on the guy's head with the force I would give a zombie. My arm aches from the resistance when it meets the hardest part of his skull, but he's hurting way worse. He drops to the ground as the life slips out of him and I don't know if he's alive or dead, but he isn't getting up anytime soon.

I rush to Ryan, taking his shoulders as he slumps forward. "Are you okay?"

"Yeah," he groans. "I'll be okay. Hurts, though."

"Getting stabbed usually does. Can you stand?"

He tries to stand up straight, but winces and crumbles before he can make it. "Maybe not right now."

I growl in frustration, searching the men and women fighting around me. I spot Trent as he grabs a guy's wrist and then spins him around. The guy screams before Trent lets him fall to the ground, the guy clutching his arm as it dangles uselessly from the socket.

Trent is the only familiar face I can find.

"Where's Ali? You need a doctor."

"I'll be fine for now. Just don—Mmm," he moans for a second, leaning harder against me. "Just don't let anyone kill me, okay?"

"You got it."

"Joss!"

I sigh with relief when I see Sam come running down the master staircase. Where Sam is, Ali can't be far away.

"Sam, where's Ali? Ryan needs her."

He shakes his head, his eyes desperate. "I can't find her. I was hoping you'd seen her."

My heart plummets. "No. I haven't seen her since the boat."

Sam curses. "I screwed up. We were together going through the guest house when we saw people sneaking away over the hill. She freaked and ran off, chasing them. They ran back into the house, but I can't find her. She was convinced she saw Westbrook."

"Then what are you worried about? Let her kill him. It's what she wants. It's why we're here!"

"I don't think she really saw him."

"Did it not look like him?"

"I don't know, I've never seen him. But Ali can't tell… She doesn't…" Sam curses again, tearing at his hair. "She sees things that aren't there."

"Are you kidding me?" I ask incredulously.

He shakes his head. "Hears things too. Not all the time, but when she's stressed it can get bad."

"Like during a war?!" I shout angrily.

Why would they do this to her? Why bring her here?

"Or surrounded by zombies for the first time in years, yeah."

"Or losing Crenshaw," Ryan grunts. He's starting to sweat. I need to get him out of here.

"Well, screw it," I say gruffly. I wedge myself

under Ryan's arm so he's leaning heavy on me and I start to walk him forward. "I'm getting Ryan out of here. Can you cover us?"

"Can I use your ASP?" Sam asks, a tiny grin on his face.

I roll my eyes as I hand it over to him. "Yeah, whatever."

We make it two steps. Two labored, difficult steps until we're stopped dead by the scariest sound I've heard in a long time. A sound so terrifying and strange it makes me scream loud and long.

A gunshot.

I throw Ryan to the ground, then throw myself on top of him. He shouts in pain and surprise as my body pins his roughly, but I don't care. I know it hurts him and I'm sorry for that, but a bullet will hurt worse and that's not happening to him. Not on my watch. Not while I'm still breathing.

Everyone else in the room reacts to the sound in almost exactly the same way. Most hit the deck, and those who don't, jump back and cower. Even the Vashons.

"Enough!" Alvarez shouts into the newly silent room.

He's standing in the doorway. There's a fine mist of dust floating down on top of him like snow. He's holding a pistol in the air pointed at the sky and I realize the dust is bits of the ceiling he just blew a hole in. He looks around the room, surveying the situation. There are now eight bodies on the ground. The majority are obviously dead. Only one looks to be a Vashon.

Ryan and I sit up slowly. I'm not eager to make

any sudden moves and spook the gun, but I need to get off him and ease up on his wound.

"Where is he?" Alvarez asks the room quietly.

No one answers. He lowers his weapon, aiming it at one of only two Colonists left standing.

"Where... is... he?" he repeats slowly.

"Far from here," one of the men says with a wicked smile. "So far you'll never find him. He is chosen to survive. To lead. To purify what has been tain—"

Alvarez shoots him in the thigh.

He shifts the gun to the other Colonist before repeating, "Where is he?"

"We'll never tell you," the man replies defiantly, but his eyes are shifty. He's scared.

I can't say I blame him. I'm a little freaked right now myself.

"Is he here?" Alvarez asks the Vashon beside him.

The guy shakes his head. "I don't know. I can't tell."

"Joss, the body there by you and Ryan. The build is about right. Is that him?"

"Wh—what does he look like?" I stammer, staring at the gun in Alvarez's hand. "I don't remember what you told us."

"Glasses," Ryan says breathlessly. "About sixty years old. Dark hair. Five foot ten."

"Not anymore."

There's a *whoosh* from above us, then a sickening, wet *smack*. Everyone jumps, Ryan and I stumbling backwards to get away from the mass that's just dropped down onto the gleaming floor in front of us. Red splatters and white specks shoot in every direction. I'm hit in the hand by something yellow, small, and hard. It's a tooth. I stare at it completely confused until my eyes figure it out. I drag them to the mass in the middle of the floor. Then I start to gag.

It's a severed human head.

"What the—" Ryan begins in amazement, his eyes rising to the landing one floor above us.

There stands Ali. She's coated in blood, looking creepily like a cannibal, a long hatchet dangling loosely from her hand.

Her eyes black as coal, she grins crookedly. "I'd say he's closer to five foot four now."

Chapter Twenty Four

They're attaching Westbrook's head to a spike on the front of the boat. Ryan, Trent, and I are sitting on lounge chairs just off the dock, enjoying the warm afternoon sunshine, and watching one of the most disturbing things I've seen a human being ever do. Andy eating Marlow is solidly Number One, but this isn't falling far behind.

"The southern Colony is still burning," Trent observes casually.

He's right—smoke is rising from across the water, where the Colony still burns and the zombies still roam. I doubt there's a living person left in that place, and if there is, I imagine they wish they weren't.

I think it's all pretty depressing.

"I wish they'd finish it off already," I say sourly.

"I wish they'd take that head down," Ryan grumbles.

"I don't want to get on that boat."

"It's the only way home."

I grin at him. "We could swim."

He chuckles, but it turns into a cough and I feel bad for making the joke. "Not even on a good day."

Ali checked him out before putting the disgusting star on her Christmas tree. She said he'll be fine. Infection is his only real concern and she found plenty of med supplies in the mansion. She patched him up and told him to rest, so that's what we're doing. Vashons are ransacking the mansion, taking everything that's not nailed down, and anything that is will burn. They're hell-bent on destroying this place and making sure another Westbrook doesn't rise up to take this one's place.

I may not agree with everything they're doing, but that much I can get behind.

"They're not bad people, Joss," Ryan says quietly.

I zoned out staring at the boat, my face pinched with disgust.

"They look like bad people."

"Good people can do bad things. No one is perfect."

"I liked them," I admit sadly. "When we first met them I really liked them. I liked them right up until they sealed the gate on the southern Colony."

"I know."

"Do you still like them?"

"Some of them."

"Sam?"

"And Ali. And Alvarez."

I shake my head in disbelief but I keep my mouth shut. I wish I still liked Ali.

"You'll like them again someday," Trent tells me.

I grin at him, not even mad he's telling me my own feelings. "Oh yeah?"

"Yeah. They're your kind of people. You just caught them on a bad day. If I judged you by your bad days, I wouldn't like you."

I snort. "Pretty bad day."

"They'll be more good than bad. Give it time."

"I'll never forget this, no matter how long I wait."

"No, but someday you'll forgive it. At the very least you'll understand it."

I look at him quizzically. "Do you still like them?"

He smiles. "Who said I ever did?"

***

We ride at the back of the boat as far away from the head mount as we can. We took the lounge chairs with us and I have to admit, I'm pretty excited about them. They are comfy! Despite the nightmare on the front of the boat, I'm pretty happy sitting back here in the breeze under the sun with Ryan and Trent. The Vashons are driving the boat up over the city, through an inlet, and out into the Sound. We'll pass over the MOHAI and I wonder if Vin has taken it or if my friend is dead. Part of me is worried, but a bigger part—the part that knows him best—believes what I told Crenshaw: that man is too wicked to die.

We don't dip down into the cul-de-sac the

MOHAI sits in, but Trent helps me find it with the binoculars as we pass. I can't see anyone on the outside, but the building is intact and they're not flying a Hive flag, so I breathe a little easier.

When we pass by The Hive, a few men come out to stand on the dock and watch us go by. Their expressions are unreadable.

"And this is why they're parading Westbrook's head," Ryan tells me from his spot on his chair. His eyes are closed against the sun. He looks so peaceful I almost worry about him.

"Why?"

"It's a warning."

"Hmm. They couldn't have sent a letter?"

He smiles. "Who can afford postage these days?"

Next stop is the stadiums. That is a totally different experience than cruising by the empty MOHAI or the indifferent Hive. People come pouring out of the stadiums to swarm the shoreline. They scream and shout, clapping and waving to us like we're heroes. And maybe to them we are. The Colonists here have been set free by the people on this boat. They've gotten their lives back and I'm glad I get to see this. It gives me hope that maybe this wasn't all a mistake. I'll never regret what we've done, but the sour taste I have in my mouth over what happened in the southern Colony is sweetened a little by the joy we see from the Colonists.

No, not Colonists. The people. The men and women re-released to the wild.

Trent shoves his binoculars against my chest

roughly. "Don't lose these."

"Oh, okay," I say, unsure why he's brusquely pawning them off on me.

When I get my answer, I still don't understand.

Trent goes back a few steps, crouches down, then sprints forward. He leaps into the air, up and over the side of the boat, and right down into the cold water of the Sound.

"Trent!" I shout, rushing forward to look over the edge.

I wait for a few breathless seconds but he finally appears, his blond hair bright against the dark water. He takes long, powerful strokes away from the boat, swimming for the shore.

"Did he jump?" Ryan asks, sounding shocked.

I turn to face him, my mouth hanging open. "I—he—"

I lift the binoculars to follow Trent as he swims the distance to the shore. I'm nervous the entire time. When he finds land and begins to stride purposefully out of the water, I breathe a sigh of relief.

Then I gasp in shock.

"What?" Ryan demands. "Is he okay?"

Trent walks onto the shore, pushes through the crowd patting him on the back, and makes his way directly to a girl—a tall girl with chestnut brown hair and a sweet smile.

Then he straight-up kisses her.

"What's happening?!" Ryan shouts at me, getting annoyed.

"Trent kissed a girl!"

"Very funny. Is he okay?"

I turn to Ryan, laughing. "Come here. I know it hurts to stand, but you have to see this! Trent is kissing a girl!"

Ryan moves quick for a guy with a stab wound. He takes the binoculars from me, finds where I'm pointing, and nearly drops them into the water.

"Holy shit," he mutters numbly.

"Right?"

"Who is that?"

"Amber."

"Who's Amber?"

"My friend from the kitchens in the Colony. Trent has met her like one time! Maybe two."

"I guess he liked what he saw."

I snatch the binoculars back. "Quit hogging them. I want to see this."

"Pervert."

"Yes," I whisper happily.

I watch Trent bend Amber over backwards, dipping her until she's nearly horizontal. The best part about it? She's holding onto him tightly. She's kissing him back.

"Joss."

"What?"

When he doesn't answer me I lower the binoculars.

His warm eyes are glowing with excitement. "Let's do it."

"Do what? Jump overboard?"

"No," he laughs, "the woods. The park. Let's really do it. Let's live there. Together."

The air is too thin. It pinches in my lungs, getting lost down in my stomach and making it bubble nervously.

"You don't want that," I protest weakly.

"Yes, I do," he replies seriously. "I want that more than anything."

Me too, I think.

So why can't I say it?

"I'd make a crap roommate."

He grins. "No worse than Trent."

I take a step closer to him, my hand gliding along the metal railing toward his. "I can be a jerk."

"I can handle it."

I slide my hand closer. My fingertips brush against his. "I can't cook."

"I'd never ask you to."

He slips his fingers between mine, weaving them together.

I blink rapidly. "I can't live in Crenshaw's house. I don't think I can ever set foot in there again."

"I'll build you a new one," he promises, tugging me toward him.

I go willingly, stepping into his space. "I'll help."

He smiles. "Is that a yes?"

I take a deep breath, pulling in the air, the sunshine, the water, his eyes. The world. I let it in and I let myself be in it.

I nod my head. I smile.

"Yes."

He looks so ridiculously happy then, and my heart clenches with a strange joy knowing that I did that. I make him feel that. He looks relieved and light. He looks young, the way he's supposed to be, the way we're both supposed to be, and I feel it standing there smiling with him. I feel so many things I never thought I would or could.

I feel loved.

Free.

Wild.

Alive.

Thank you for reading the Survival Series!
I hope you enjoyed it. If you did, please consider leaving a review for this or any of the books in the series on Amazon.

If you'd like to read more of my work, go to the next page for Chapter One of my highly rated Sci-Fi Romance novel, <u>Sleepless</u>

Prologue

Nick

The first time I saw her, I was dead.

I was rolling down the river with two coins for the Ferryman, heading out onto the infinite, black sea. Worst of all, I was going without a fight.

How she found me is still a mystery or a miracle, depending on your perspective. Any way you slice it, I'm lucky she was there, though showing gratitude for it wouldn't come easy for a long time after. How she put up with me for as long as she did is pure miracle, no mystery about it. She's as close to an angel as I'll ever get. Whenever I think of her, I always remember the way she looked there by the river; long auburn hair, glistening hazel eyes and a T-shirt that read *Zombies Hate Fast Food.*

When she reached out and took my hand, it shattered my world. Her eyes and the warm press of her skin against mine changed everything. Suddenly I was gasping for breath, fighting for life, and as she lowered her face to within inches of mine, I felt my heart slam painfully in my chest. She parted her lips, making me believe she would kiss me goodbye. If that had been the last sensation I experienced in this world I would have died a lucky man. Instead, she whispered one word against my mouth. One word that would press air into my lungs and pull me back from the void.

"Breathe."

Then she was gone.

Chapter One

Alex

I wake with a start. My eyes immediately find the black sparrow decals flying across the white paint of the wall beside my bed, calming my racing heart. I trace one with my fingers, smiling at the familiar feel of its edges. This is what I always do. This is how they tell me that I'm home.

I actually hate birds. They're too quick and erratic with their sharp claws and beaks. They're like flying, disease carrying knives. But more than anything I hate them because they remind me of the Dragon.

"Are you here?" Cara calls.

"Present and accounted for." I drop my hand from the bird just as my bedroom door swings open. My sister stands in the doorway. Watching.

"You okay?"

"Yeah, I'm good."

"I'm glad you're home."

I chuckle quietly. It could go without saying but she says it every time. "Me too."

"Where'd you go? Do I want to know?"

"Transylvania," I lie.

"Okay, so I don't want to know."

I shake my head. No. She doesn't want to know.

"I had the Dragon Dream," I tell her, changing the subject. "It brought me home."

"The Jabberwocky," she corrects me quickly.

I roll my eyes. "It's not the Jabberwocky."

"I have shown you the pictures. It looks exactly as you described."

"I know, but—"

"Is it or is it not the spitting image of the Jabberwocky?"

"It is," I concede, "but how would I have started dreaming of the Jabberwocky when I was four years old? We never had the book."

"You saw the movie."

"We've talked about this," I groan. "The Disney *Alice* doesn't have the Jabberwocky in it. There's no way. It's not him, it's just a dragon."

"It'd be cool if you could dream about *Pete's Dragon*."

"Jesus, don't put the idea in my head!"

"What? He's friendly! And it's not like you can Slip to Passamaquody."

Slip is our word for what I do. For my tendency to fall asleep, dream of New York City and wake up in Times Square in my underwear. My parents called it sleep walking though it's not at all

5

accurate. It just made it sound normal, made it easier for them. I don't stand up and walk out the door. When I Slip, I dream of a place then there I am. The base of the Eiffel Tower. The shore on the coast of Ireland. The third baseline at Wrigley Field. While it can take my mind a millisecond to raise familiar images of the Las Vegas strip, it will take me days to return my body home from it. I don't understand how it happens. No one does. It's mind over matter to the nth degree. It is unpredictable, terrifying, and most of all, annoying.

"He kicked my ass," I tell her glumly, thinking of the Dragon. I rub my leg even though there's no wound on it. Not anymore. Not now that I'm awake.

"Jabberwocky's are the worst."

"It's not the Jabberwocky!"

"Sure. Hey, what are we doing tonight? Did you decide?"

I throw my arm across my face. "Nothing, we are doing nothing."

"No," she insists, pulling my arm away. "We were going to do nothing if you Slipped away to Antarctica. But you didn't. You're here and we need to celebrate."

"It's not a big one. Can't we just let it slide?"

"Every birthday until your twenty-second is a big one. Your twenty-second is a bust. From there on out you receive no new liberties, other than the right to grow old."

"That's depressing."

"It is, so enjoy the good ones while you can. You're turning twenty! This is a big deal." She takes my hand in hers and squeezes it affectionately. "Plus, you got shafted pretty hard on your last few birthdays. They should have been special and I know they really weren't. Let's use this year to make up for it."

For my Sweet Sixteen my parents gave me an eviction notice and a new car. Worst Showcase Showdown ever. Since then birthdays have held little appeal to me seeing as I now associate them with abandonment and hush money.

My sister is eight years older than I am and was already an established, responsible adult when I got the boot. She's a Certified Public Accountant making good money and was more than happy to take me in. She knew what was wrong with me, knew she'd have to support me because I can't hold down a job, but she didn't care. When I showed up at her door, a lost, crying mess, she promised that she'd always watch out for me. Then she went to our parent's house, took my things, gave them a piece of her mind and never looked back. She's fiercely protective of me and I want to say it bothers me and that I can take care of myself, but after growing up with a mother who kept me at a distance, knowing someone has my back is indescribable.

"Can we egg their house?" I ask, referring to our parents.

"No. But I will buy a big ass Margarita and let you take hits off it."

"Deal."

∞

7

I'm standing on the bank of the Missouri River in Omaha, wondering why I work so hard to stay here. I should embrace the escape and let my mind Slip me far, far away to a place that is warm. My hands are freezing and my toes would ache if they could remember what it was like to feel.

Cara brought me here to try and use her old driver's license to get me into the casinos, but I'm having doubts. Doubts I like to call Mango Margarita: The Devil's Drink. Or El Bebir Del Diablo? I don't know, I didn't do well in high school Spanish. I Slipped to Mexico once and it was a complete disaster. Turns out *hambre* and *hombre* are easily confused and when you adamantly insist in broken Spanglish that you be in possession of one, it doesn't always get you a burrito. Sometimes it gets you a male prostitute. Who knew brothels had a lunch menu?

Cara is up at the car waiting for her work friends to join us while I and my dubious stomach have taken a walk to the river in case of emergency. I'm not fond of the idea of barfing in the parking lot in plain view of everyone. At the moment, I am not fond of anything.

I'm surveying the frozen beach, looking for somewhere to sit and wait out my troubles, when I spot the body. It's a man, ghostly white and lying in the shallow waters of the freezing river. Before my brain knows what's happening, I'm rushing down the shore, tripping over mounds of snow and ice slicked rocks until I collapse on my knees beside him.

He looks to be about my age, his pale skin

8

contrasting sharply with his buzzed black hair. He's naked except for a black Speedo-esque swimsuit. Even to my drunk mind, that seems like weird attire for December in Nebraska. I quickly strip off my heavy coat and throw it over his chest, shivering immediately in just my T-shirt. I don't see his chest rising or falling so I grab for his hand to take his pulse. Relief floods through me when I find his skin is relatively warm and pliant. I'm hoping this means he's not dead yet.

The second I touch him, he lurches forward as though I shocked him. His arms and legs spasm wildly before he leans over to cough. He ends up puking almost directly into my lap. It's all liquid but I smell something chemical in it, something vaguely familiar. I wonder if it's some kind of alcohol. He drops back down hard onto the rocks, but they don't make a sound with the impact. I watch as he stares unblinking at the sky, lying so still I think he must be dead now. I may have just witnessed death throws.

I rub his hand between both of mine and lean in close, so close our noses are almost touching and my hair falls around us. His eyes latch onto mine. I gasp at how bright they are. How brilliantly green. How utterly alive.

I whisper one word to him, the only thing I can think to say.

"Breathe."

He vanishes. My coat is lying on wet stones, my hand is holding cold air.

My heart stops beating. My breath freezes in my lungs. I clench my hands tightly, feeling them

9

tingle and itch where my skin met his. He was real. I held his hand and I'm awake. I know that I'm awake. There's no way that was a dream.

"What the hell?" I whisper, my voice quivering.

This is it. This is insanity taking hold. I'm breaking from reality. I'm losing my mind, though it never fully felt like mine to begin with.

Trembling from the cold, shock and a growing fear, I grab my jacket to pull it on. I can't get my hands to work right. The zipper feels painfully cold between my fingertips and I abandon any hope of closing it. Standing quickly, I run back across the rocks and up the bank to my sister's car. By the time I get there I'm nearly hyperventilating.

Her friends have arrived and they're standing in a halo of streetlight, clouds of warm breath rising around them in the cold air. Cara sees me and my anxiety must be on my face because she rushes over.

"What's wrong? Were you sick?" she asks, touching my arm. She frowns and pulls her hand back. "Your coat is wet."

"Yeah."

"Did you puke on your coat?" she asks, her face disgusted.

I think of the guy leaning over and throwing up river water.

"Yeah," I mumble.

"Gross. I think you're done for the night."

"Me too," I say eagerly. I nod but it's more of a convulsion and I practically run for the car.

Cara says a hasty goodbye to her friends who

laugh in understanding. Once inside, she cranks the heat and eyes me, watching me shake.

"You sure you're okay?"

"I just want to go to sleep."

"That's a first," she says, but leaves it at that.

Over the years Cara has learned that I don't like to talk about half the stuff that goes on when I'm asleep. I've seen things and been places that I don't like to revisit, waking or otherwise.

"What's that smell?" she asks suddenly.

"My dinner's second coming."

"No, you smell like a swimming pool." She scrunches up her nose and glances sideways at me. "Like chlorine."

This night is getting weirder by the second. I vow to never drink again.

About the Author

I was born in Eugene, Oregon and studied English Literature at the University of Oregon (Go Ducks!) I'm married to my best friend and an Airman in the United States Air Force, I'm the mother of the greatest little boy on the planet and a rescue dog with more soul than most humans, and I'll read books in just about any genre as long as the story is good. I started writing when I was a kid and finally decided to self-publish when I read one too many books centered around disturbingly Alpha males and the sniveling women who inexplicably love them. There are strong women and gentle men out there, and a beautiful love story can be woven between them. I want to tell those stories.

Visit my website for more information on upcoming releases, www.traceywardauthor.com

Made in the USA
San Bernardino, CA
01 November 2014